Buffy THE VAMPIRE SLAYER™
BAD BLOOD

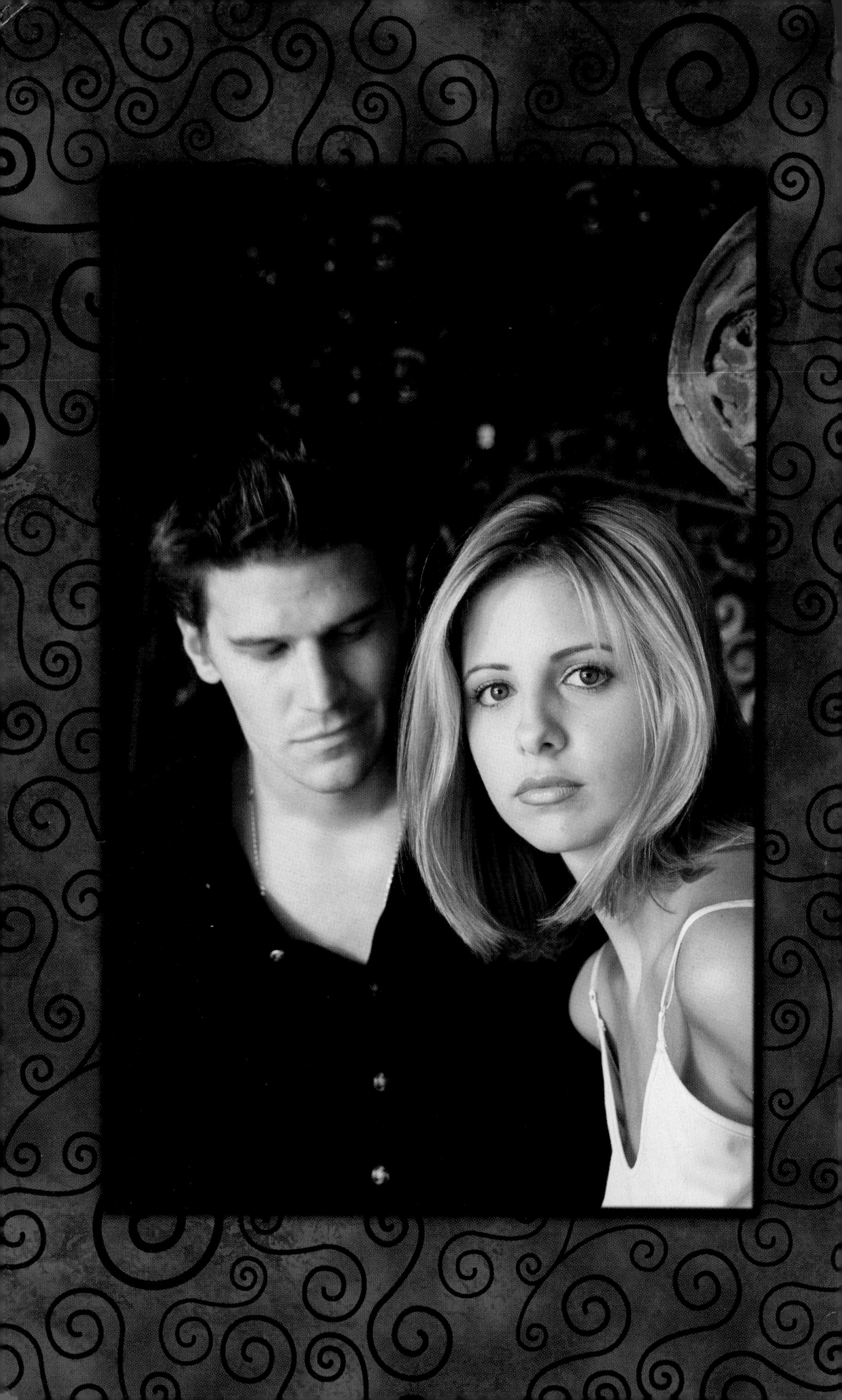

Buffy the Vampire Slayer™
BAD BLOOD

based on the television series created by
JOSS WHEDON

writer **ANDI WATSON**

penciller **JOE BENNET**

inker **RICK KETCHAM**

colorist **GUY MAJOR**

letterer **JANICE CHIANG**

and featuring "Hello, Moon"

written by **CHRISTOPHER GOLDEN** *and* **DANIEL BRERETON**

penciller **JOE BENNET**

inker **JIM AMASH**

colorist **GUY MAJOR**

letterer **CLEM ROBINS**

These stories take place during Buffy the Vampire Slayer's third season.

DARK HORSE COMICS®

publisher
MIKE RICHARDSON

editor
SCOTT ALLIE
with ADAM GALLARDO *and* BEN ABERNATHY

collection designer
KEITH WOOD

art director
MARK COX

special thanks to
DEBBIE OLSHAN AT FOX LICENSING,
CAROLINE KALLAS AND GEORGE SNYDER AT *BUFFY THE VAMPIRE SLAYER*,
AND DAVID CAMPITI AT GLASS HOUSE GRAPHICS.

PUBLISHED BY
DARK HORSE COMICS, INC.
10956 SE MAIN STREET
MILWAUKIE, OR 97222

FIRST EDITION
APRIL 2000
ISBN: 1 - 56971 - 445 - 2

1 3 5 7 9 10 8 6 4 2

printed in canada.

introduction

Last fall, just months after Angel's return from Hell, Buffy Summers' holidays were ruined by a new vampire in town—the beautiful Selke. On Halloween a group of bloodsuckers kidnapped Willow Rosenburg. When Buffy came for her best friend, only Selke escaped, spared by an off-the-mark stake from the Slayer. On Thanksgiving Selke returned, much worse for wear, and managed to take Buffy captive. Buffy got out by the skin of her teeth after setting fire to the rotted wood and scattered coffins of Selke's mausoleum home, leaving the wounded vampire to die in flames …*

Selke wasn't that lucky, though. The fire didn't kill her, but it gave her another reason to track down the Slayer and her friends, and kill them all.

As if being seniors weren't hard enough.

*See *Buffy the Vampire Slayer: The Remaining Sunlight*

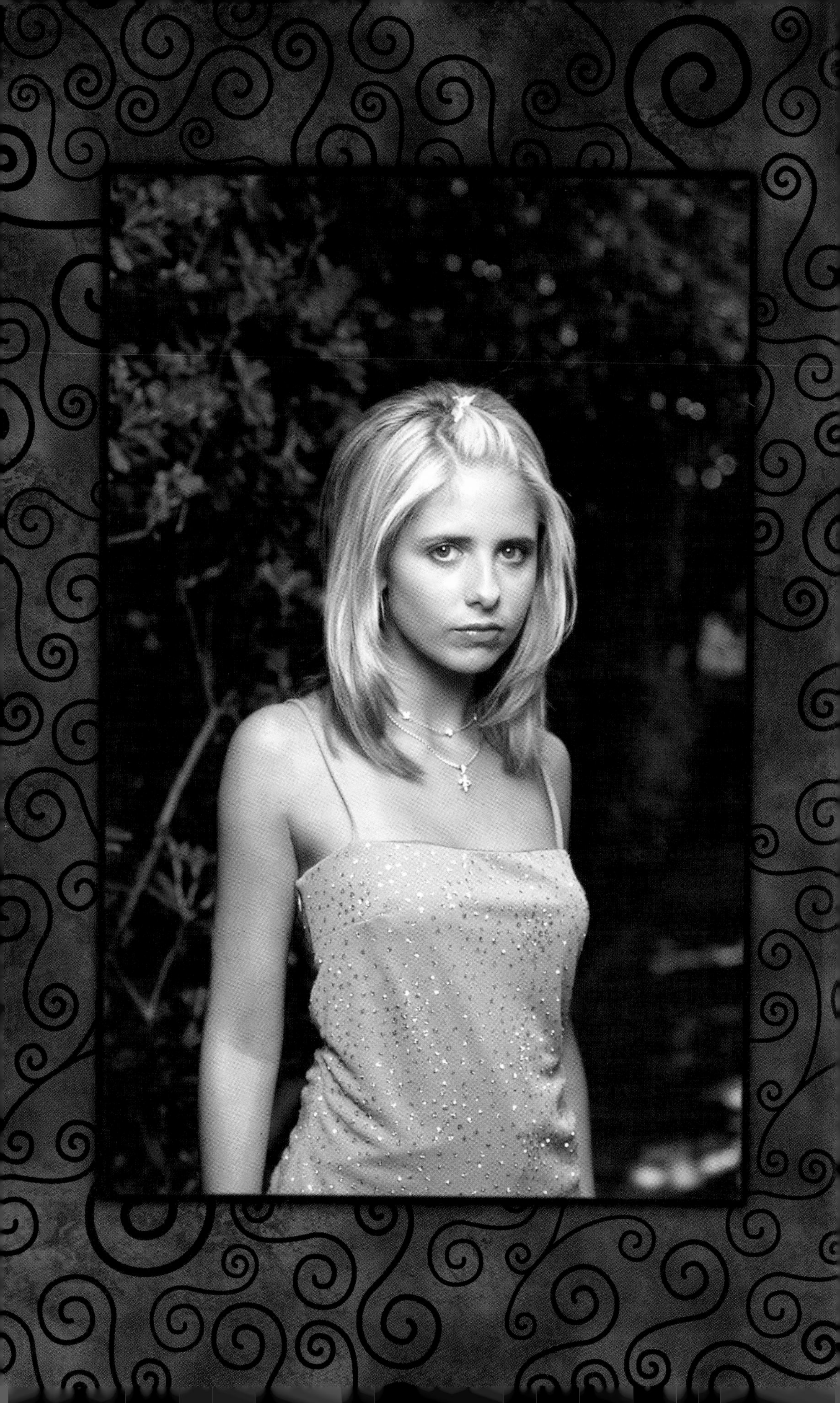

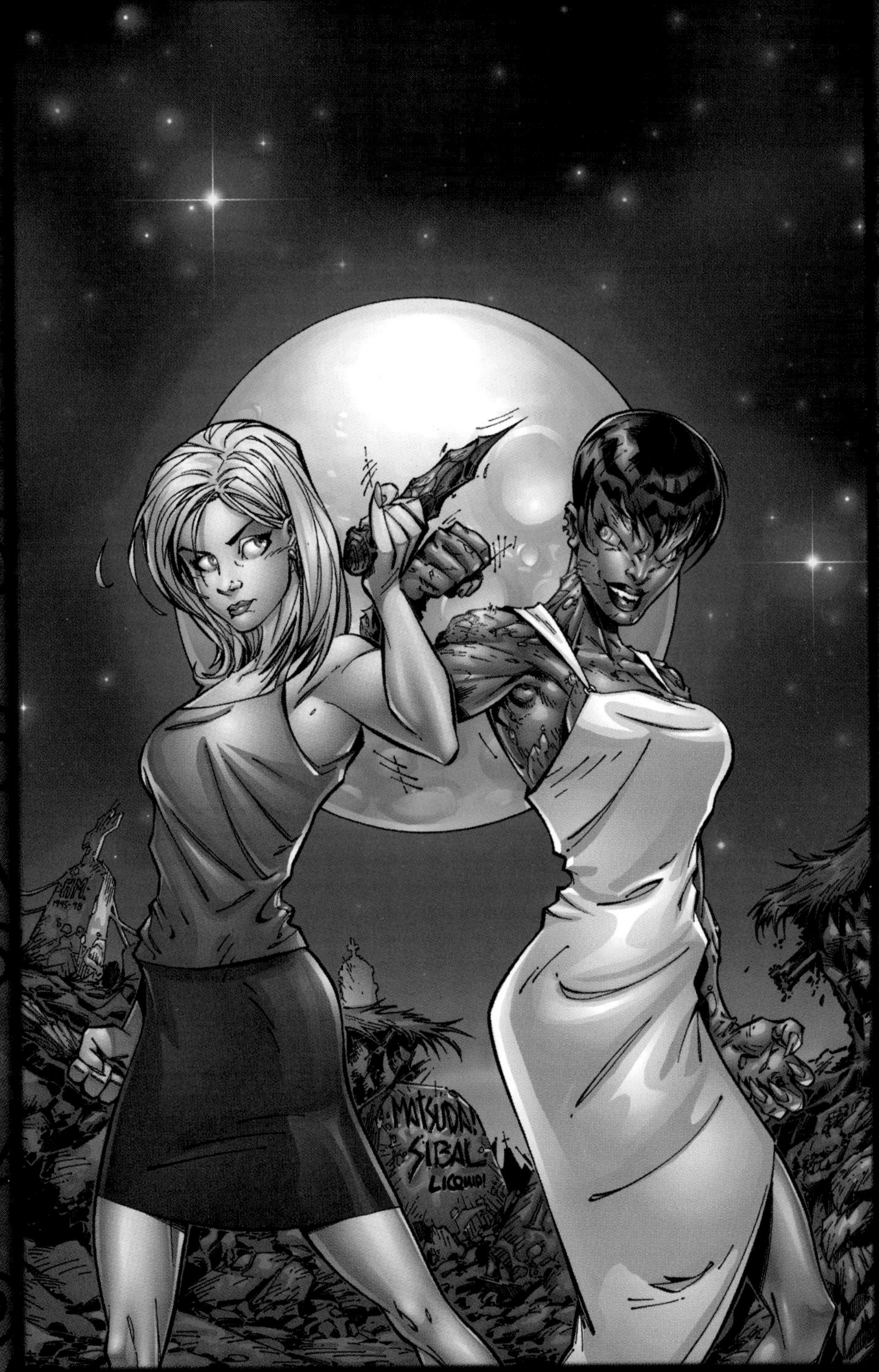
MATSUDA!
SIBAL

Art by JEFF MATSUDA *and* JON SIBAL
Colors by LIQUID!

HEY, GOOD LOOKIN'

PART I

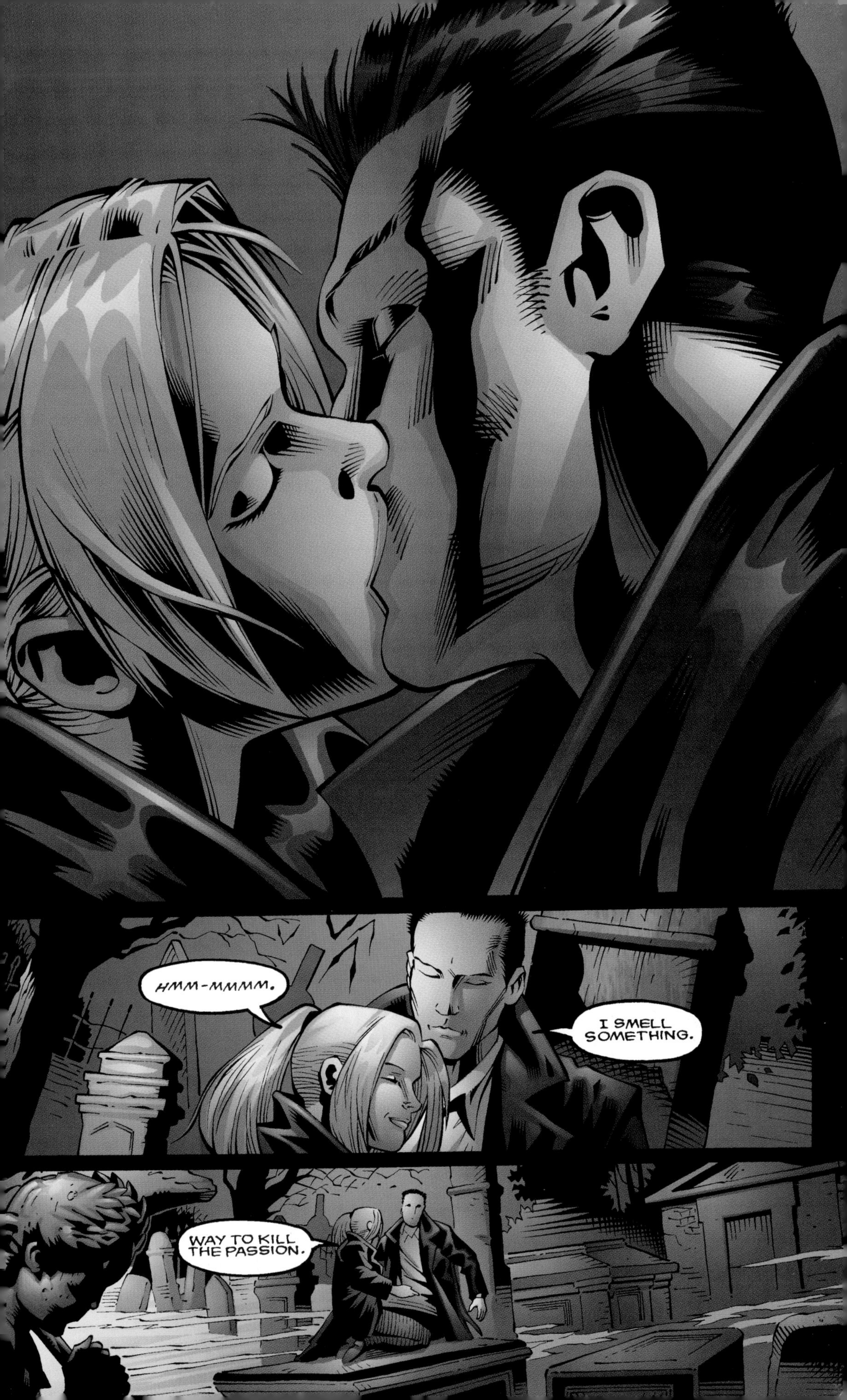
HMM-MMMM.
I SMELL SOMETHING.
WAY TO KILL THE PASSION.

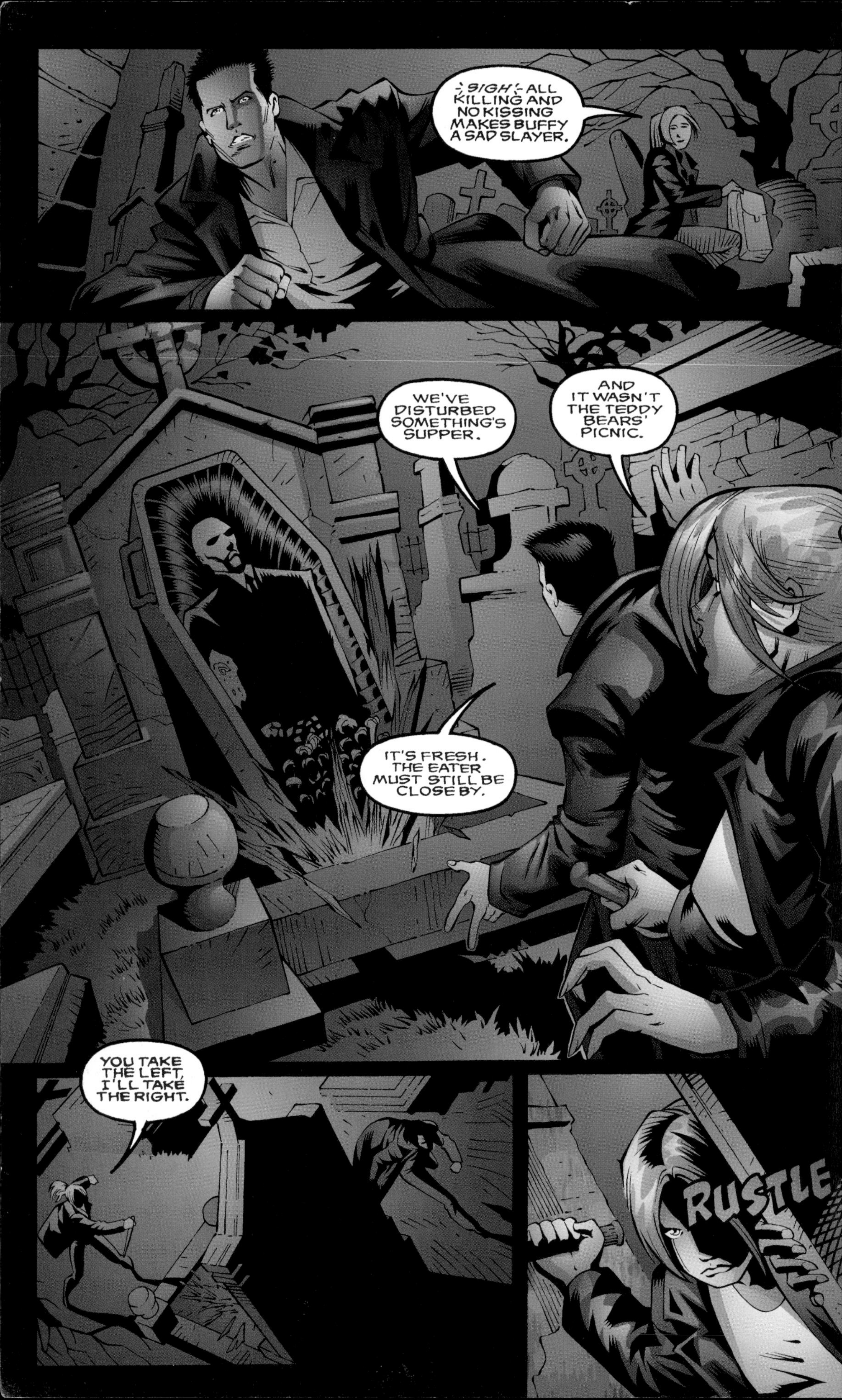
-; SIGH ;- ALL KILLING AND NO KISSING MAKES BUFFY A SAD SLAYER.
WE'VE DISTURBED SOMETHING'S SUPPER.
AND IT WASN'T THE TEDDY BEARS' PICNIC.
IT'S FRESH. THE EATER MUST STILL BE CLOSE BY.
YOU TAKE THE LEFT, I'LL TAKE THE RIGHT.
RUSTLE

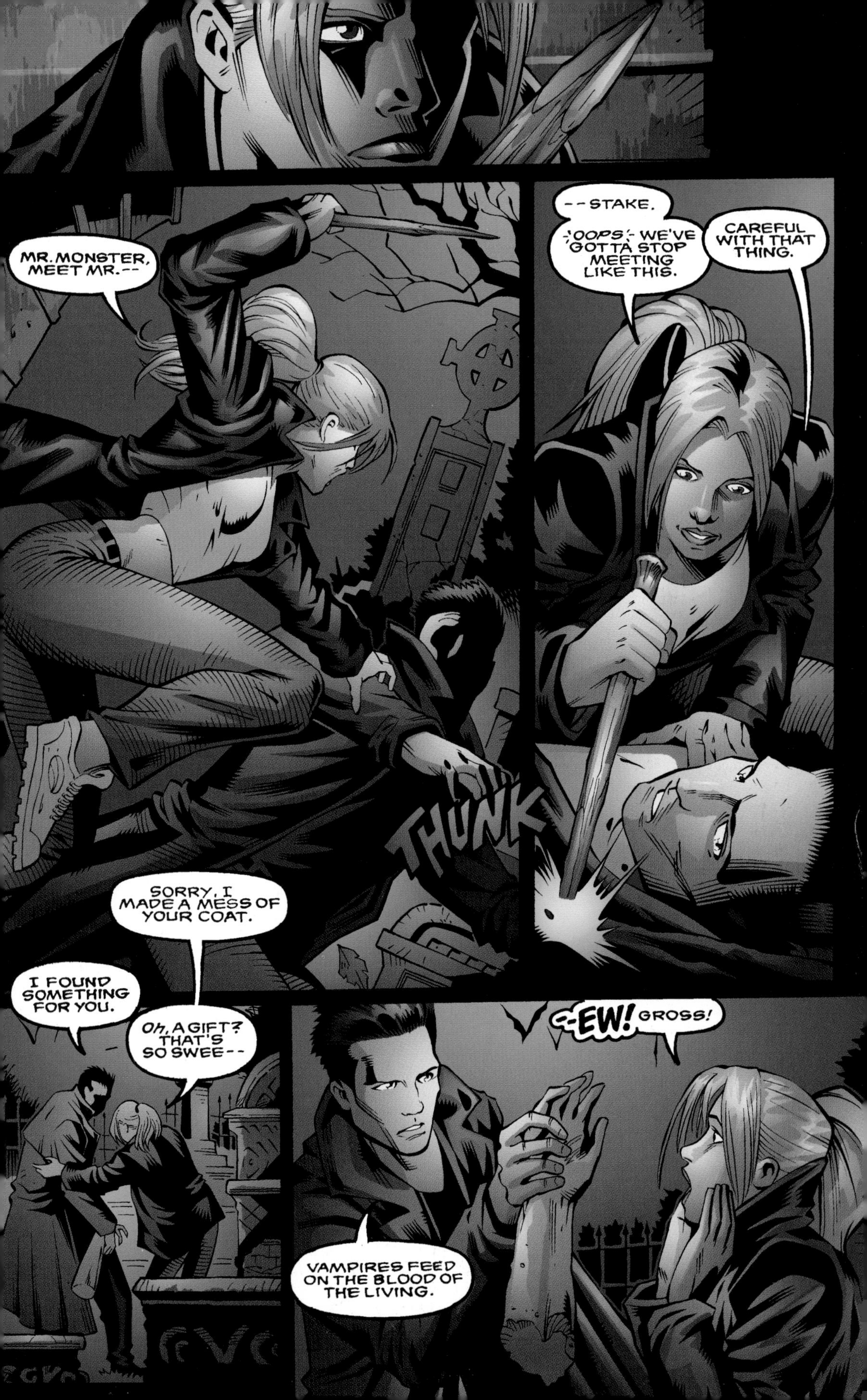
MR. MONSTER, MEET MR.--
--STAKE.
-OOPS- WE'VE GOTTA STOP MEETING LIKE THIS.
CAREFUL WITH THAT THING.
THUNK
SORRY, I MADE A MESS OF YOUR COAT.
I FOUND SOMETHING FOR YOU.
Oh, A GIFT? THAT'S SO SWEE--
--EW! GROSS!
VAMPIRES FEED ON THE BLOOD OF THE LIVING.

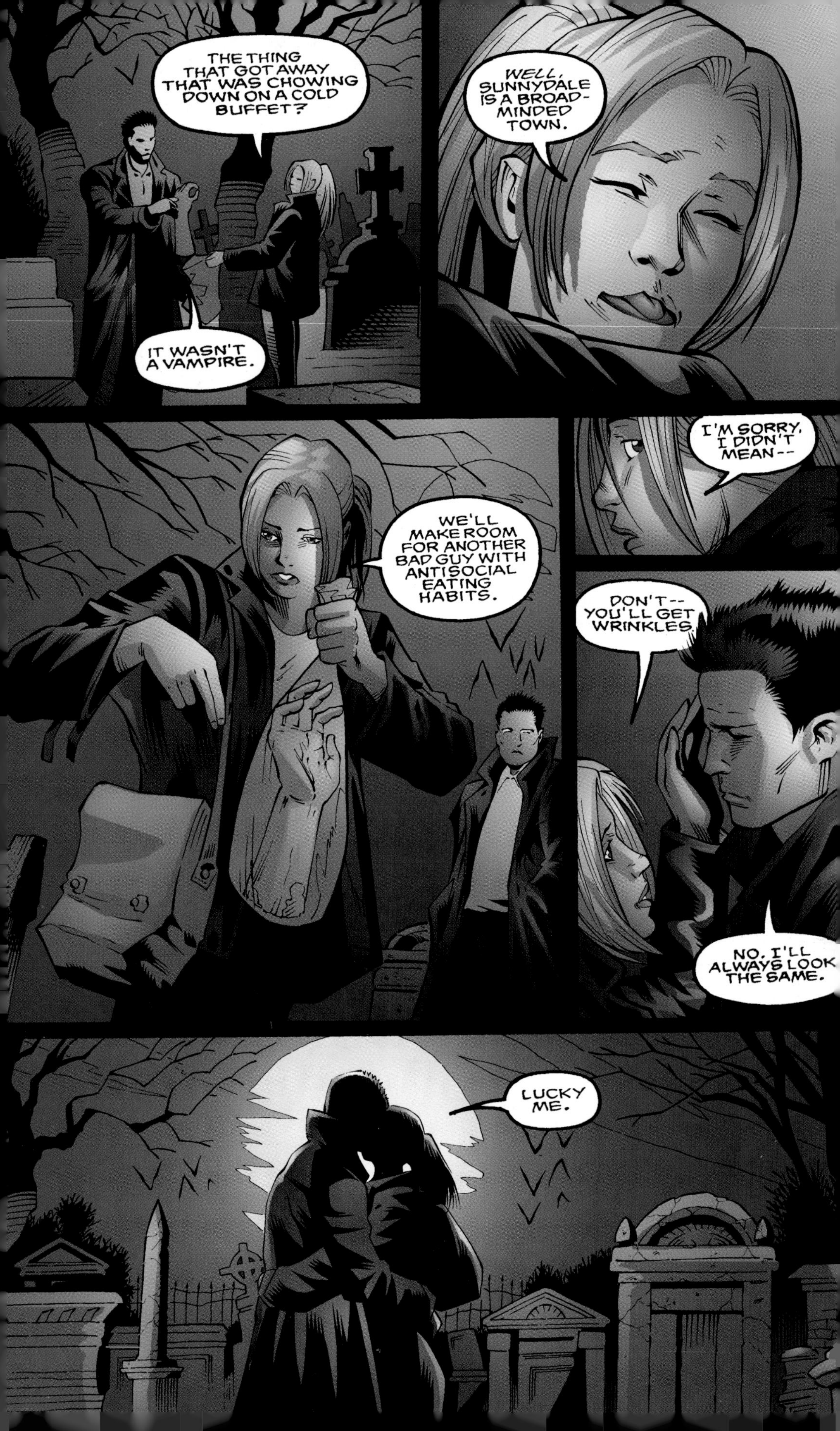
THE THING THAT GOT AWAY THAT WAS CHOWING DOWN ON A COLD BUFFET?
IT WASN'T A VAMPIRE.
WELL, SUNNYDALE IS A BROAD-MINDED TOWN.
WE'LL MAKE ROOM FOR ANOTHER BAD GUY WITH ANTISOCIAL EATING HABITS.
I'M SORRY, I DIDN'T MEAN--
DON'T-- YOU'LL GET WRINKLES.
NO. I'LL ALWAYS LOOK THE SAME.
LUCKY ME.

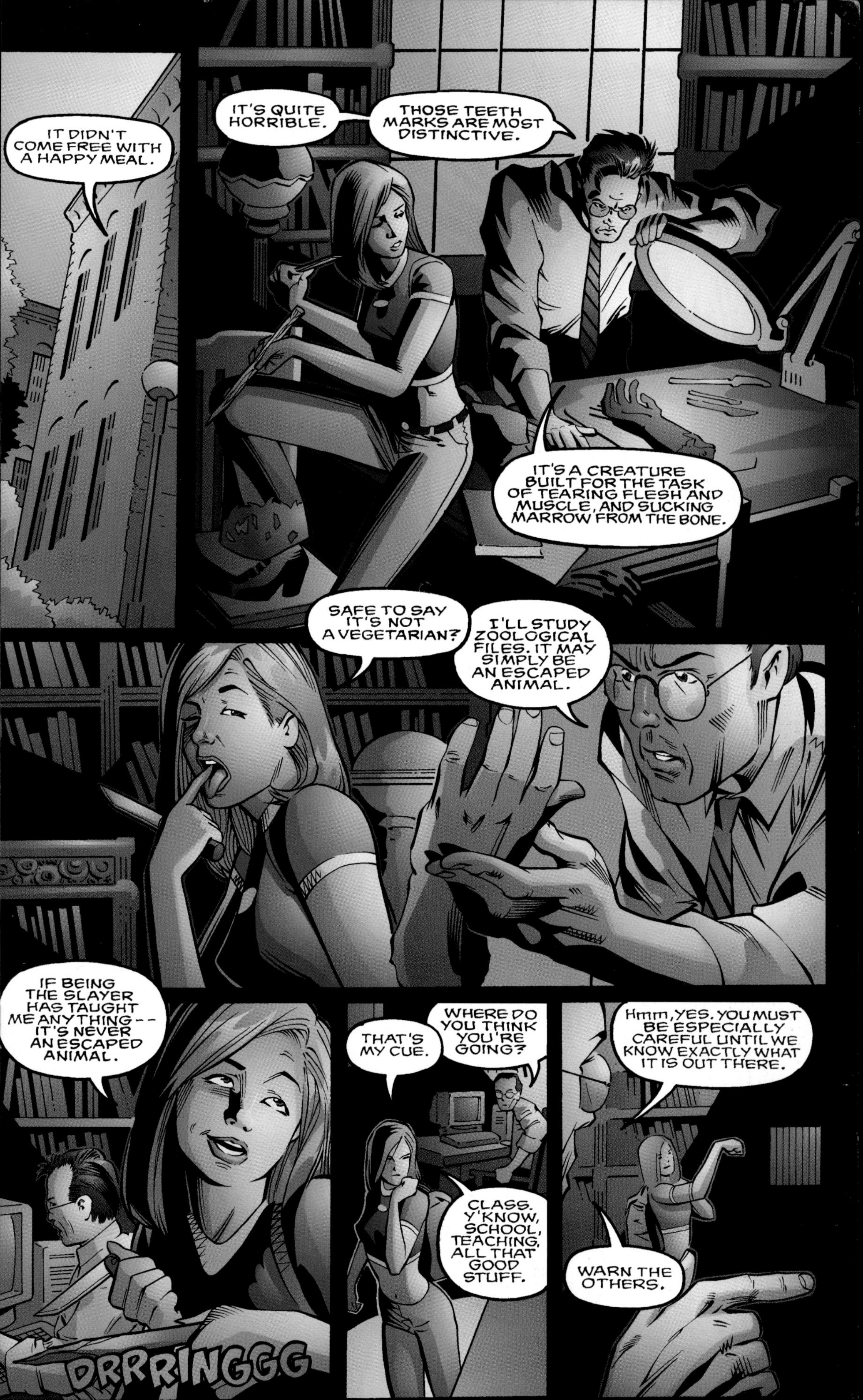
IT DIDN'T COME FREE WITH A HAPPY MEAL.
IT'S QUITE HORRIBLE.
THOSE TEETH MARKS ARE MOST DISTINCTIVE.
IT'S A CREATURE BUILT FOR THE TASK OF TEARING FLESH AND MUSCLE, AND SUCKING MARROW FROM THE BONE.
SAFE TO SAY IT'S NOT A VEGETARIAN?
I'LL STUDY ZOOLOGICAL FILES. IT MAY SIMPLY BE AN ESCAPED ANIMAL.
IF BEING THE SLAYER HAS TAUGHT ME ANYTHING-- IT'S NEVER AN ESCAPED ANIMAL.
DRRRINGGG
THAT'S MY CUE.
WHERE DO YOU THINK YOU'RE GOING?
CLASS. Y'KNOW, SCHOOL, TEACHING, ALL THAT GOOD STUFF.
Hmm, YES. YOU MUST BE ESPECIALLY CAREFUL UNTIL WE KNOW EXACTLY WHAT IT IS OUT THERE.
WARN THE OTHERS.

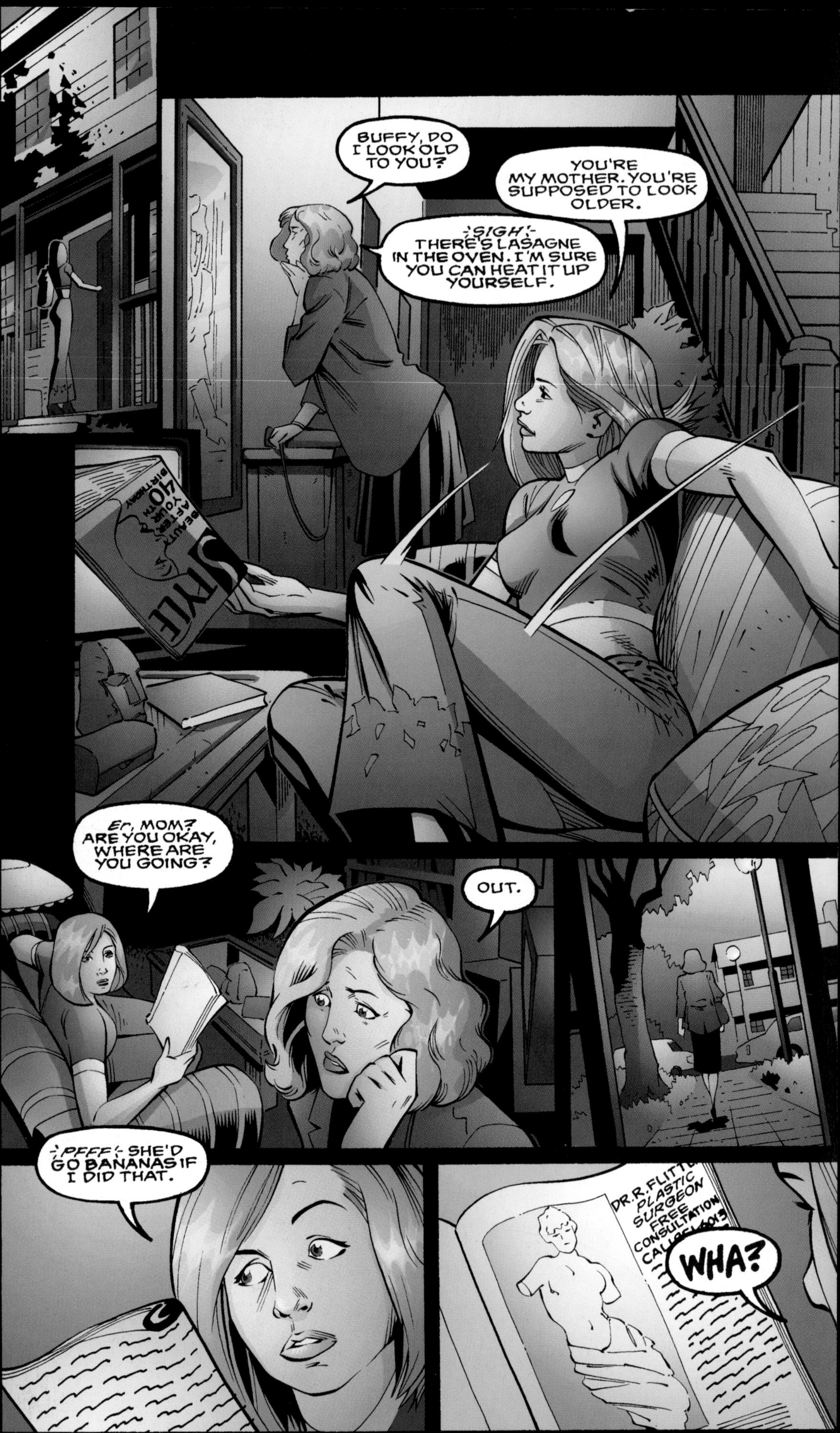
BUFFY, DO I LOOK OLD TO YOU?
YOU'RE MY MOTHER. YOU'RE SUPPOSED TO LOOK OLDER.
-SIGH- THERE'S LASAGNE IN THE OVEN. I'M SURE YOU CAN HEAT IT UP YOURSELF.
STYLE
BEAUTY AFTER YOUR 40TH BIRTHDAY
Er, MOM? ARE YOU OKAY, WHERE ARE YOU GOING?
OUT.
-PFFF- SHE'D GO BANANAS IF I DID THAT.
DR. R. FLITT
PLASTIC SURGEON
FREE CONSULTATION
WHA?

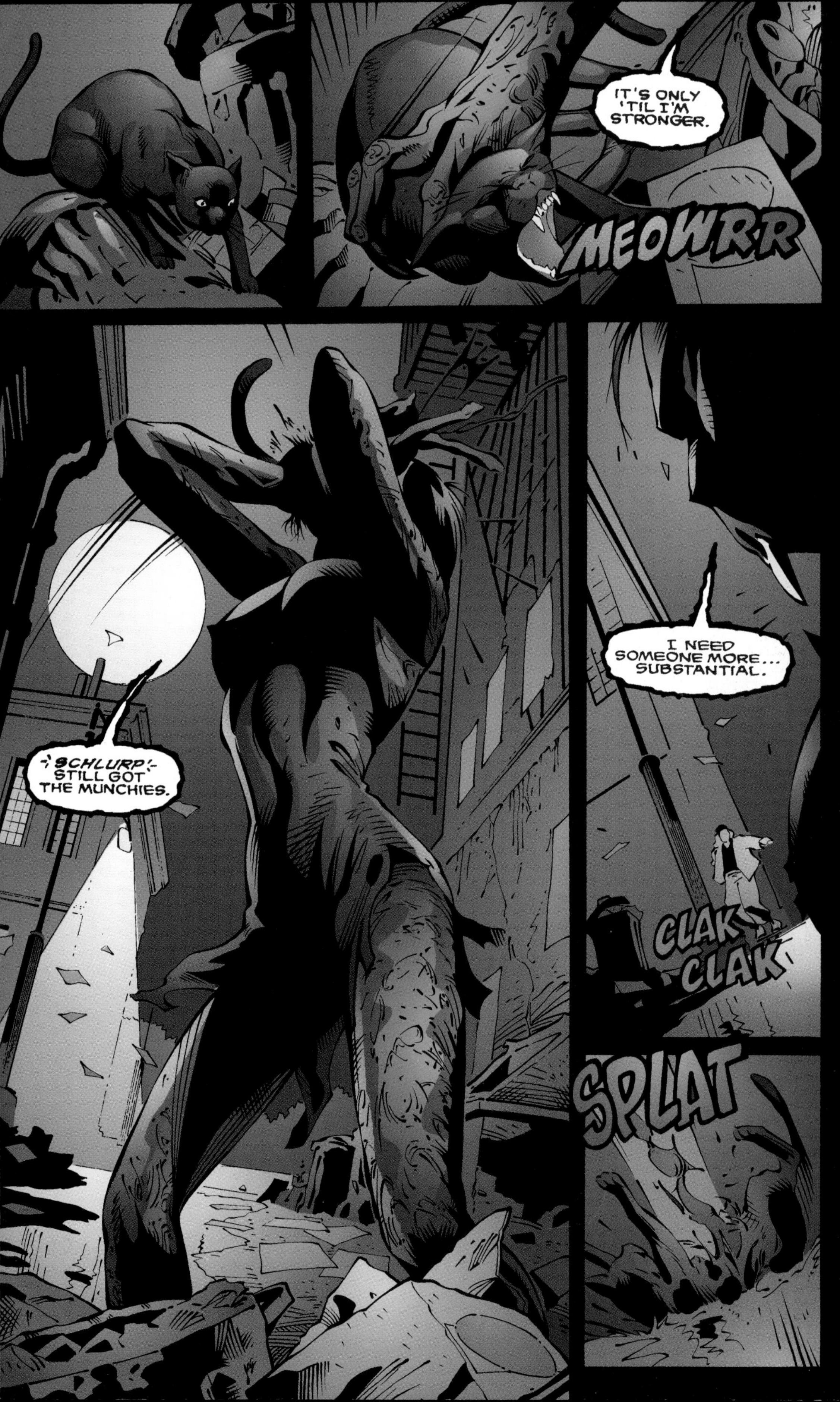
IT'S ONLY 'TIL I'M STRONGER.
MEOWRR
-SCHLURP- STILL GOT THE MUNCHIES.
I NEED SOMEONE MORE... SUBSTANTIAL.
CLAK CLAK
SPLAT

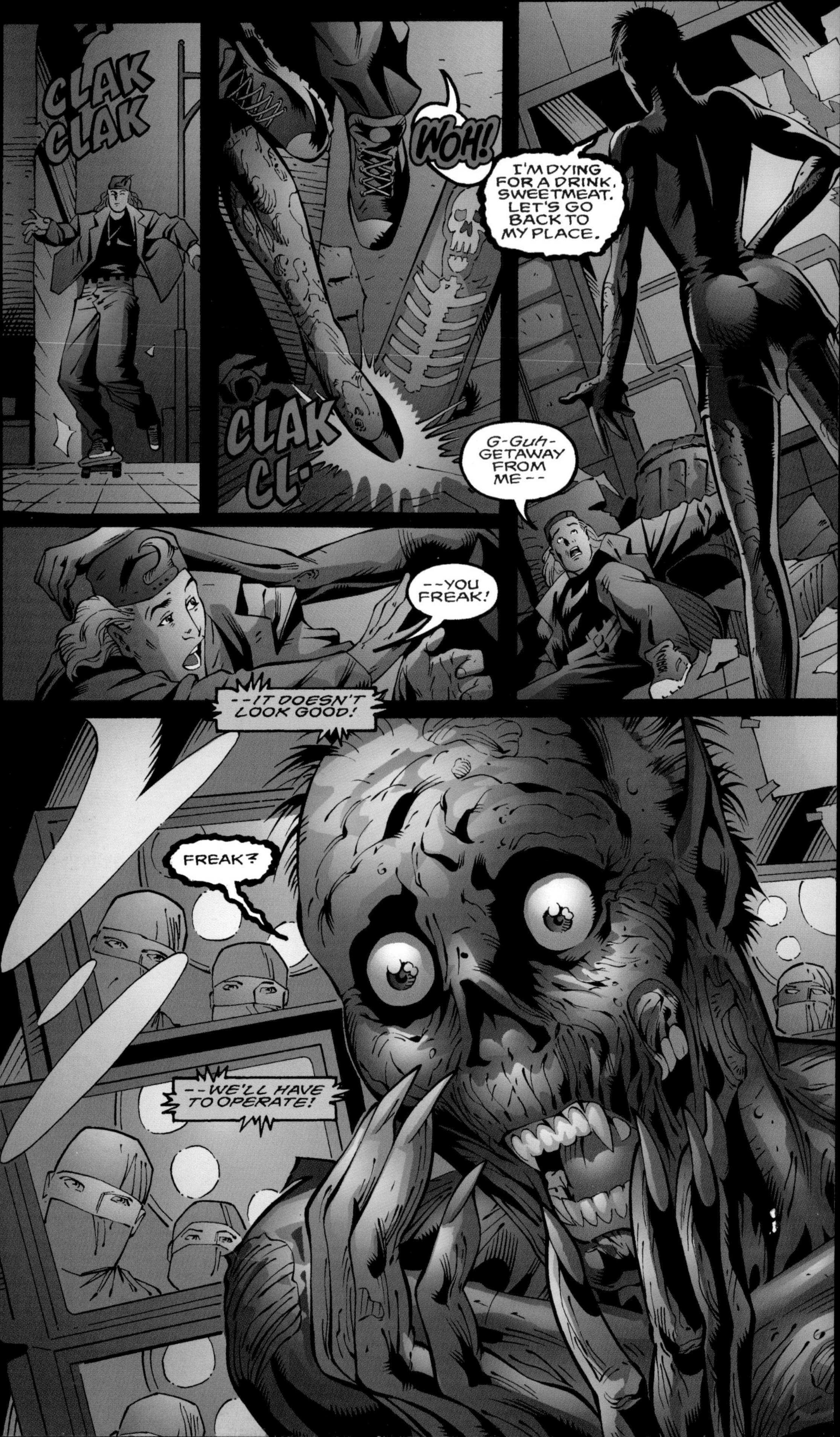
CLAK CLAK
WOH!
I'M DYING FOR A DRINK, SWEETMEAT. LET'S GO BACK TO MY PLACE.
CLAK CL-
G-Guh- GETAWAY FROM ME--
--YOU FREAK!
--IT DOESN'T LOOK GOOD!
FREAK?
--WE'LL HAVE TO OPERATE!

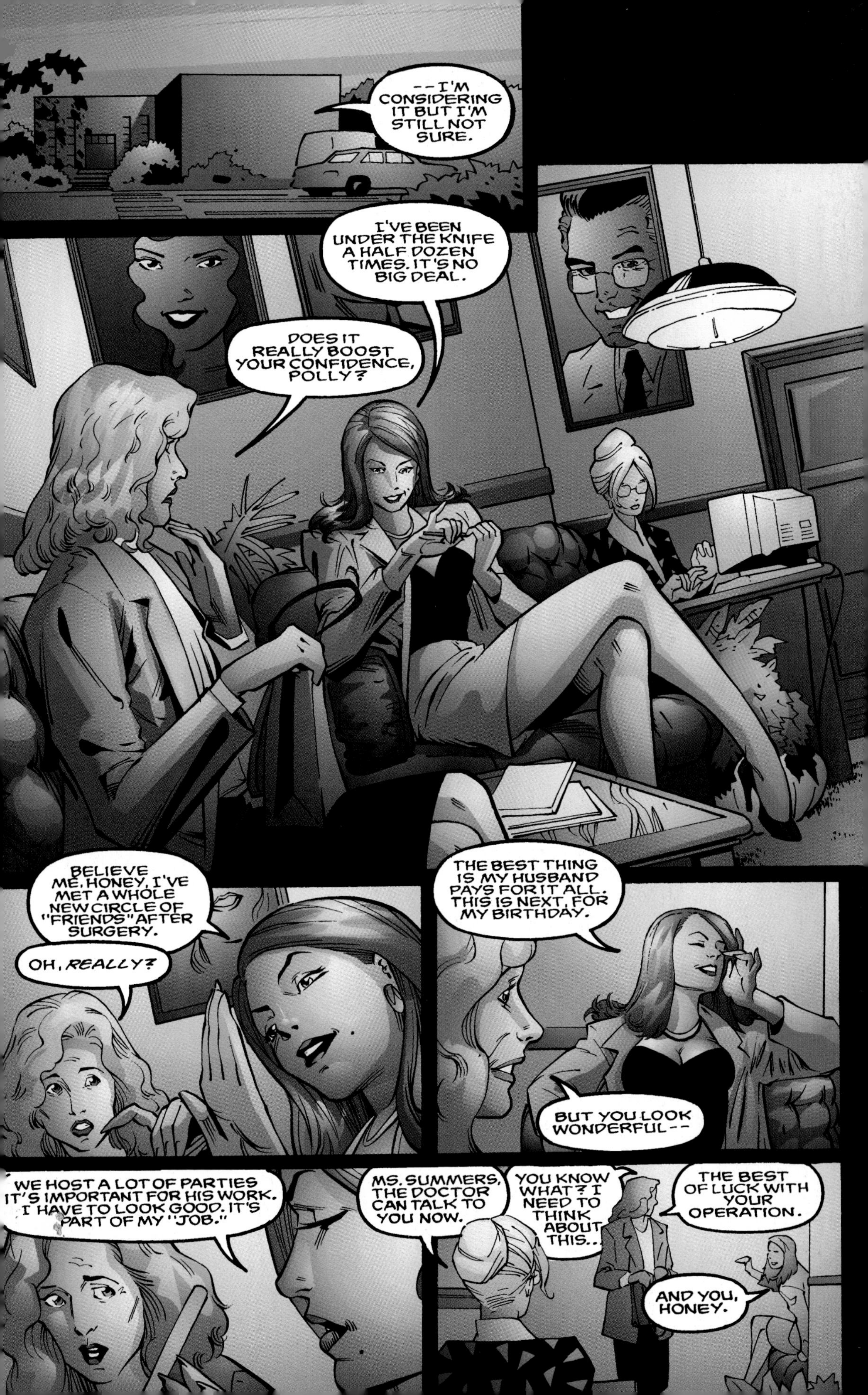
--I'M CONSIDERING IT BUT I'M STILL NOT SURE.
I'VE BEEN UNDER THE KNIFE A HALF DOZEN TIMES. IT'S NO BIG DEAL.
DOES IT REALLY BOOST YOUR CONFIDENCE, POLLY?
BELIEVE ME, HONEY, I'VE MET A WHOLE NEW CIRCLE OF "FRIENDS" AFTER SURGERY.
OH, *REALLY?*
THE BEST THING IS MY HUSBAND PAYS FOR IT ALL. THIS IS NEXT, FOR MY BIRTHDAY.
BUT YOU LOOK WONDERFUL--
WE HOST A LOT OF PARTIES IT'S IMPORTANT FOR HIS WORK. I HAVE TO LOOK GOOD. IT'S PART OF MY "JOB."
MS. SUMMERS, THE DOCTOR CAN TALK TO YOU NOW.
YOU KNOW WHAT? I NEED TO THINK ABOUT THIS..
THE BEST OF LUCK WITH YOUR OPERATION.
AND YOU, HONEY.

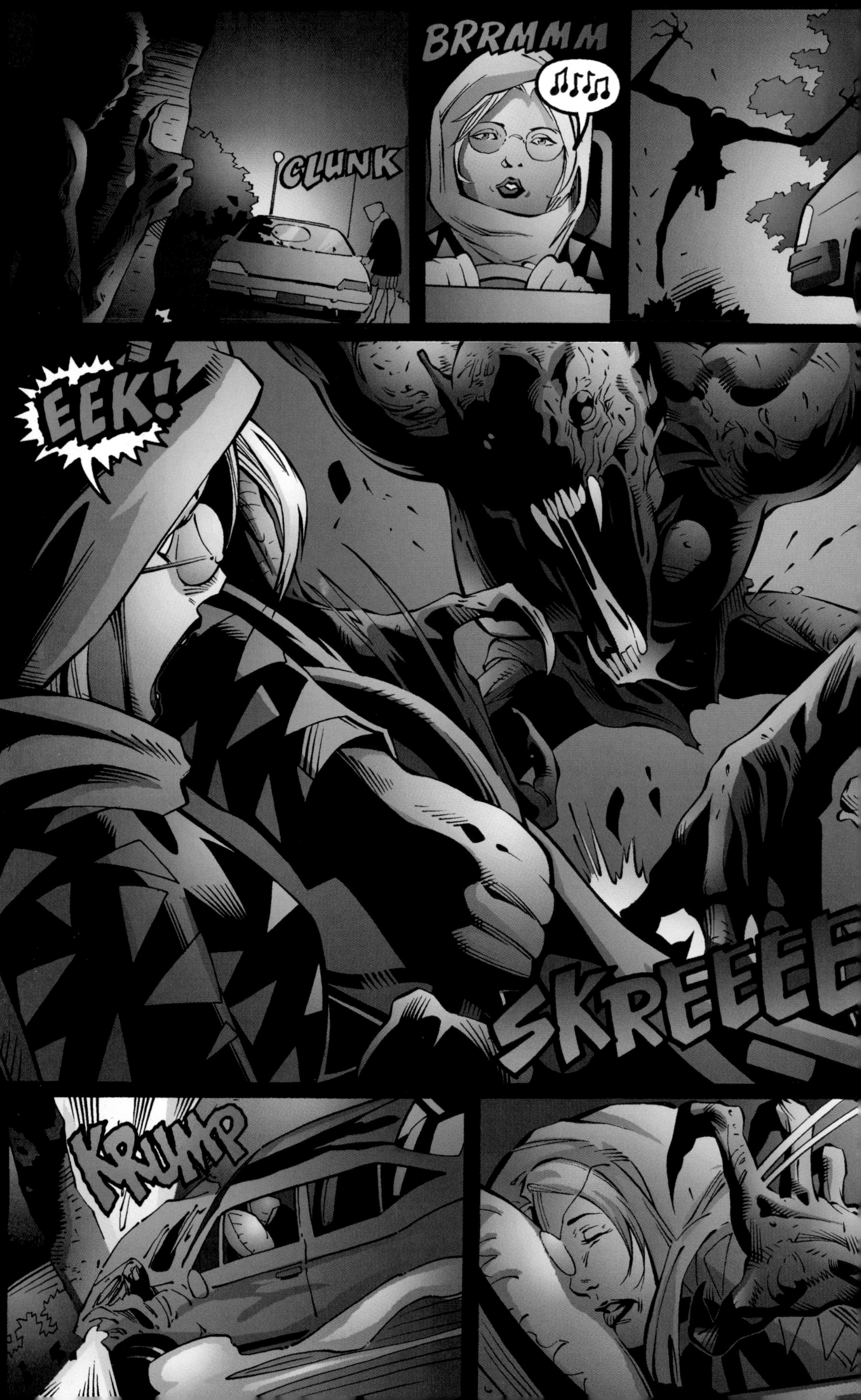
CLUNK
BRRMMM
♫♫♫
EEK!
SKREEEE
KRUMP

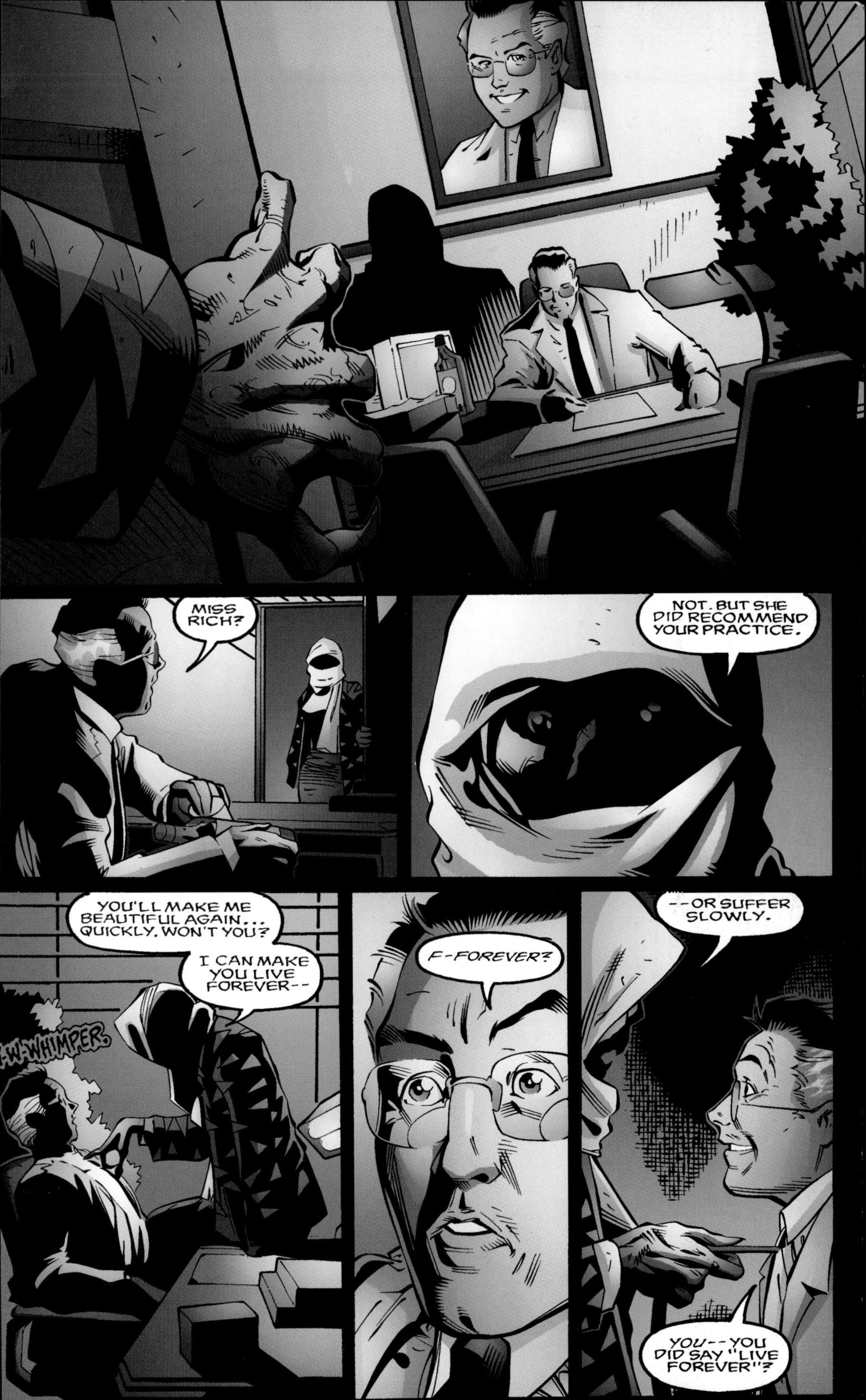
MISS RICH?
NOT. BUT SHE DID RECOMMEND YOUR PRACTICE.
YOU'LL MAKE ME BEAUTIFUL AGAIN... QUICKLY. WON'T YOU?
I CAN MAKE YOU LIVE FOREVER--
W-WHIMPER.
F-FOREVER?
--OR SUFFER SLOWLY.
YOU--YOU DID SAY "LIVE FOREVER"?

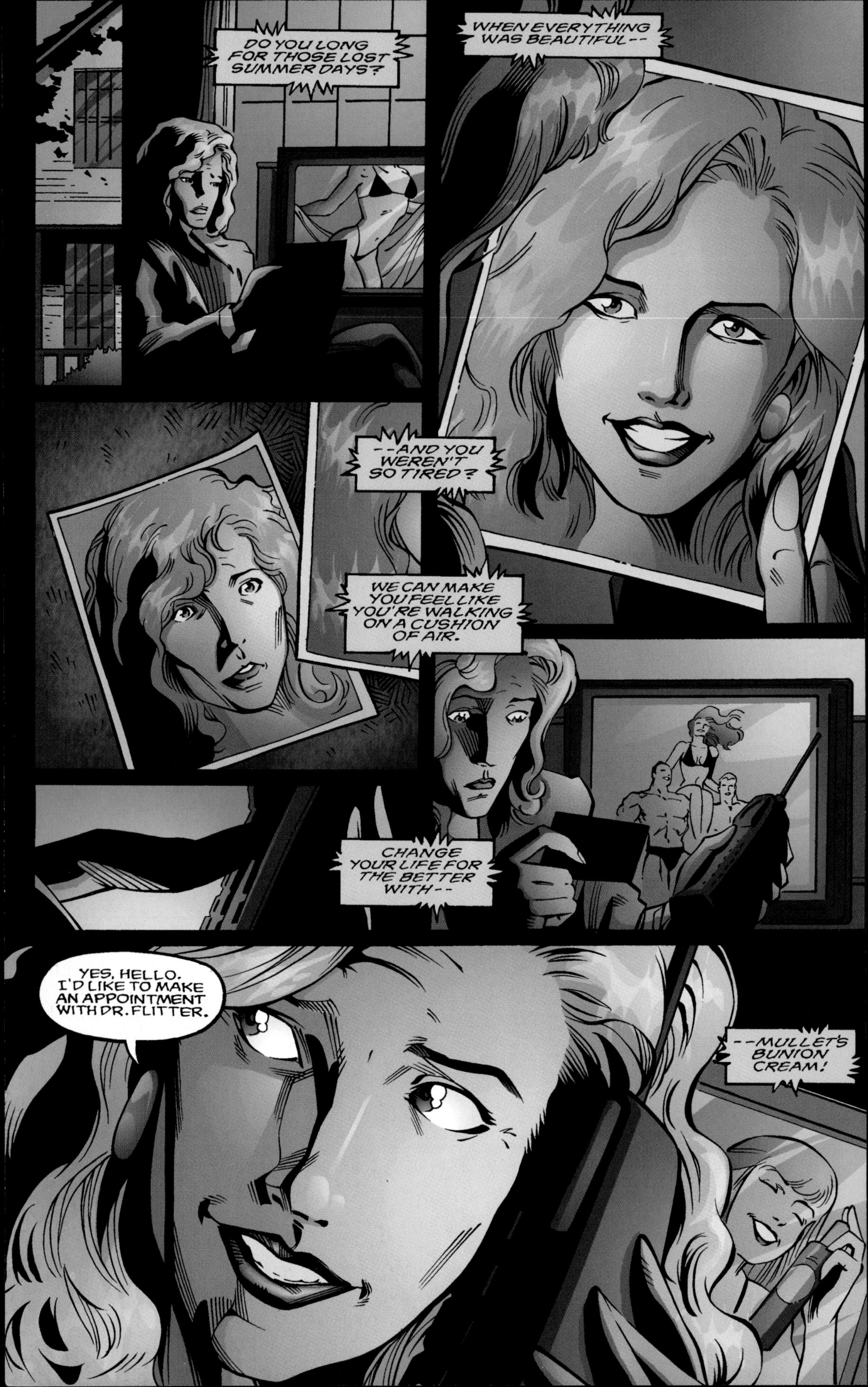
DO YOU LONG FOR THOSE LOST SUMMER DAYS?
WHEN EVERYTHING WAS BEAUTIFUL--
--AND YOU WEREN'T SO TIRED?
WE CAN MAKE YOU FEEL LIKE YOU'RE WALKING ON A CUSHION OF AIR.
CHANGE YOUR LIFE FOR THE BETTER WITH--
YES, HELLO. I'D LIKE TO MAKE AN APPOINTMENT WITH DR. FLITTER.
--MULLET'S BUNION CREAM!

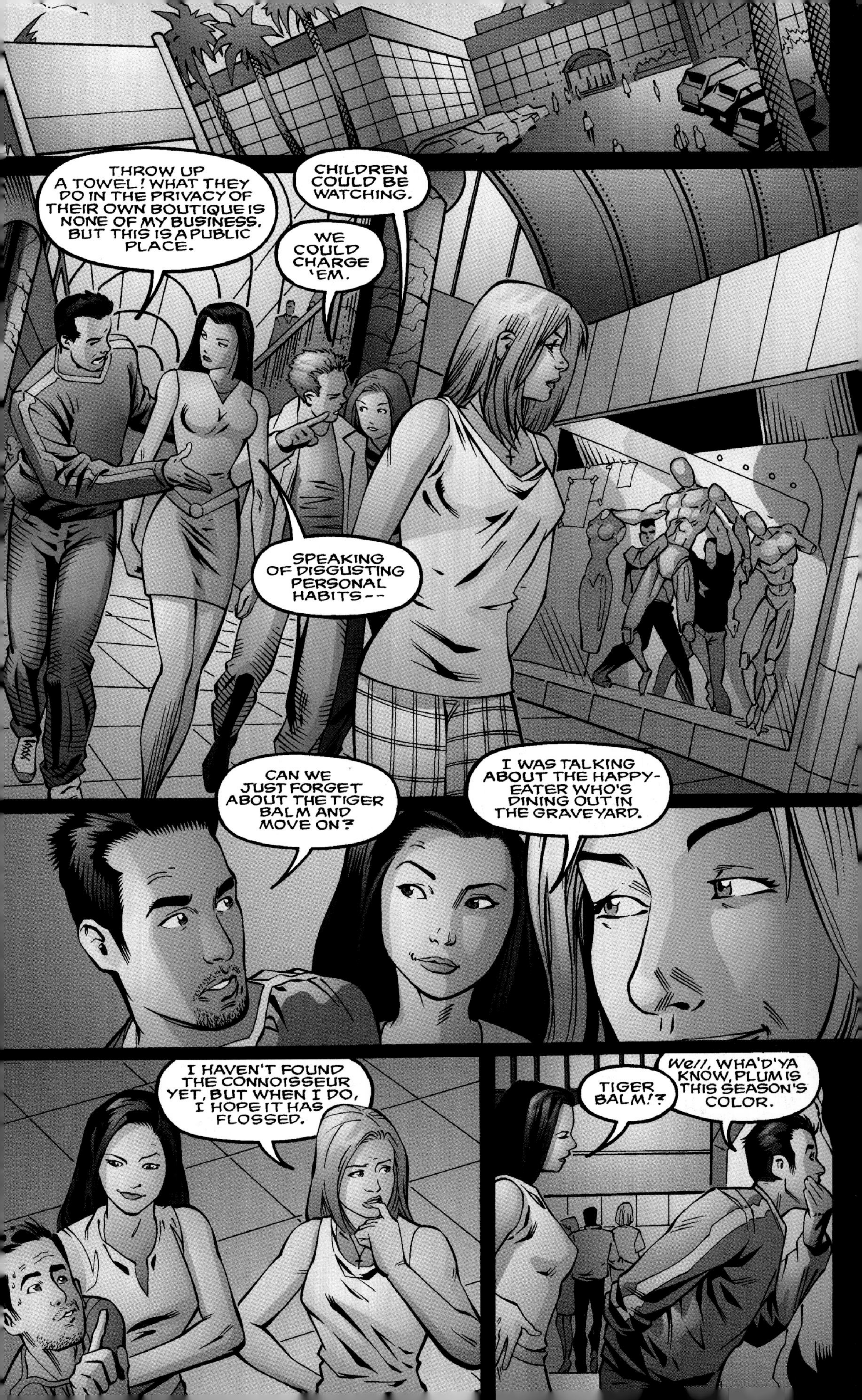
THROW UP A TOWEL! WHAT THEY DO IN THE PRIVACY OF THEIR OWN BOUTIQUE IS NONE OF MY BUSINESS, BUT THIS IS A PUBLIC PLACE.
CHILDREN COULD BE WATCHING.
WE COULD CHARGE 'EM.
SPEAKING OF DISGUSTING PERSONAL HABITS--
CAN WE JUST FORGET ABOUT THE TIGER BALM AND MOVE ON?
I WAS TALKING ABOUT THE HAPPY-EATER WHO'S DINING OUT IN THE GRAVEYARD.
I HAVEN'T FOUND THE CONNOISSEUR YET, BUT WHEN I DO, I HOPE IT HAS FLOSSED.
TIGER BALM!?
Well, WHA'D'YA KNOW, PLUM IS THIS SEASON'S COLOR.

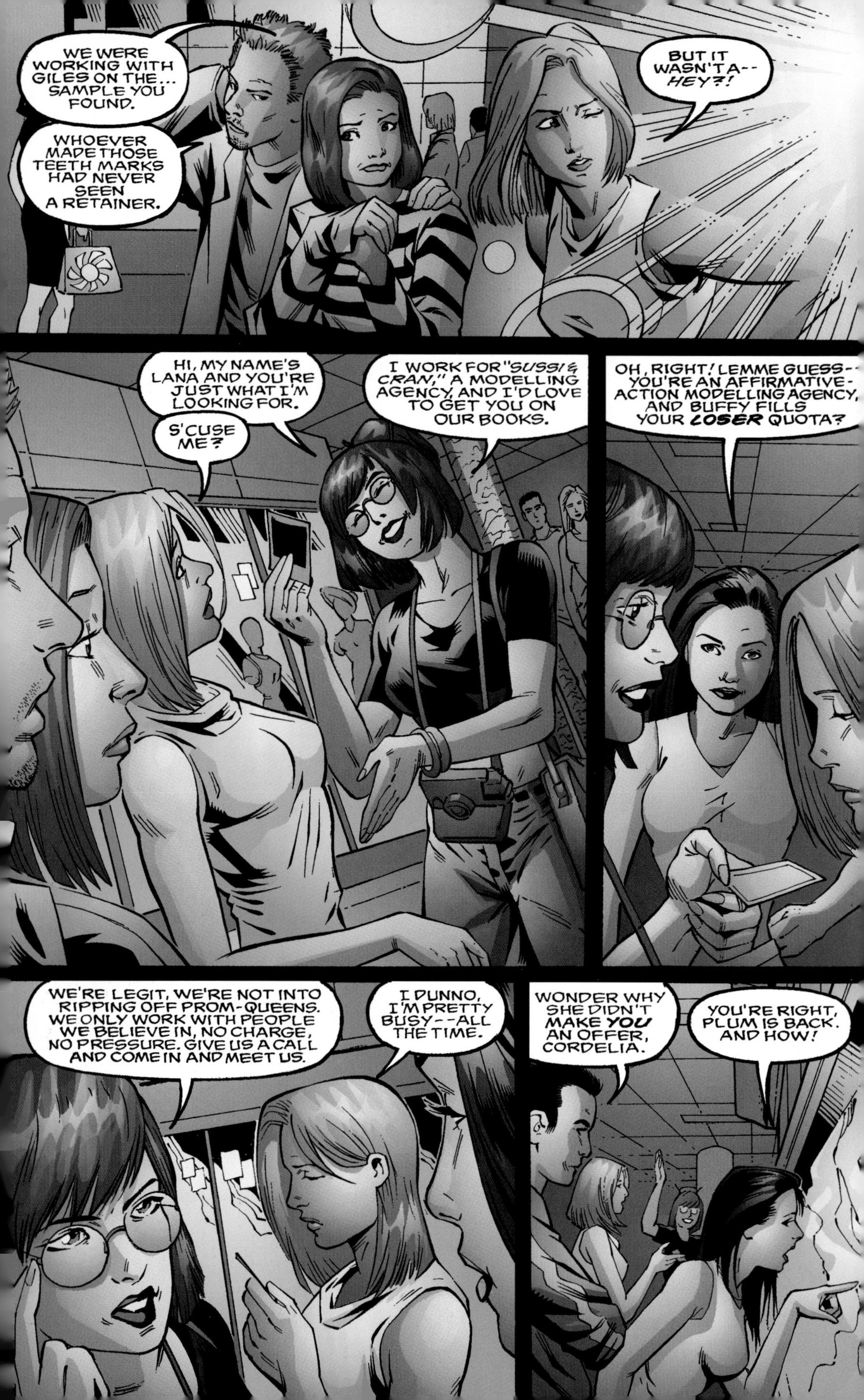
WE WERE WORKING WITH GILES ON THE... SAMPLE YOU FOUND.
WHOEVER MADE THOSE TEETH MARKS HAD NEVER SEEN A RETAINER.
BUT IT WASN'T A-- HEY?!
HI, MY NAME'S LANA AND YOU'RE JUST WHAT I'M LOOKING FOR.
S'CUSE ME?
I WORK FOR "SUSSI & CRAN," A MODELLING AGENCY, AND I'D LOVE TO GET YOU ON OUR BOOKS.
OH, RIGHT! LEMME GUESS-- YOU'RE AN AFFIRMATIVE-ACTION MODELLING AGENCY, AND BUFFY FILLS YOUR LOSER QUOTA?
WE'RE LEGIT, WE'RE NOT INTO RIPPING OFF PROM-QUEENS. WE ONLY WORK WITH PEOPLE WE BELIEVE IN, NO CHARGE, NO PRESSURE. GIVE US A CALL AND COME IN AND MEET US.
I DUNNO, I'M PRETTY BUSY--ALL THE TIME.
WONDER WHY SHE DIDN'T MAKE YOU AN OFFER, CORDELIA.
YOU'RE RIGHT, PLUM IS BACK. AND HOW!

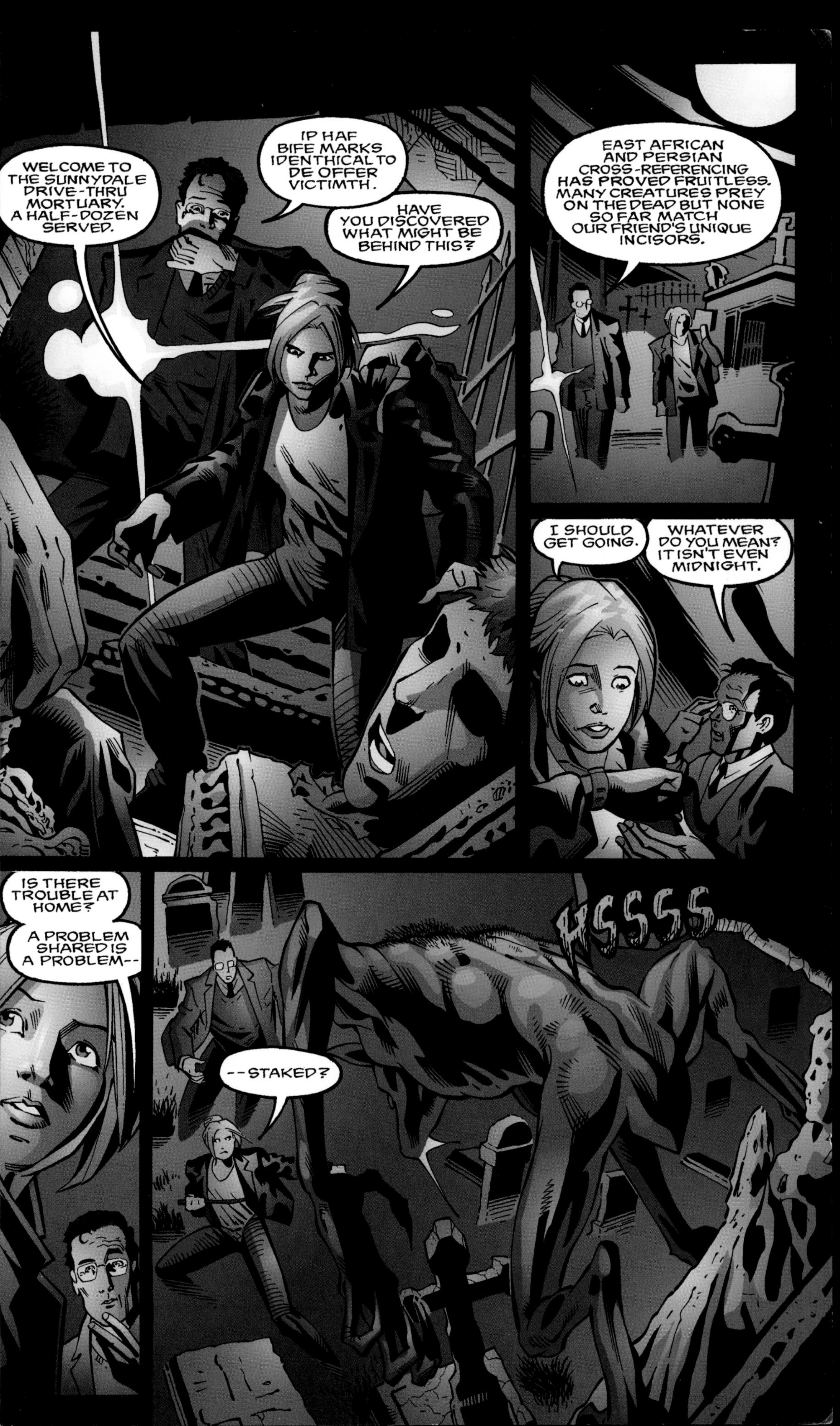

WELCOME TO THE SUNNYDALE DRIVE-THRU MORTUARY. A HALF-DOZEN SERVED.
IP HAF BIFE MARKS IDENTHICAL TO DE OFFER VICTIMTH.
HAVE YOU DISCOVERED WHAT MIGHT BE BEHIND THIS?
EAST AFRICAN AND PERSIAN CROSS-REFERENCING HAS PROVED FRUITLESS. MANY CREATURES PREY ON THE DEAD BUT NONE SO FAR MATCH OUR FRIEND'S UNIQUE INCISORS.
I SHOULD GET GOING.
WHATEVER DO YOU MEAN? IT ISN'T EVEN MIDNIGHT.
IS THERE TROUBLE AT HOME?
A PROBLEM SHARED IS A PROBLEM--
--STAKED?
HSSSSS

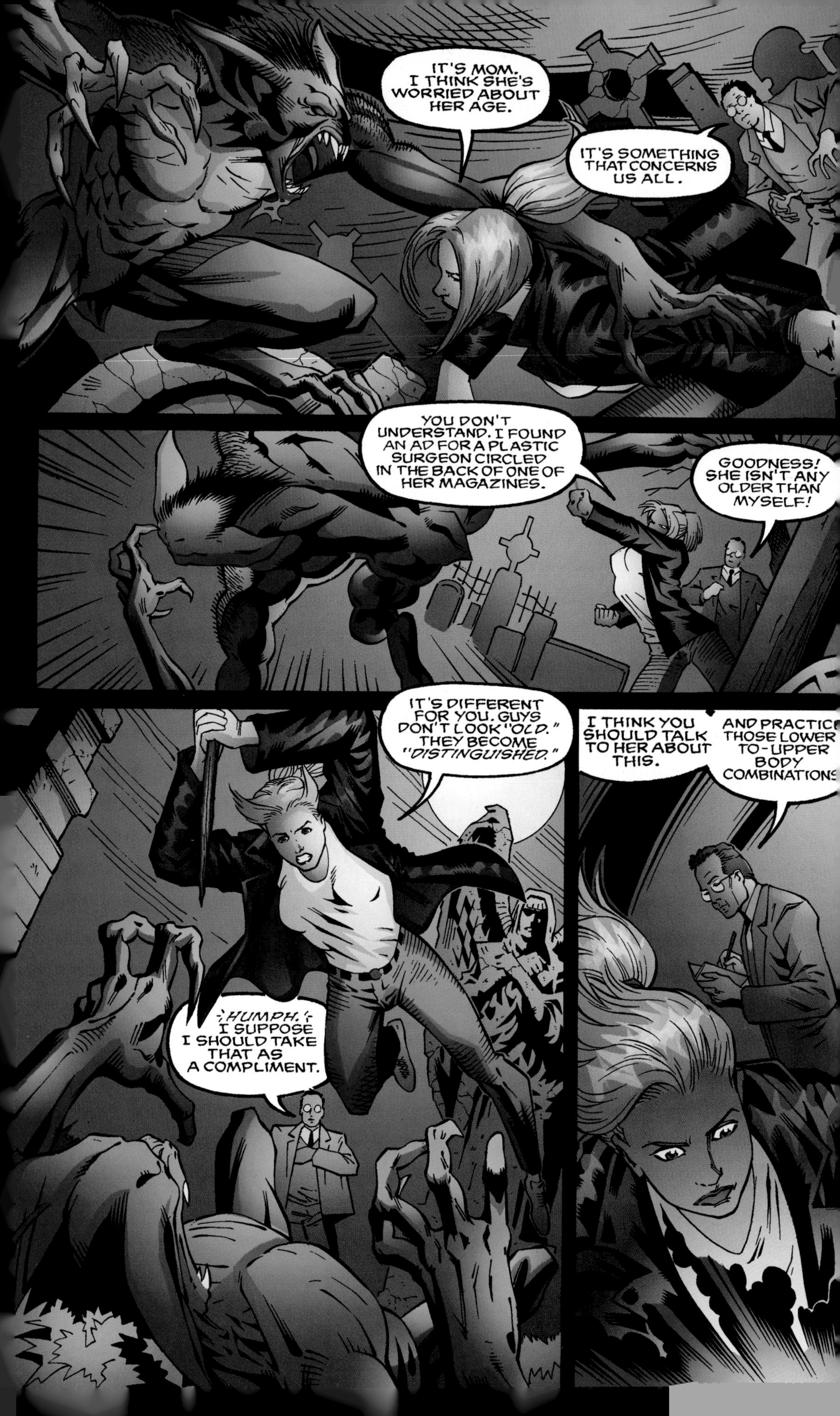
IT'S MOM. I THINK SHE'S WORRIED ABOUT HER AGE.
IT'S SOMETHING THAT CONCERNS US ALL.
YOU DON'T UNDERSTAND. I FOUND AN AD FOR A PLASTIC SURGEON CIRCLED IN THE BACK OF ONE OF HER MAGAZINES.
GOODNESS! SHE ISN'T ANY OLDER THAN MYSELF!
IT'S DIFFERENT FOR YOU. GUYS DON'T LOOK "OLD." THEY BECOME "DISTINGUISHED."
HUMPH. I SUPPOSE I SHOULD TAKE THAT AS A COMPLIMENT.
I THINK YOU SHOULD TALK TO HER ABOUT THIS.
AND PRACTIC THOSE LOWER TO-UPPER BODY COMBINATIONS

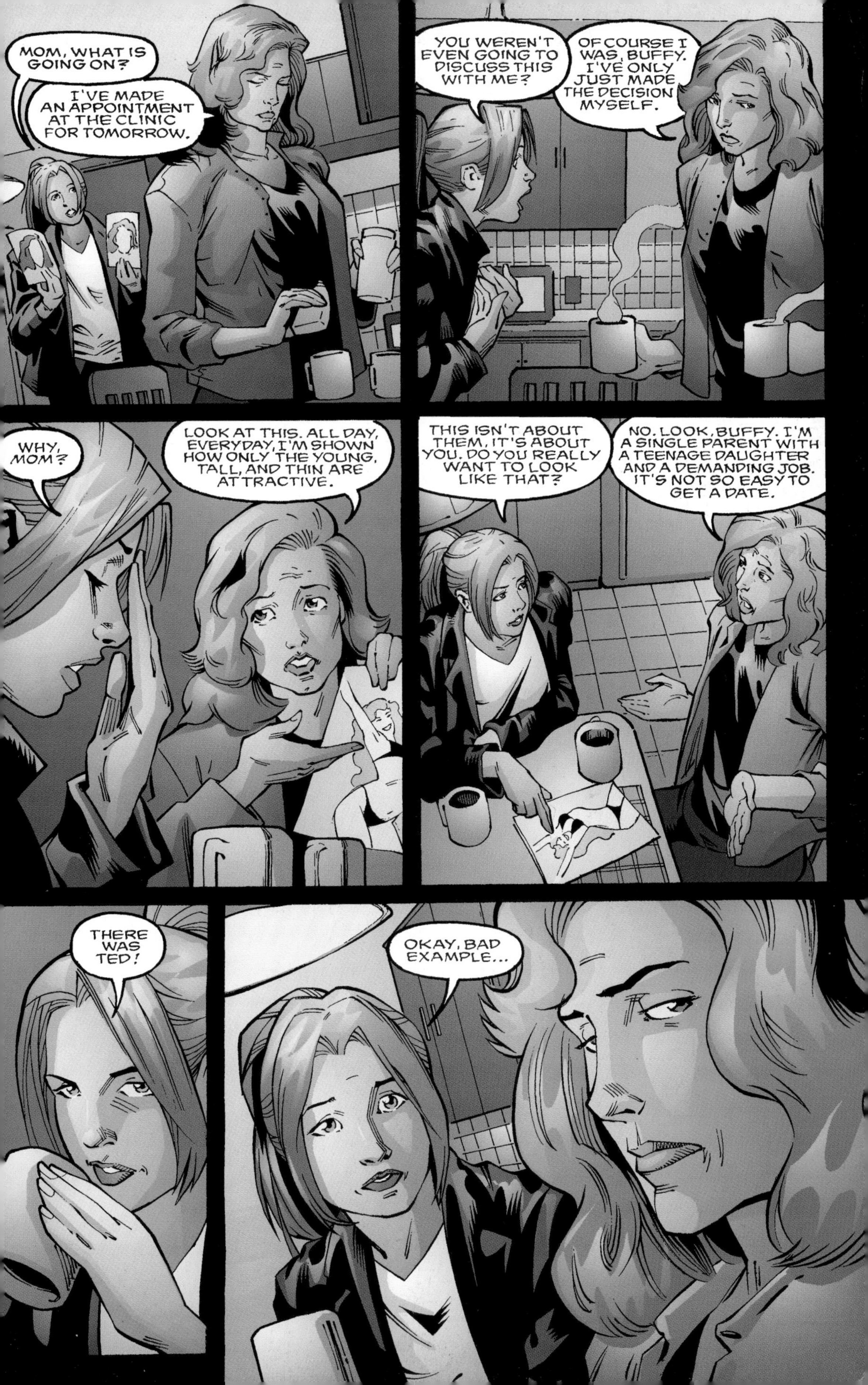
MOM, WHAT IS GOING ON?
I'VE MADE AN APPOINTMENT AT THE CLINIC FOR TOMORROW.
YOU WEREN'T EVEN GOING TO DISCUSS THIS WITH ME?
OF COURSE I WAS, BUFFY. I'VE ONLY JUST MADE THE DECISION MYSELF.
WHY, MOM?
LOOK AT THIS. ALL DAY, EVERYDAY, I'M SHOWN HOW ONLY THE YOUNG, TALL, AND THIN ARE ATTRACTIVE.
THIS ISN'T ABOUT THEM, IT'S ABOUT YOU. DO YOU REALLY WANT TO LOOK LIKE THAT?
NO. LOOK, BUFFY. I'M A SINGLE PARENT WITH A TEENAGE DAUGHTER AND A DEMANDING JOB. IT'S NOT SO EASY TO GET A DATE.
THERE WAS TED!
OKAY, BAD EXAMPLE...

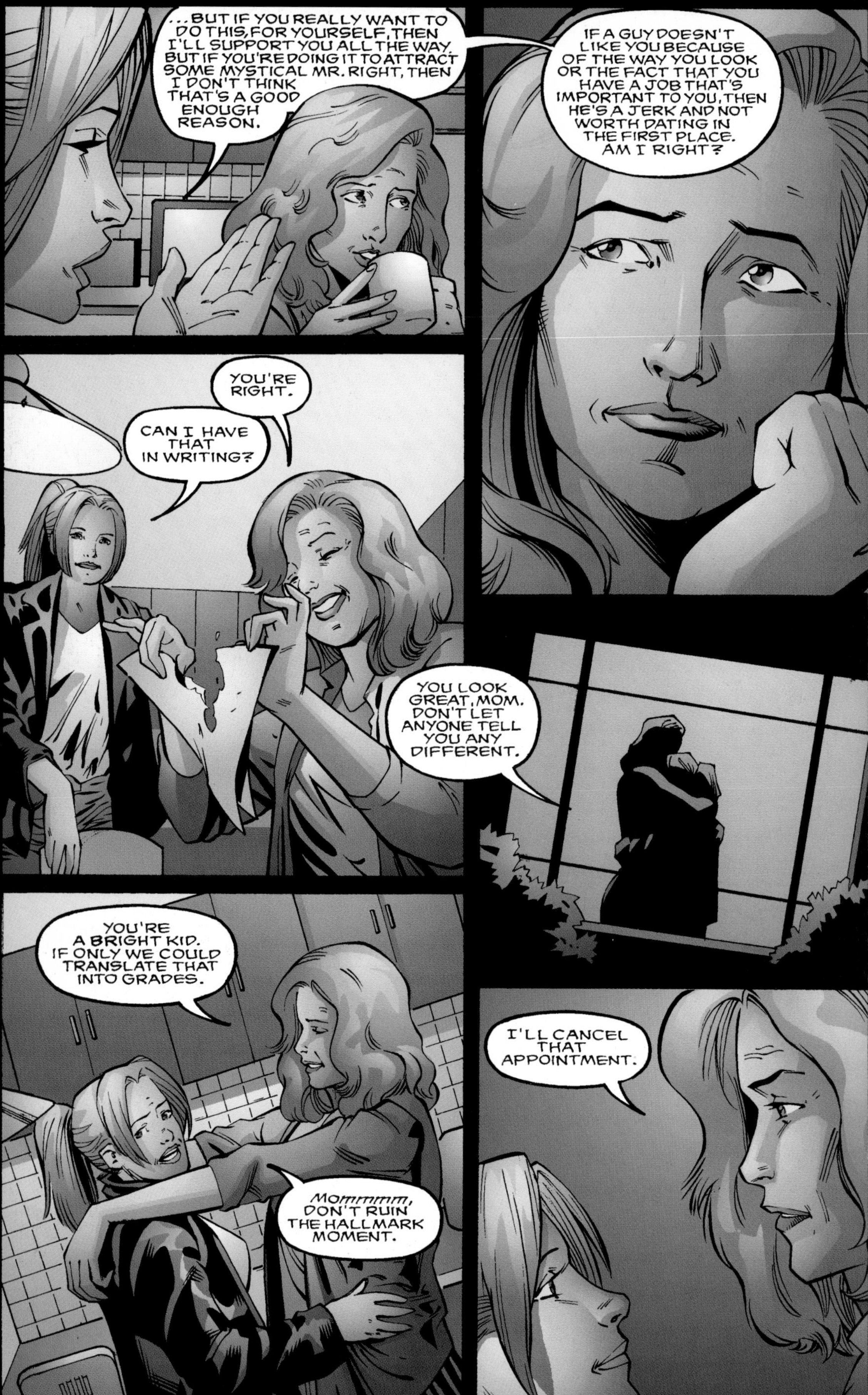
...BUT IF YOU REALLY WANT TO DO THIS, FOR YOURSELF, THEN I'LL SUPPORT YOU ALL THE WAY. BUT IF YOU'RE DOING IT TO ATTRACT SOME MYSTICAL MR. RIGHT, THEN I DON'T THINK THAT'S A GOOD ENOUGH REASON.
IF A GUY DOESN'T LIKE YOU BECAUSE OF THE WAY YOU LOOK OR THE FACT THAT YOU HAVE A JOB THAT'S IMPORTANT TO YOU, THEN HE'S A JERK AND NOT WORTH DATING IN THE FIRST PLACE. AM I RIGHT?
YOU'RE RIGHT.
CAN I HAVE THAT IN WRITING?
YOU LOOK GREAT, MOM. DON'T LET ANYONE TELL YOU ANY DIFFERENT.
YOU'RE A BRIGHT KID. IF ONLY WE COULD TRANSLATE THAT INTO GRADES.
Mommmmm, DON'T RUIN THE HALLMARK MOMENT.
I'LL CANCEL THAT APPOINTMENT.

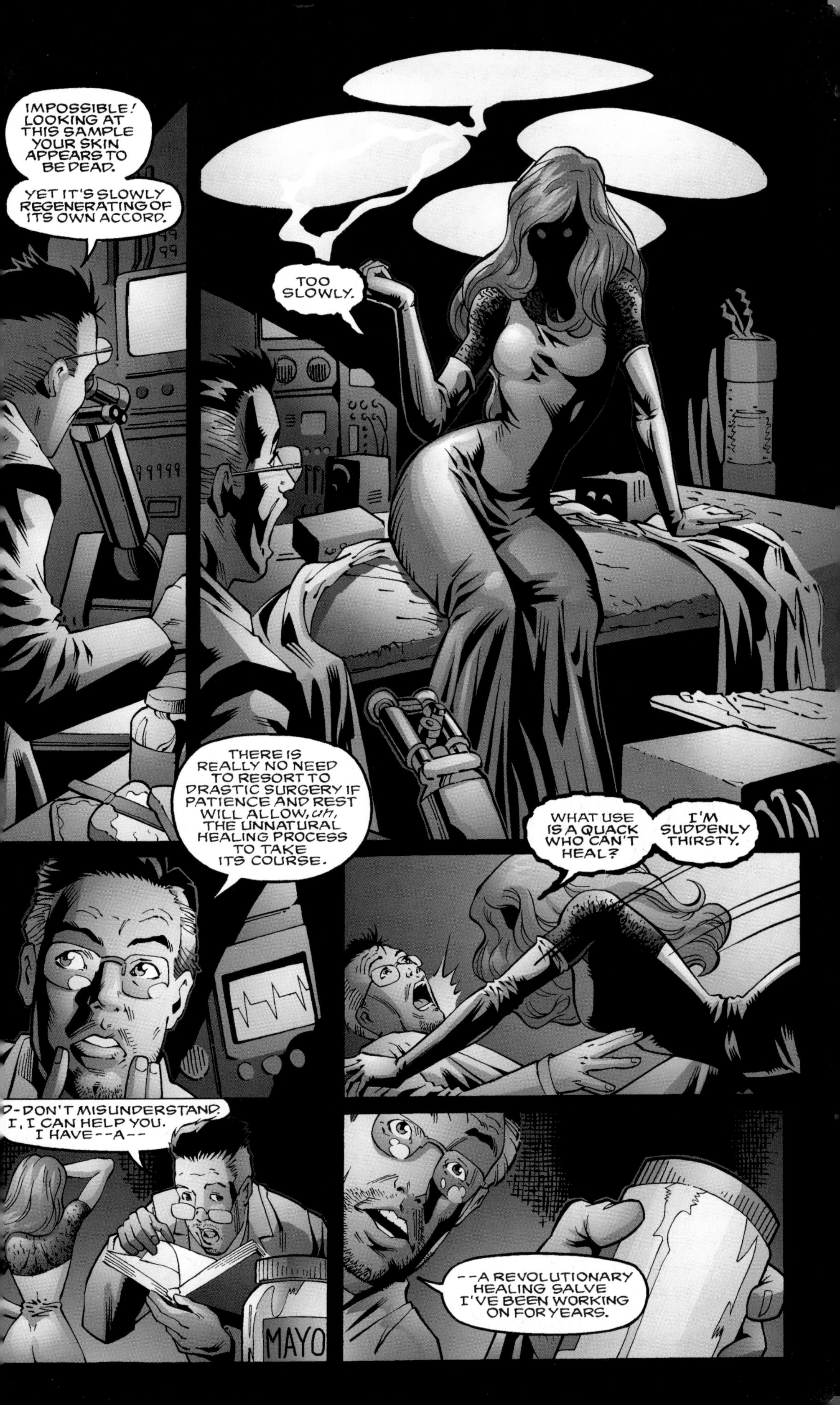

IMPOSSIBLE! LOOKING AT THIS SAMPLE YOUR SKIN APPEARS TO BE DEAD.
YET IT'S SLOWLY REGENERATING OF ITS OWN ACCORD.
TOO SLOWLY.
THERE IS REALLY NO NEED TO RESORT TO DRASTIC SURGERY IF PATIENCE AND REST WILL ALLOW, *uh*, THE UNNATURAL HEALING PROCESS TO TAKE ITS COURSE.
WHAT USE IS A QUACK WHO CAN'T HEAL?
I'M SUDDENLY THIRSTY.
D-DON'T MISUNDERSTAND. I, I CAN HELP YOU. I HAVE--A--
MAYO
--A REVOLUTIONARY HEALING SALVE I'VE BEEN WORKING ON FOR YEARS.

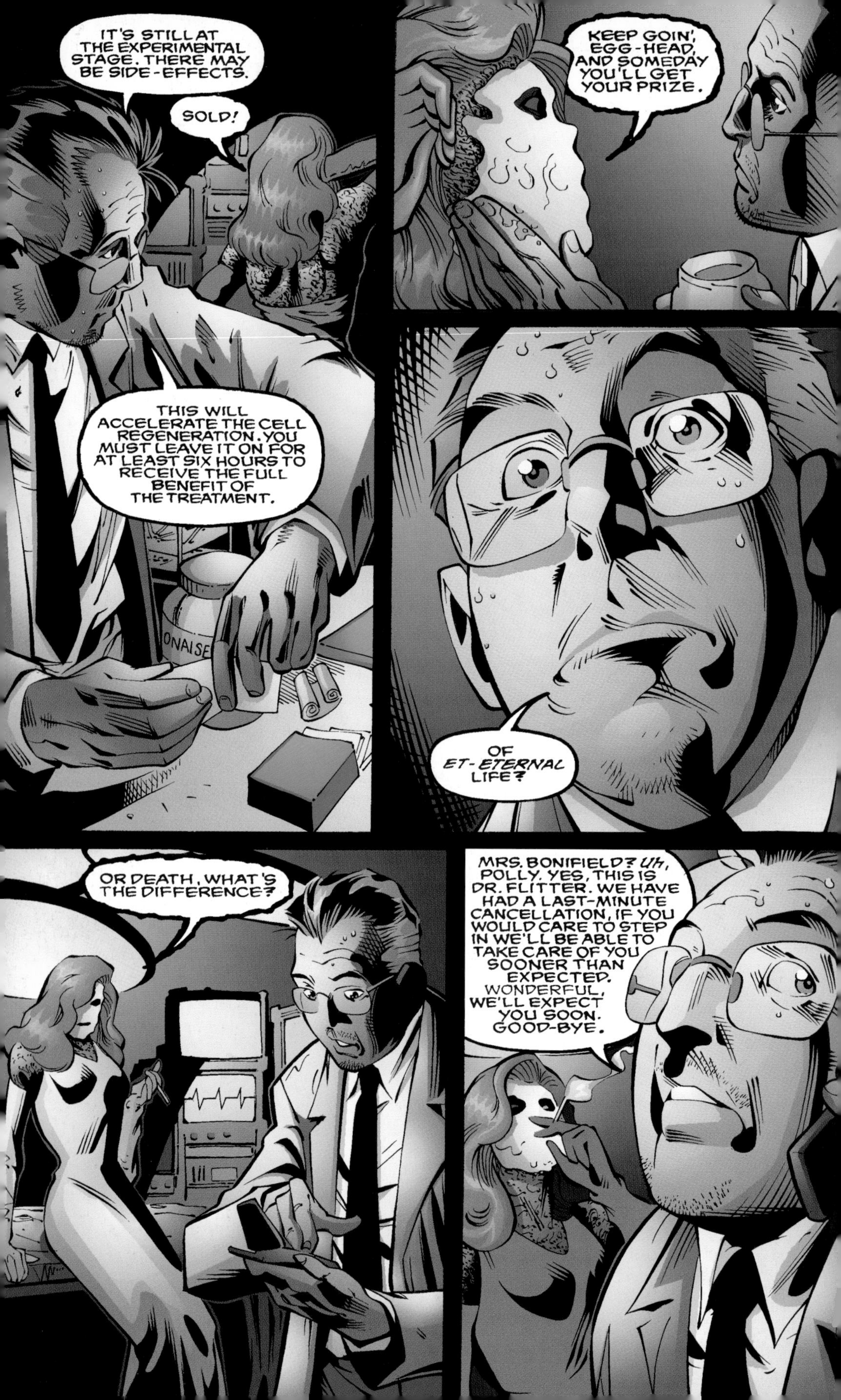
IT'S STILL AT THE EXPERIMENTAL STAGE. THERE MAY BE SIDE-EFFECTS.
SOLD!
KEEP GOIN', EGG-HEAD, AND SOMEDAY YOU'LL GET YOUR PRIZE.
THIS WILL ACCELERATE THE CELL REGENERATION. YOU MUST LEAVE IT ON FOR AT LEAST SIX HOURS TO RECEIVE THE FULL BENEFIT OF THE TREATMENT.
ONAISE
OF *ET-ETERNAL* LIFE?
OR DEATH, WHAT'S THE DIFFERENCE?
MRS. BONIFIELD? *UH*, POLLY. YES, THIS IS DR. FLITTER. WE HAVE HAD A LAST-MINUTE CANCELLATION, IF YOU WOULD CARE TO STEP IN WE'LL BE ABLE TO TAKE CARE OF YOU SOONER THAN EXPECTED. WONDERFUL, WE'LL EXPECT YOU SOON. GOOD-BYE.

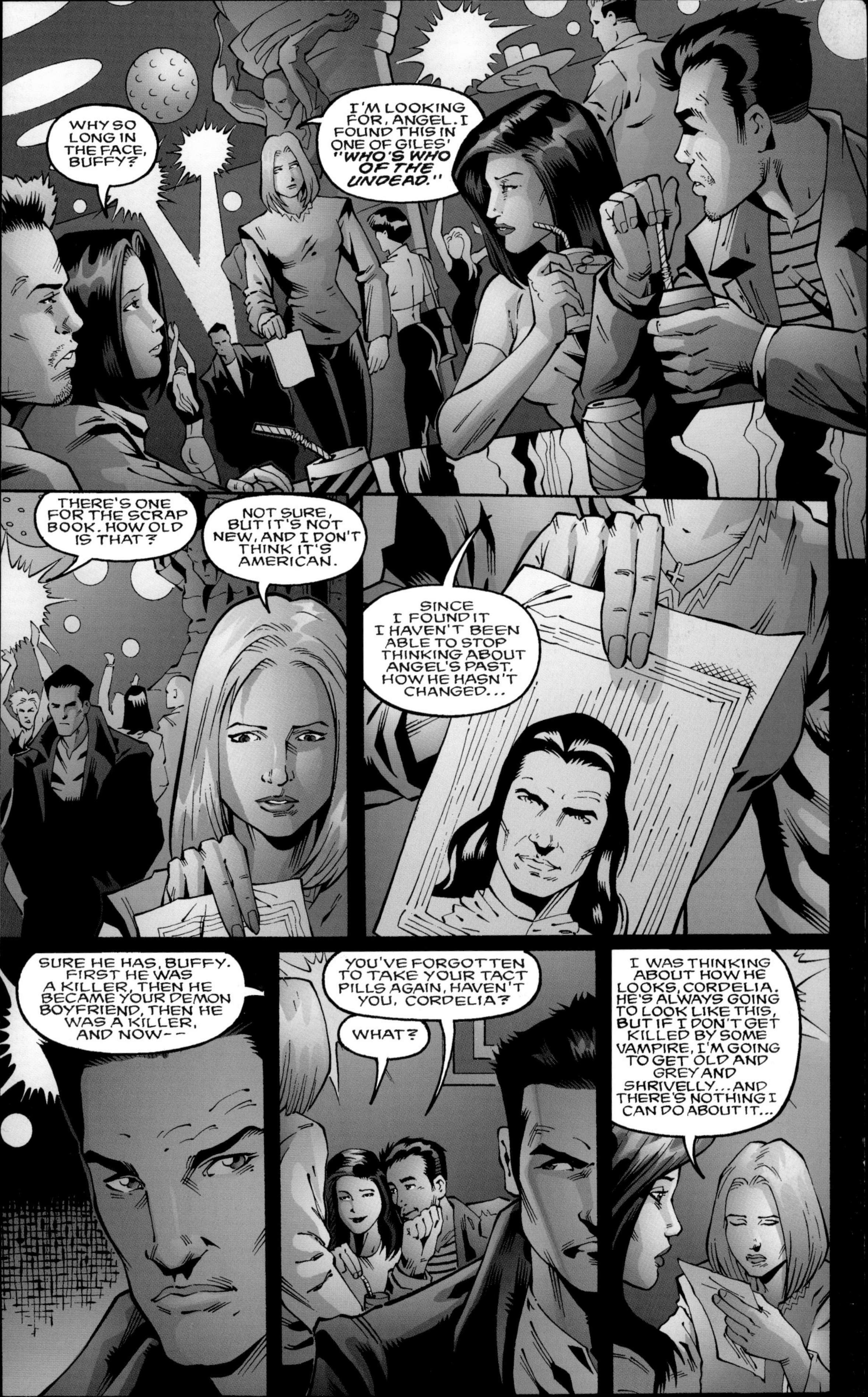
WHY SO LONG IN THE FACE, BUFFY?
I'M LOOKING FOR, ANGEL. I FOUND THIS IN ONE OF GILES' "WHO'S WHO OF THE UNDEAD."
THERE'S ONE FOR THE SCRAP BOOK. HOW OLD IS THAT?
NOT SURE, BUT IT'S NOT NEW, AND I DON'T THINK IT'S AMERICAN.
SINCE I FOUND IT I HAVEN'T BEEN ABLE TO STOP THINKING ABOUT ANGEL'S PAST, HOW HE HASN'T CHANGED...
SURE HE HAS, BUFFY. FIRST HE WAS A KILLER, THEN HE BECAME YOUR DEMON BOYFRIEND, THEN HE WAS A KILLER, AND NOW--
YOU'VE FORGOTTEN TO TAKE YOUR TACT PILLS AGAIN, HAVEN'T YOU, CORDELIA?
WHAT?
I WAS THINKING ABOUT HOW HE LOOKS, CORDELIA. HE'S ALWAYS GOING TO LOOK LIKE THIS, BUT IF I DON'T GET KILLED BY SOME VAMPIRE, I'M GOING TO GET OLD AND GREY AND SHRIVELLY... AND THERE'S NOTHING I CAN DO ABOUT IT...

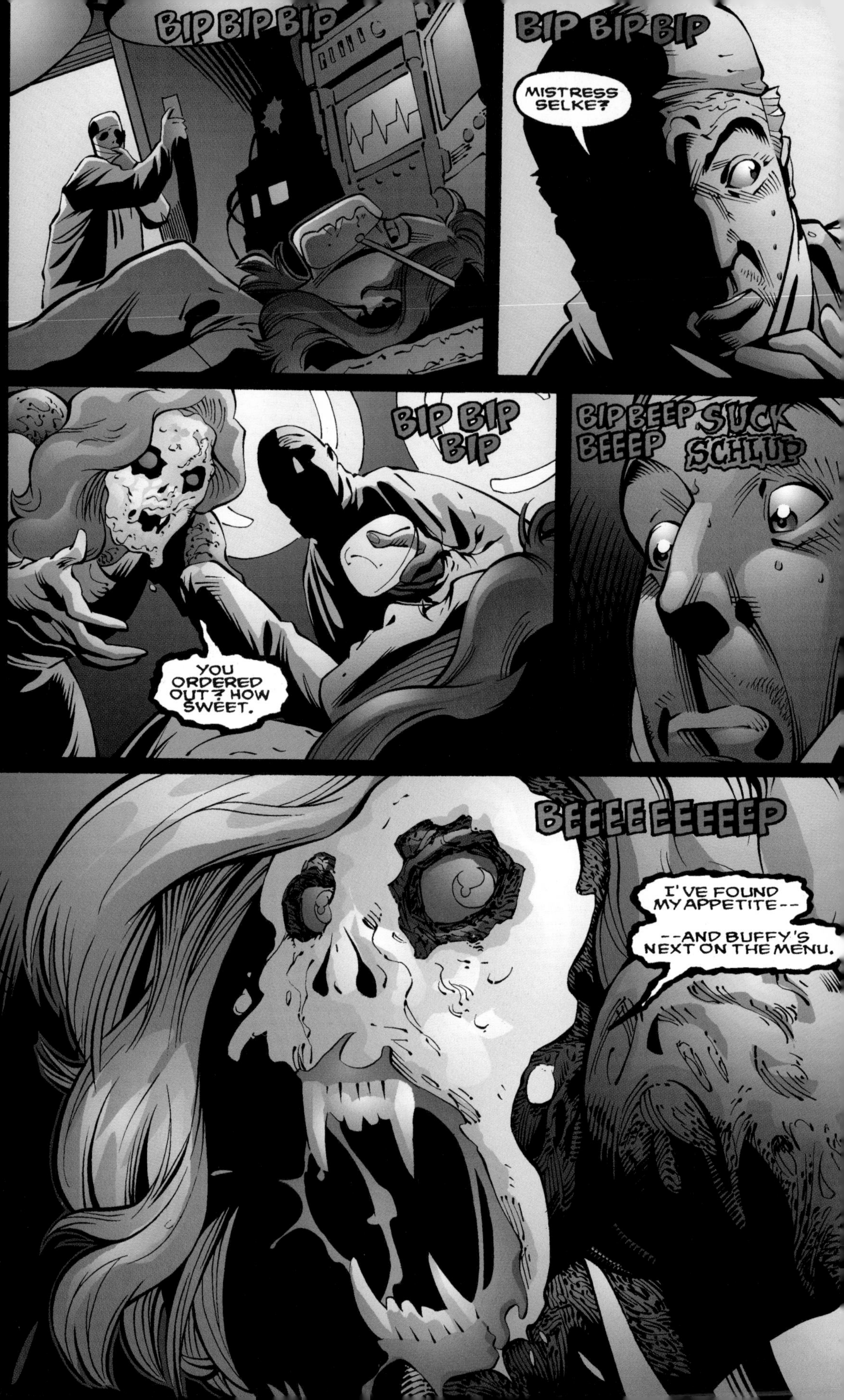
BIP BIP BIP
BIP BIP BIP
MISTRESS SELKE?
BIP BIP BIP
YOU ORDERED OUT? HOW SWEET.
BIP BEEP BEEEP
SUCK SCHLUP
BEEEE EEEEEP
I'VE FOUND MY APPETITE--
--AND BUFFY'S NEXT ON THE MENU.

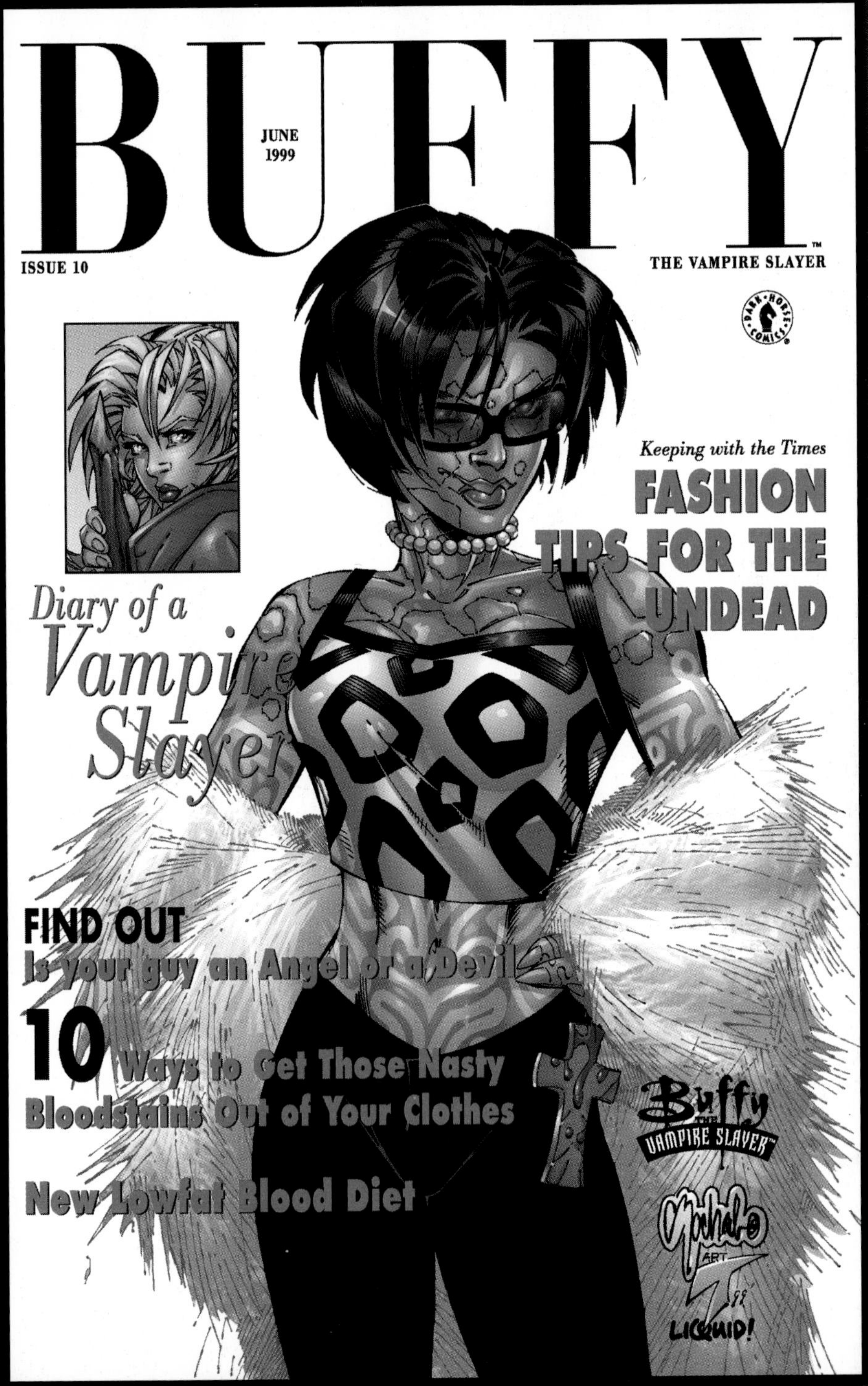
BUFFY
JUNE
1999
ISSUE 10
THE VAMPIRE SLAYER
Keeping with the Times
FASHION TIPS FOR THE UNDEAD
Diary of a Vampire Slayer
FIND OUT
Is your guy an Angel or a Devil
10 Ways to Get Those Nasty Bloodstains Out of Your Clothes
New Lowfat Blood Diet
Buffy the Vampire Slayer
LIQUID!

Art by CHRIS BACHALO *and* ART THIBERT
Colors by LIQUID!
Text layout by KRISTEN BURDA

HEY, GOOD LOOKIN'

PART II

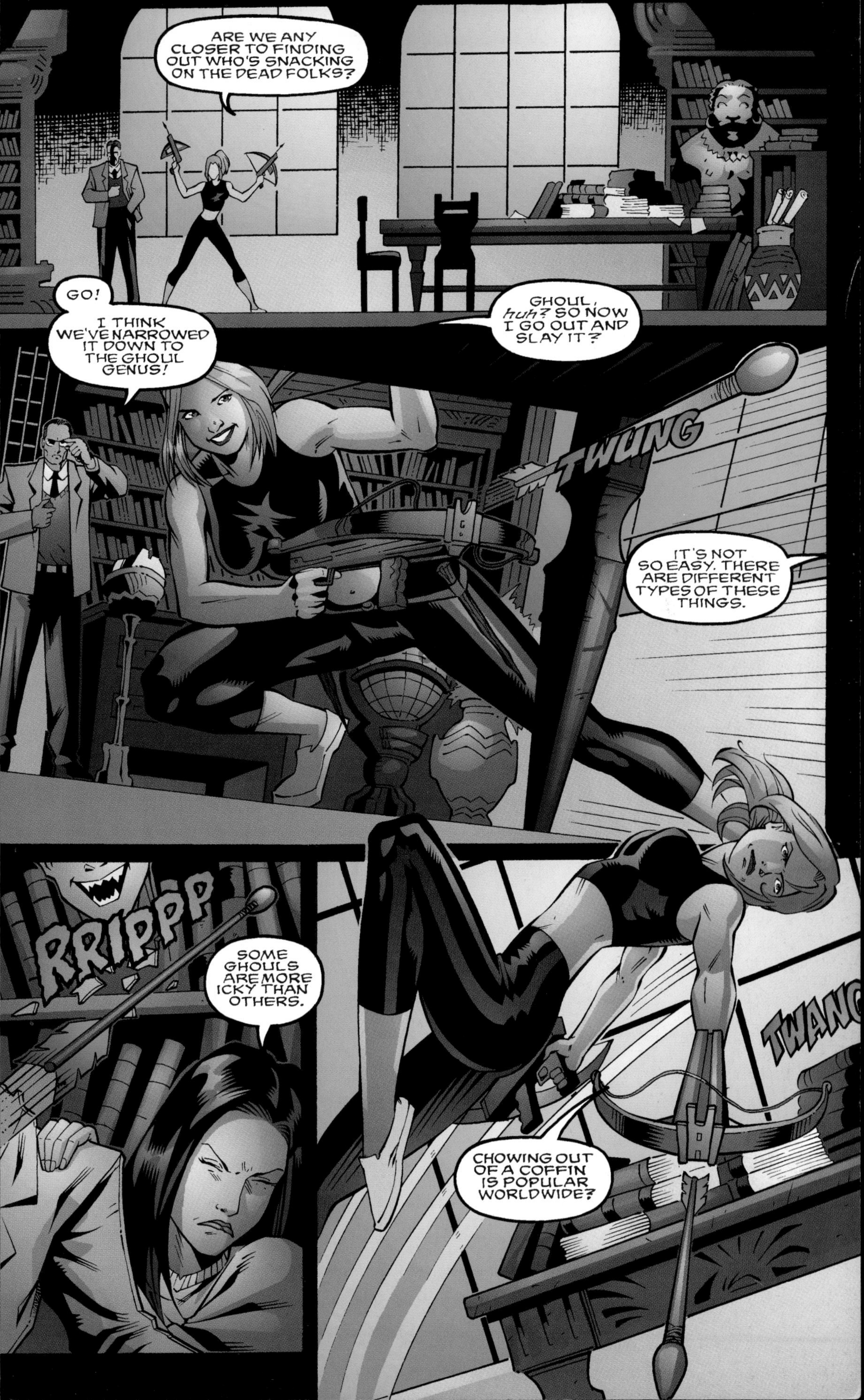
ARE WE ANY CLOSER TO FINDING OUT WHO'S SNACKING ON THE DEAD FOLKS?
GO!
I THINK WE'VE NARROWED IT DOWN TO THE GHOUL GENUS!
GHOUL, *huh?* SO NOW I GO OUT AND SLAY IT?
TWUNG
IT'S NOT SO EASY. THERE ARE DIFFERENT TYPES OF THESE THINGS.
RRIPPP
SOME GHOULS ARE MORE ICKY THAN OTHERS.
TWANG
CHOWING OUT OF A COFFIN IS POPULAR WORLDWIDE?

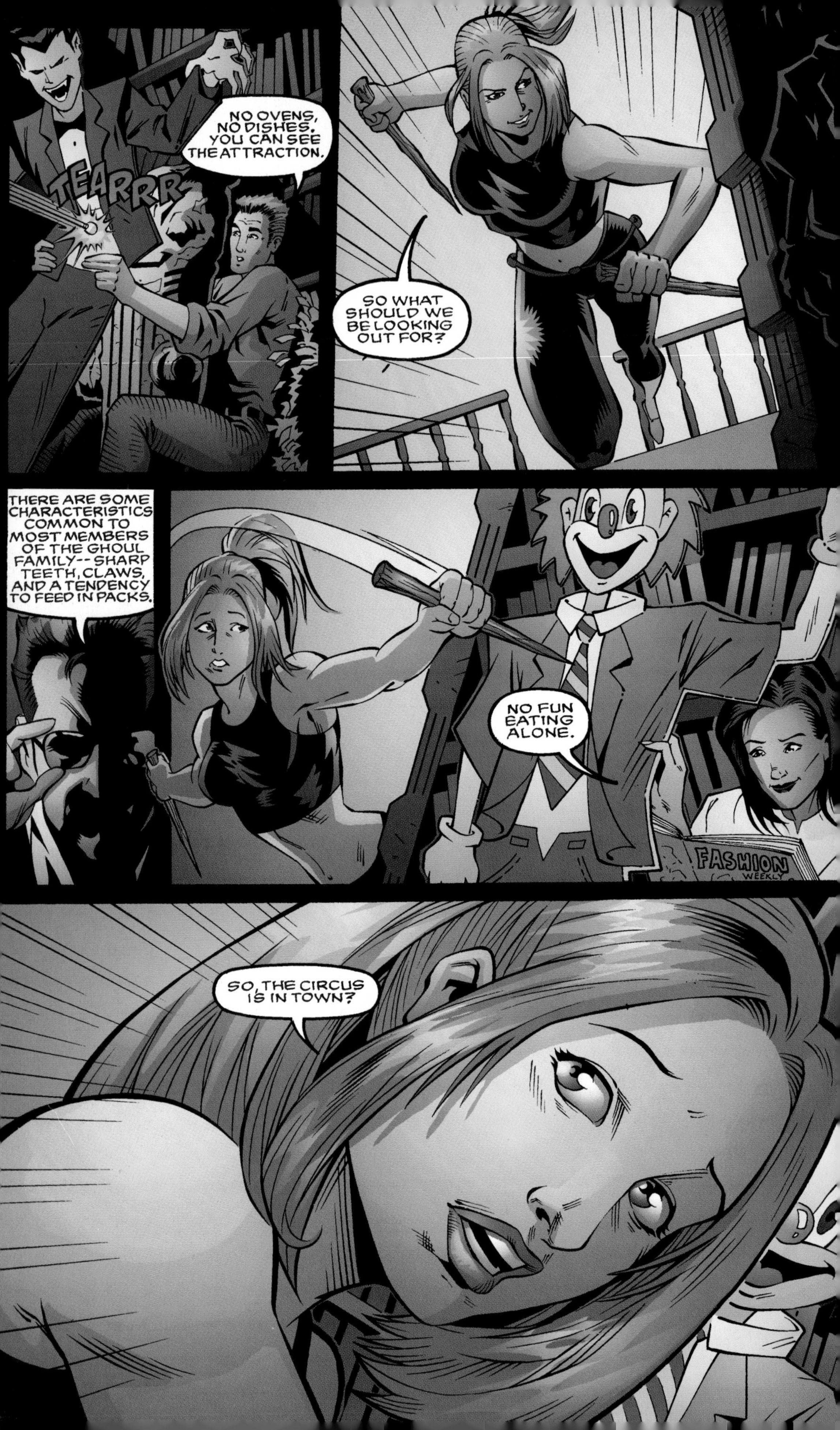
NO OVENS, NO DISHES. YOU CAN SEE THE ATTRACTION.
TEARRR
SO WHAT SHOULD WE BE LOOKING OUT FOR?
THERE ARE SOME CHARACTERISTICS COMMON TO MOST MEMBERS OF THE GHOUL FAMILY-- SHARP TEETH, CLAWS, AND A TENDENCY TO FEED IN PACKS.
NO FUN EATING ALONE.
FASHION WEEKLY
SO, THE CIRCUS IS IN TOWN?

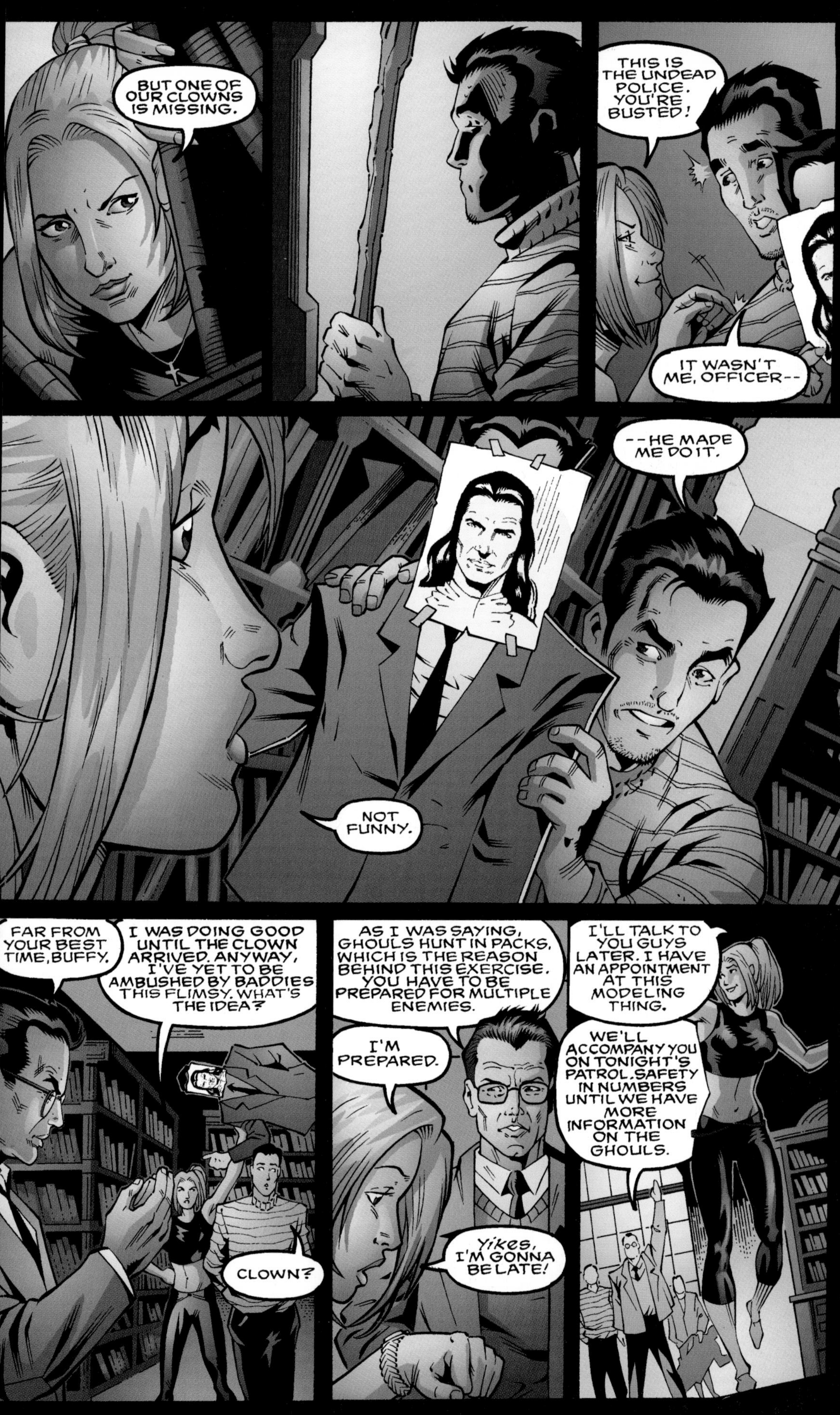
BUT ONE OF OUR CLOWNS IS MISSING.
THIS IS THE UNDEAD POLICE. YOU'RE BUSTED!
IT WASN'T ME, OFFICER--
--HE MADE ME DO IT.
NOT FUNNY.
FAR FROM YOUR BEST TIME, BUFFY.
I WAS DOING GOOD UNTIL THE CLOWN ARRIVED. ANYWAY, I'VE YET TO BE AMBUSHED BY BADDIES THIS FLIMSY. WHAT'S THE IDEA?
CLOWN?
AS I WAS SAYING, GHOULS HUNT IN PACKS, WHICH IS THE REASON BEHIND THIS EXERCISE. YOU HAVE TO BE PREPARED FOR MULTIPLE ENEMIES.
I'M PREPARED.
YIKES, I'M GONNA BE LATE!
I'LL TALK TO YOU GUYS LATER. I HAVE AN APPOINTMENT AT THIS MODELING THING.
WE'LL ACCOMPANY YOU ON TONIGHT'S PATROL, SAFETY IN NUMBERS UNTIL WE HAVE MORE INFORMATION ON THE GHOULS.

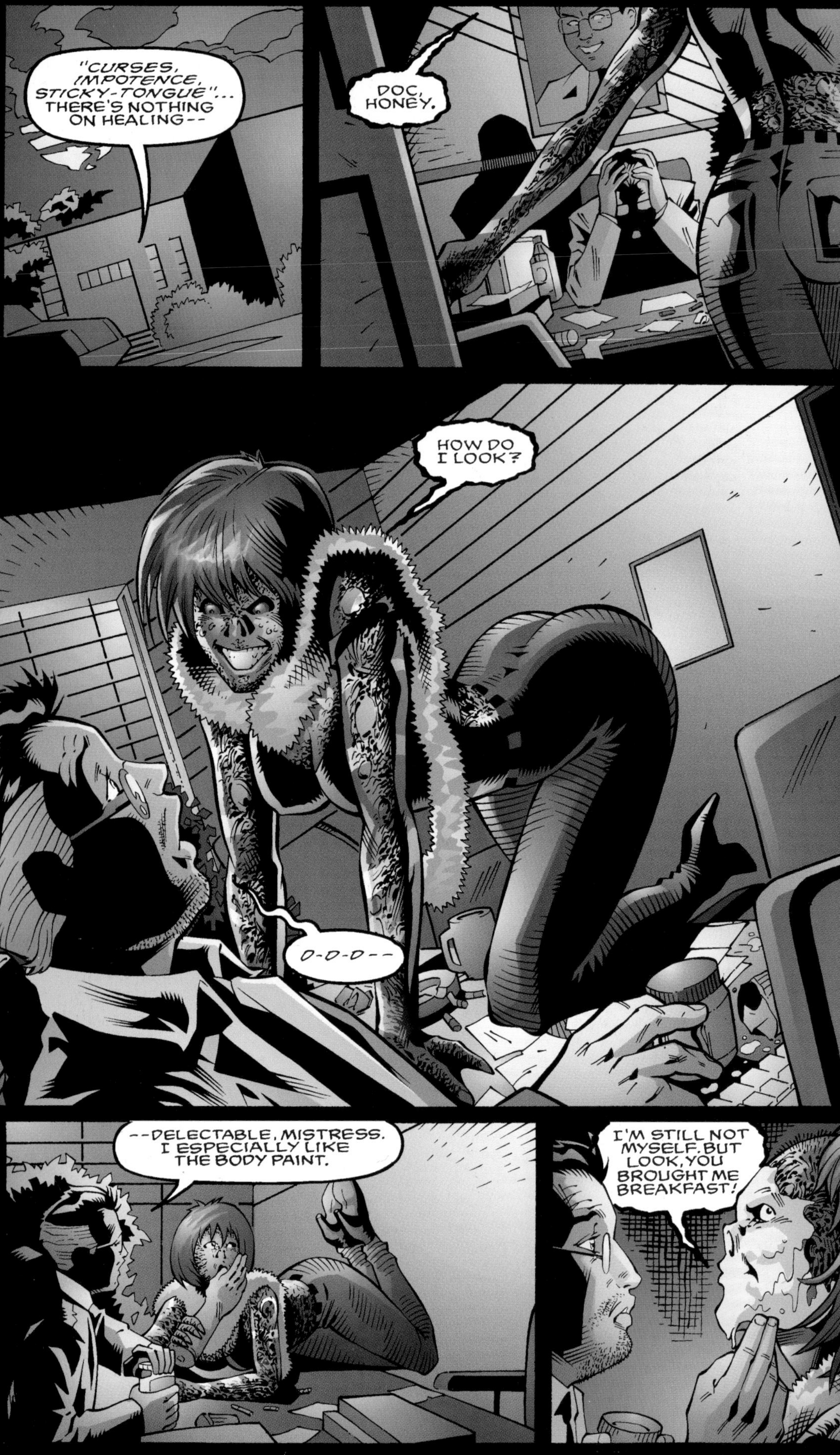
"CURSES, IMPOTENCE, STICKY-TONGUE"... THERE'S NOTHING ON HEALING--
DOC, HONEY.
HOW DO I LOOK?
O-O-O--
--DELECTABLE, MISTRESS. I ESPECIALLY LIKE THE BODY PAINT.
I'M STILL NOT MYSELF. BUT LOOK, YOU BROUGHT ME BREAKFAST!

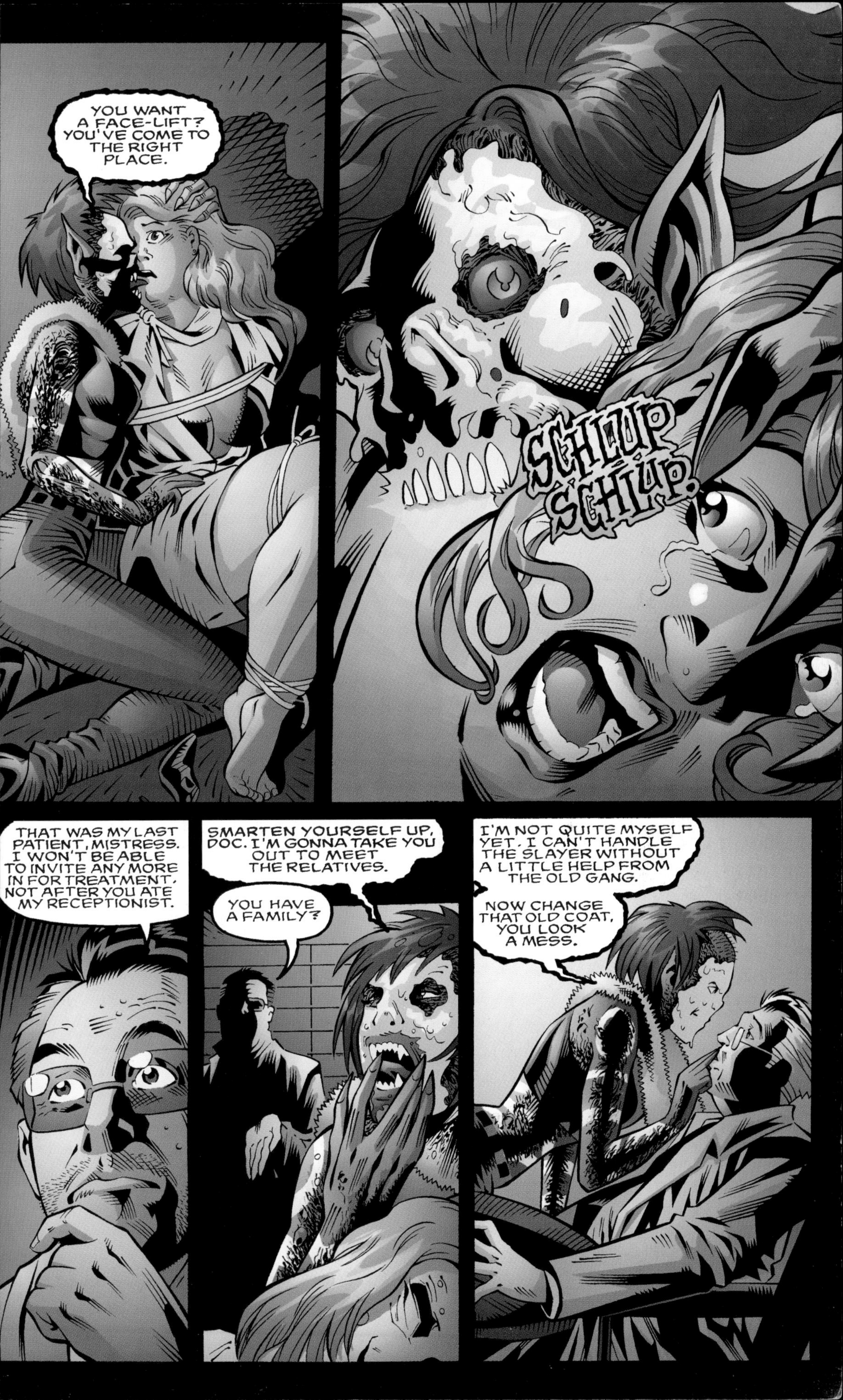
YOU WANT A FACE-LIFT? YOU'VE COME TO THE RIGHT PLACE.
SCHLUP SCHLUP.
THAT WAS MY LAST PATIENT, MISTRESS. I WON'T BE ABLE TO INVITE ANY MORE IN FOR TREATMENT, NOT AFTER YOU ATE MY RECEPTIONIST.
SMARTEN YOURSELF UP, DOC. I'M GONNA TAKE YOU OUT TO MEET THE RELATIVES.
YOU HAVE A FAMILY?
I'M NOT QUITE MYSELF YET. I CAN'T HANDLE THE SLAYER WITHOUT A LITTLE HELP FROM THE OLD GANG.
NOW CHANGE THAT OLD COAT, YOU LOOK A MESS.

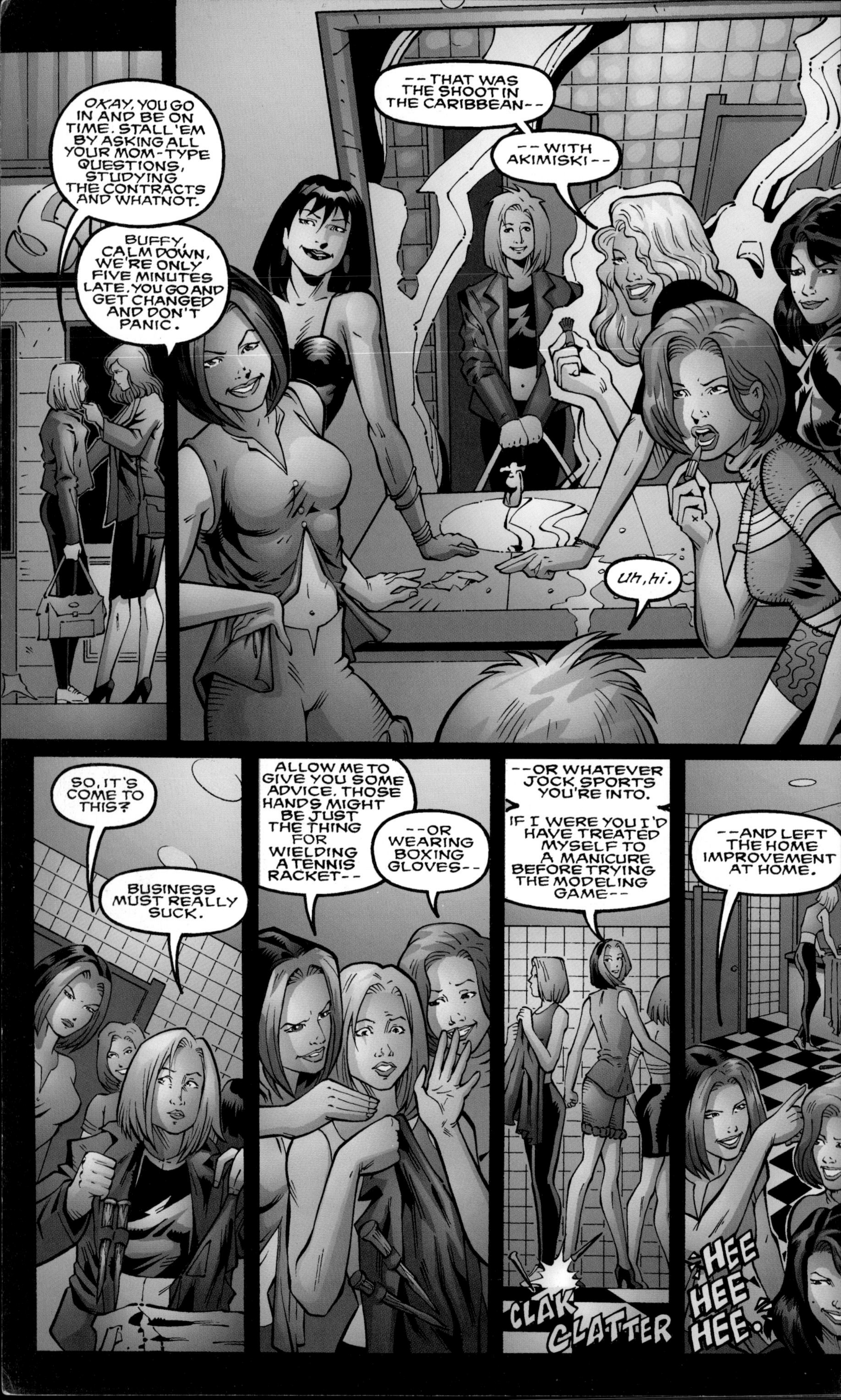
OKAY, YOU GO IN AND BE ON TIME. STALL'EM BY ASKING ALL YOUR MOM-TYPE QUESTIONS, STUDYING THE CONTRACTS AND WHATNOT.
BUFFY, CALM DOWN, WE'RE ONLY FIVE MINUTES LATE. YOU GO AND GET CHANGED AND DON'T PANIC.
--THAT WAS THE SHOOT IN THE CARIBBEAN--
--WITH AKIMISKI--
Uh, hi.
SO, IT'S COME TO THIS?
BUSINESS MUST REALLY SUCK.
ALLOW ME TO GIVE YOU SOME ADVICE. THOSE HANDS MIGHT BE JUST THE THING FOR WIELDING A TENNIS RACKET--
--OR WEARING BOXING GLOVES--
--OR WHATEVER JOCK SPORTS YOU'RE INTO.
IF I WERE YOU I'D HAVE TREATED MYSELF TO A MANICURE BEFORE TRYING THE MODELING GAME--
CLAK
CLATTER
--AND LEFT THE HOME IMPROVEMENT AT HOME.
HEE HEE HEE.

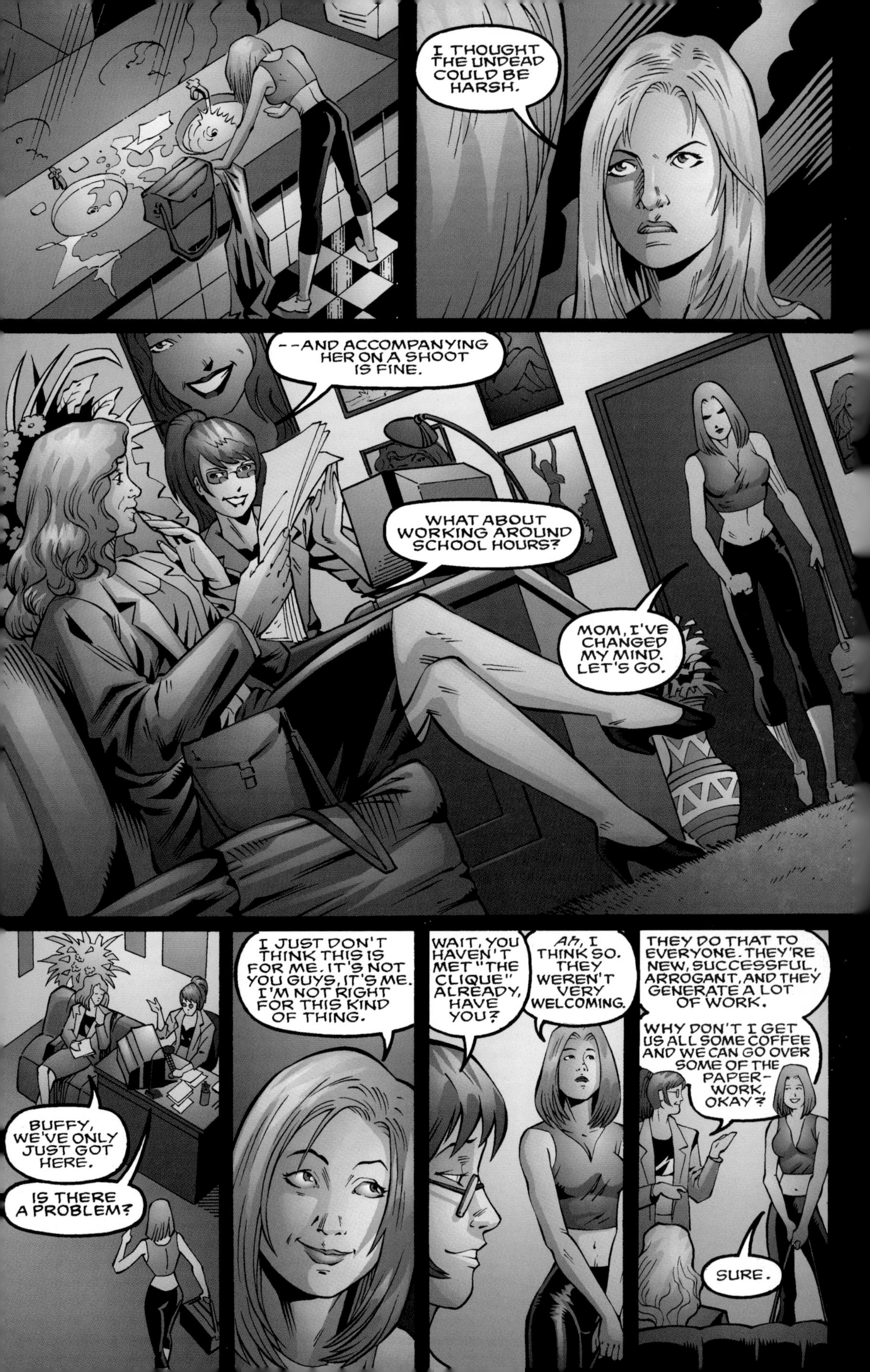
I THOUGHT THE UNDEAD COULD BE HARSH.
--AND ACCOMPANYING HER ON A SHOOT IS FINE.
WHAT ABOUT WORKING AROUND SCHOOL HOURS?
MOM, I'VE CHANGED MY MIND. LET'S GO.
BUFFY, WE'VE ONLY JUST GOT HERE.
IS THERE A PROBLEM?
I JUST DON'T THINK THIS IS FOR ME. IT'S NOT YOU GUYS, IT'S ME. I'M NOT RIGHT FOR THIS KIND OF THING.
WAIT, YOU HAVEN'T MET "THE CLIQUE" ALREADY, HAVE YOU?
Ah, I THINK SO. THEY WEREN'T VERY WELCOMING.
THEY DO THAT TO EVERYONE. THEY'RE NEW, SUCCESSFUL, ARROGANT, AND THEY GENERATE A LOT OF WORK.
WHY DON'T I GET US ALL SOME COFFEE AND WE CAN GO OVER SOME OF THE PAPER-WORK, OKAY?
SURE.

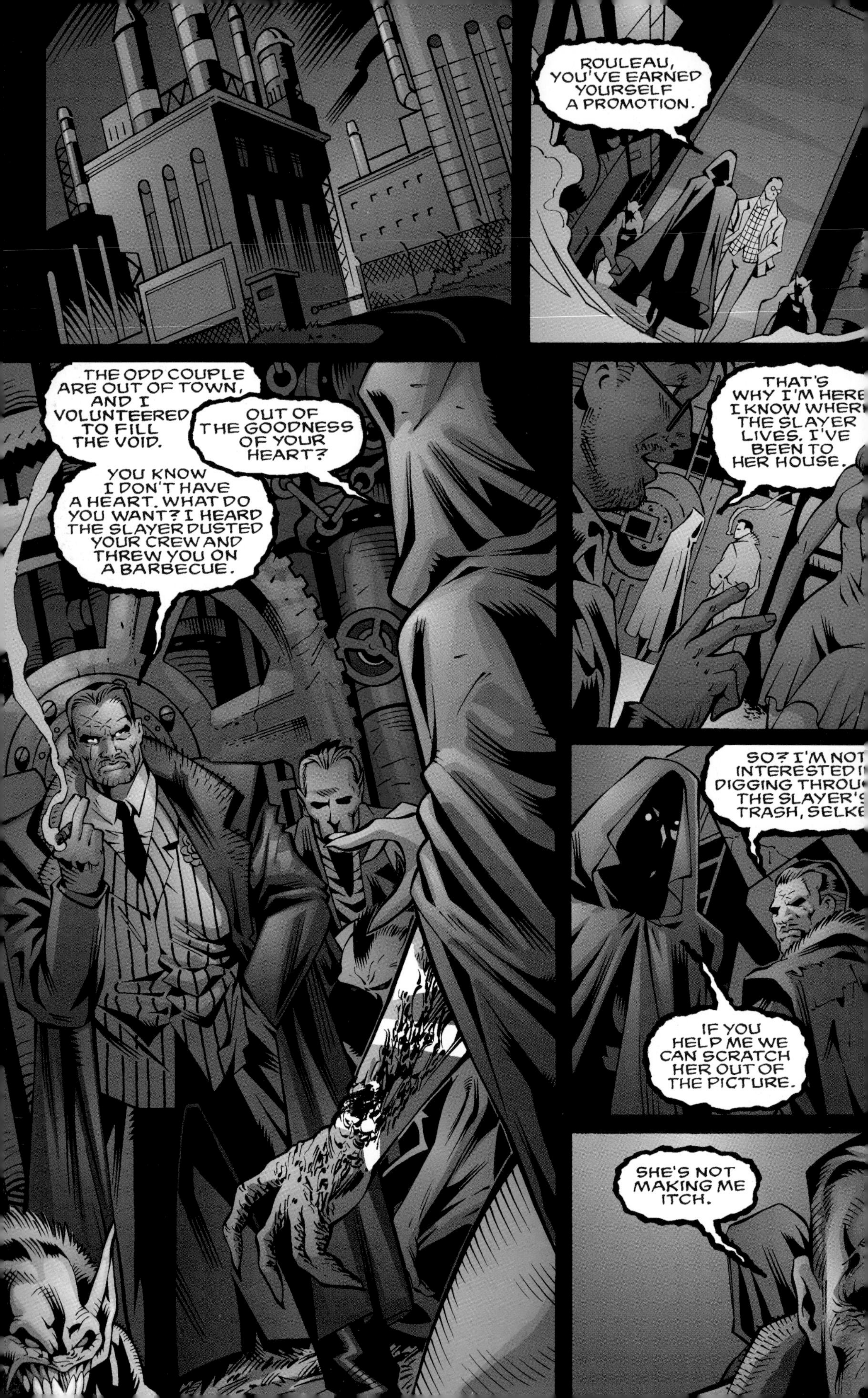
ROULEAU, YOU'VE EARNED YOURSELF A PROMOTION.
THE ODD COUPLE ARE OUT OF TOWN, AND I VOLUNTEERED TO FILL THE VOID.
OUT OF THE GOODNESS OF YOUR HEART?
YOU KNOW I DON'T HAVE A HEART. WHAT DO YOU WANT? I HEARD THE SLAYER DUSTED YOUR CREW AND THREW YOU ON A BARBECUE.
THAT'S WHY I'M HERE. I KNOW WHERE THE SLAYER LIVES. I'VE BEEN TO HER HOUSE.
SO? I'M NOT INTERESTED IN DIGGING THROUGH THE SLAYER'S TRASH, SELKE
IF YOU HELP ME WE CAN SCRATCH HER OUT OF THE PICTURE.
SHE'S NOT MAKING ME ITCH.

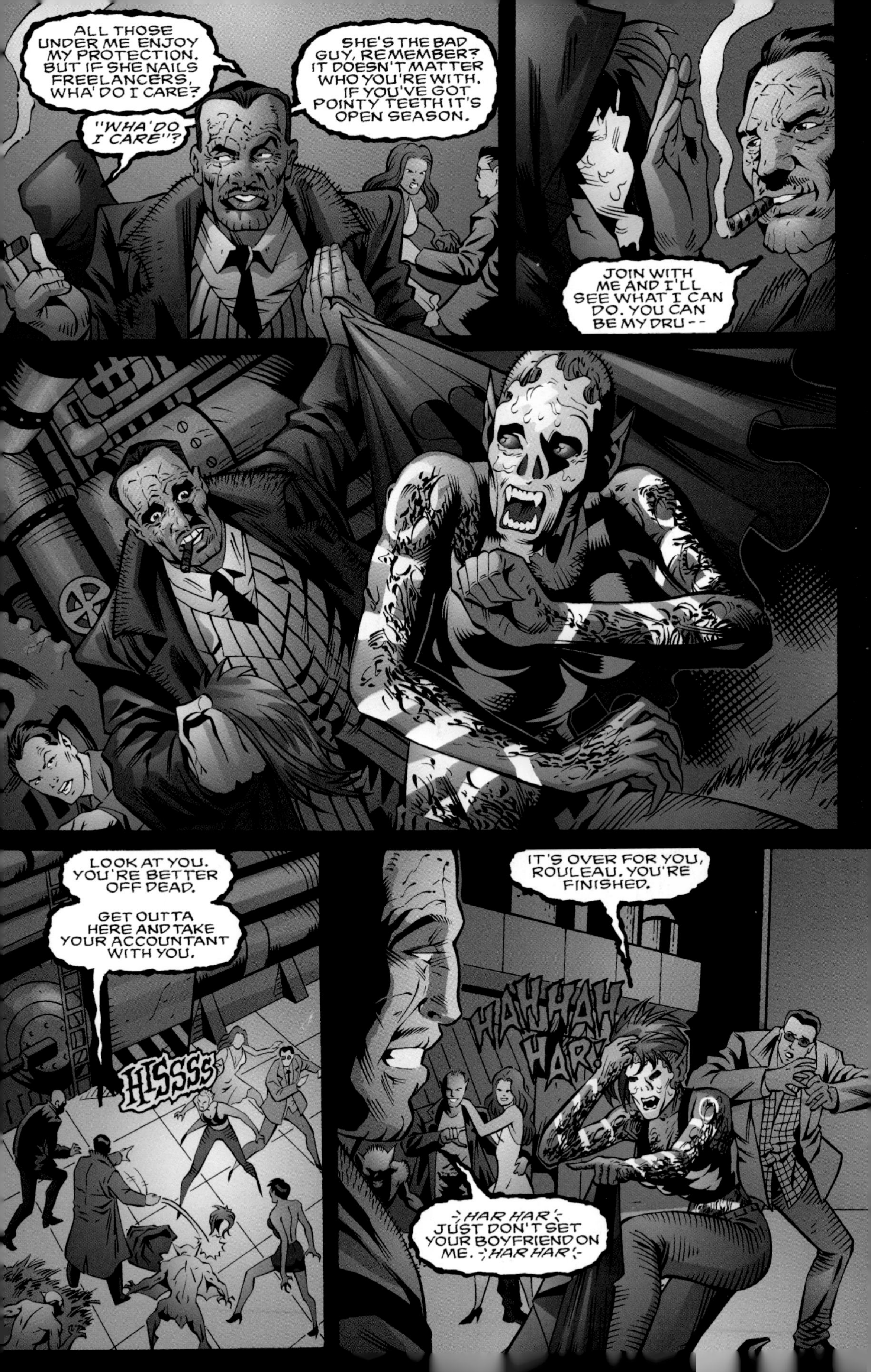
ALL THOSE UNDER ME ENJOY MY PROTECTION. BUT IF SHE NAILS FREELANCERS, WHA' DO I CARE?
"WHA'DO I CARE"?
SHE'S THE BAD GUY, REMEMBER? IT DOESN'T MATTER WHO YOU'RE WITH. IF YOU'VE GOT POINTY TEETH IT'S OPEN SEASON.
JOIN WITH ME AND I'LL SEE WHAT I CAN DO. YOU CAN BE MY DRU--
LOOK AT YOU. YOU'RE BETTER OFF DEAD.
GET OUTTA HERE AND TAKE YOUR ACCOUNTANT WITH YOU.
HISSSS
IT'S OVER FOR YOU, ROULEAU. YOU'RE FINISHED.
HAHHAH HAR!
HAR HAR JUST DON'T SET YOUR BOYFRIEND ON ME. HAR HAR

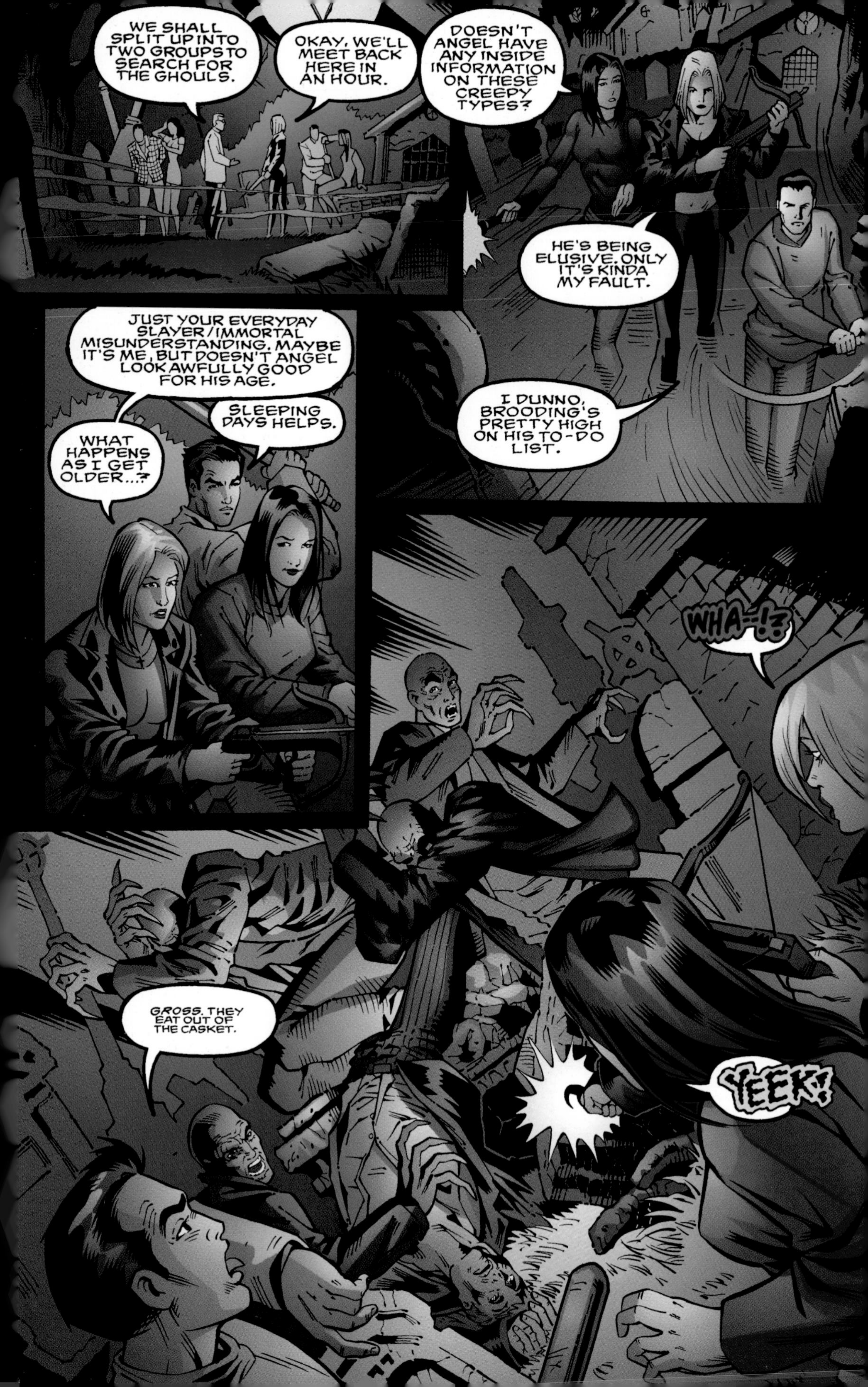
WE SHALL SPLIT UP INTO TWO GROUPS TO SEARCH FOR THE GHOULS.
OKAY, WE'LL MEET BACK HERE IN AN HOUR.
DOESN'T ANGEL HAVE ANY INSIDE INFORMATION ON THESE CREEPY TYPES?
HE'S BEING ELUSIVE. ONLY IT'S KINDA MY FAULT.
I DUNNO, BROODING'S PRETTY HIGH ON HIS TO-DO LIST.
JUST YOUR EVERYDAY SLAYER/IMMORTAL MISUNDERSTANDING. MAYBE IT'S ME, BUT DOESN'T ANGEL LOOK AWFULLY GOOD FOR HIS AGE.
SLEEPING DAYS HELPS.
WHAT HAPPENS AS I GET OLDER...?
WHA-!?
GROSS. THEY EAT OUT OF THE CASKET.
YEEK!

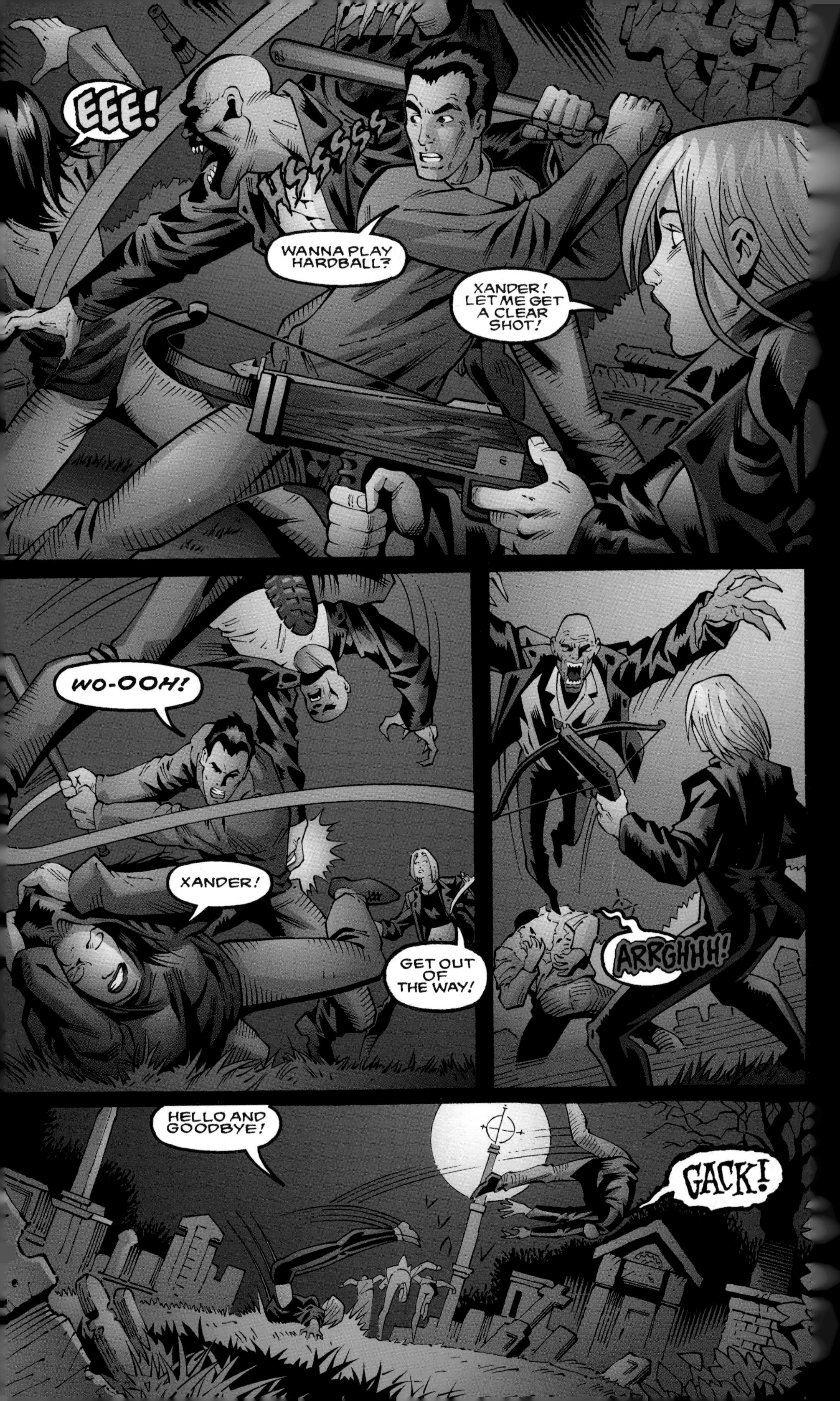
EEE!
HSSSSSS
WANNA PLAY HARDBALL?
XANDER! LET ME GET A CLEAR SHOT!
WO-OOH!
XANDER!
GET OUT OF THE WAY!
ARRGHHH!
HELLO AND GOODBYE!
GACK!

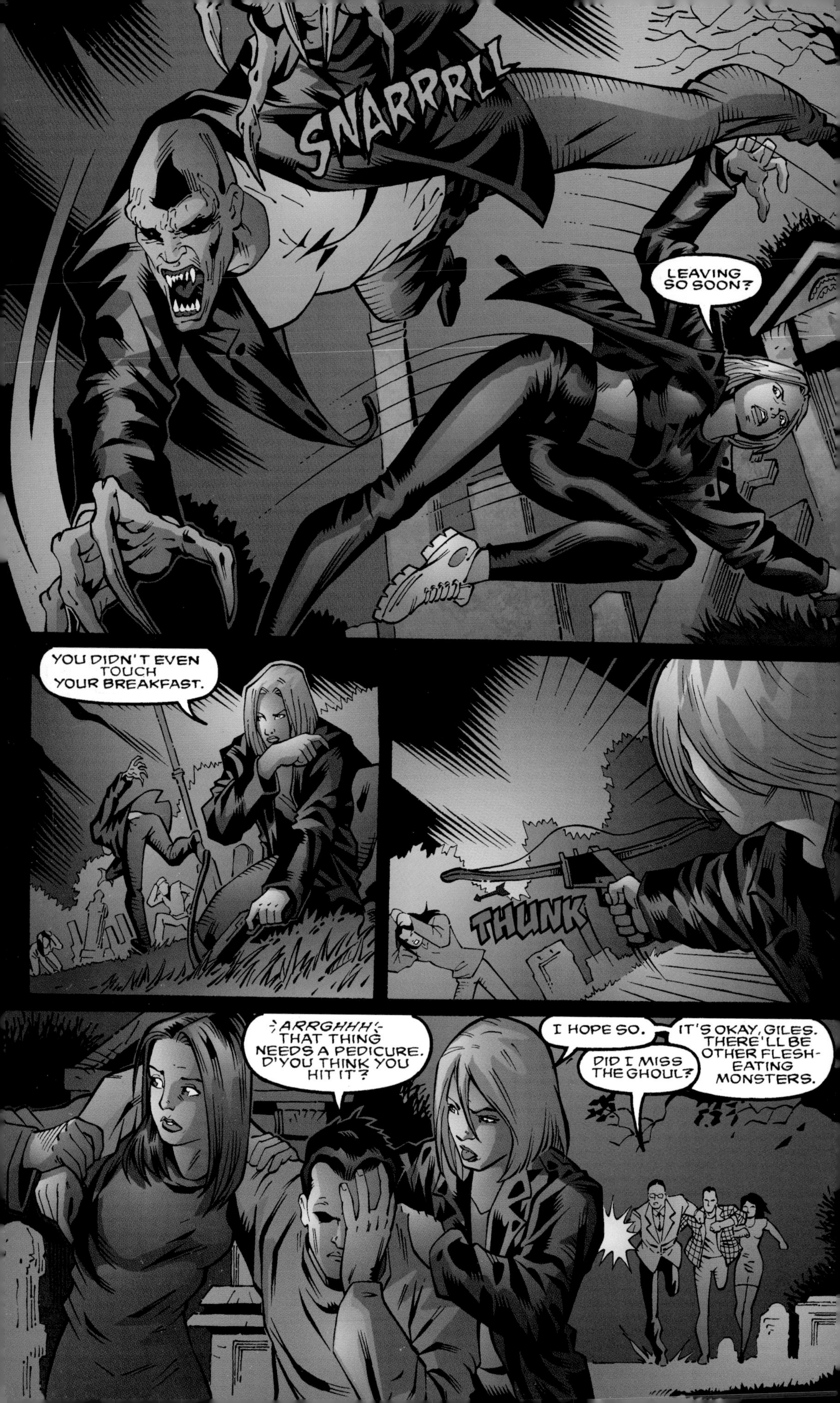
SNARRRLL
LEAVING SO SOON?
YOU DIDN'T EVEN TOUCH YOUR BREAKFAST.
THUNK
ARRGHHH! THAT THING NEEDS A PEDICURE. D'YOU THINK YOU HIT IT?
I HOPE SO.
DID I MISS THE GHOUL?
IT'S OKAY, GILES. THERE'LL BE OTHER FLESH-EATING MONSTERS.

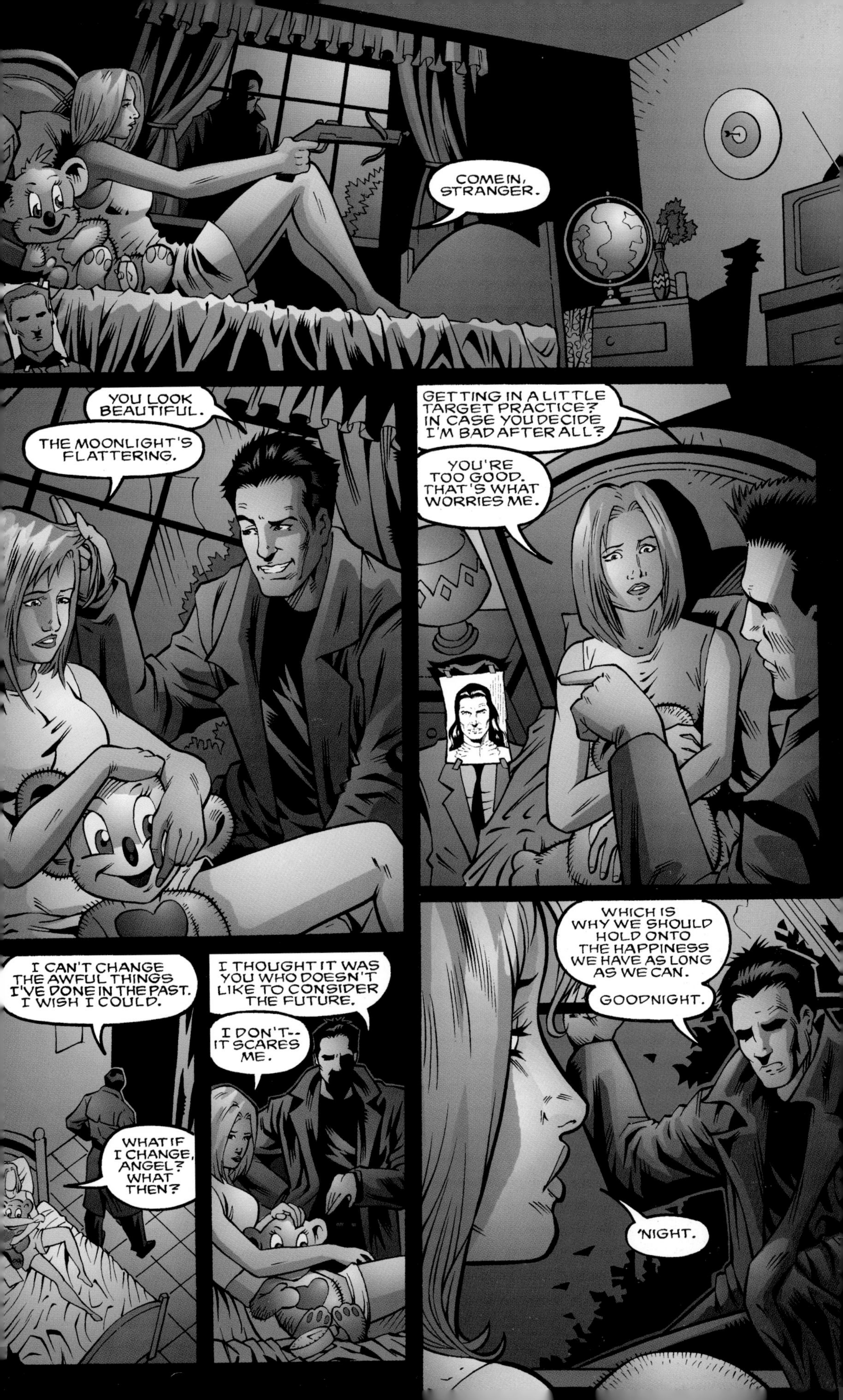
COME IN, STRANGER.
YOU LOOK BEAUTIFUL.
THE MOONLIGHT'S FLATTERING.
GETTING IN A LITTLE TARGET PRACTICE? IN CASE YOU DECIDE I'M BAD AFTER ALL?
YOU'RE TOO GOOD. THAT'S WHAT WORRIES ME.
I CAN'T CHANGE THE AWFUL THINGS I'VE DONE IN THE PAST. I WISH I COULD.
WHAT IF I CHANGE, ANGEL? WHAT THEN?
I THOUGHT IT WAS YOU WHO DOESN'T LIKE TO CONSIDER THE FUTURE.
I DON'T-- IT SCARES ME.
WHICH IS WHY WE SHOULD HOLD ONTO THE HAPPINESS WE HAVE AS LONG AS WE CAN.
GOODNIGHT.
'NIGHT.

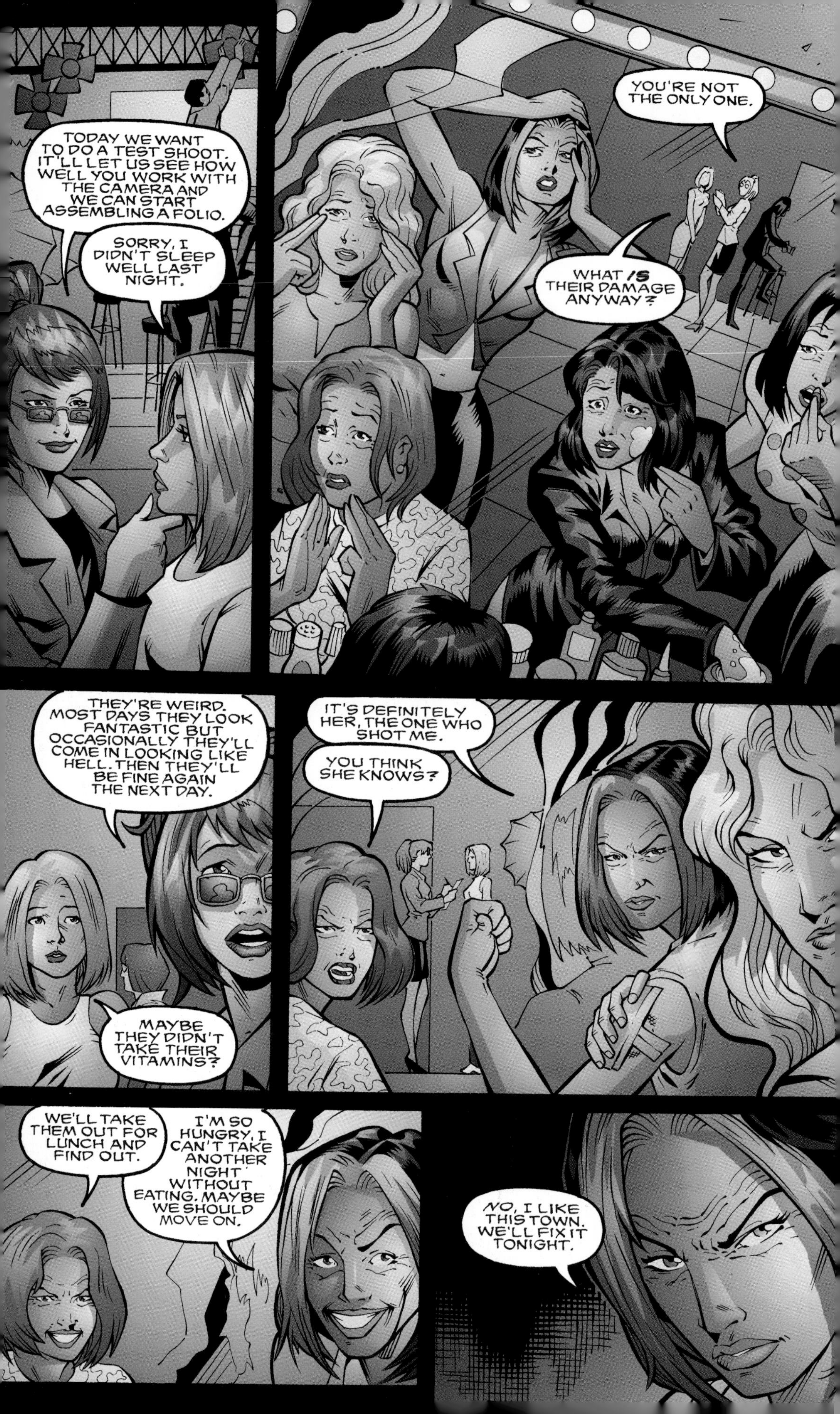
TODAY WE WANT TO DO A TEST SHOOT. IT'LL LET US SEE HOW WELL YOU WORK WITH THE CAMERA AND WE CAN START ASSEMBLING A FOLIO.
SORRY, I DIDN'T SLEEP WELL LAST NIGHT.
YOU'RE NOT THE ONLY ONE.
WHAT IS THEIR DAMAGE ANYWAY?
THEY'RE WEIRD. MOST DAYS THEY LOOK FANTASTIC BUT OCCASIONALLY THEY'LL COME IN LOOKING LIKE HELL. THEN THEY'LL BE FINE AGAIN THE NEXT DAY.
MAYBE THEY DIDN'T TAKE THEIR VITAMINS?
IT'S DEFINITELY HER, THE ONE WHO SHOT ME.
YOU THINK SHE KNOWS?
WE'LL TAKE THEM OUT FOR LUNCH AND FIND OUT.
I'M SO HUNGRY, I CAN'T TAKE ANOTHER NIGHT WITHOUT EATING. MAYBE WE SHOULD MOVE ON.
NO, I LIKE THIS TOWN. WE'LL FIX IT TONIGHT.

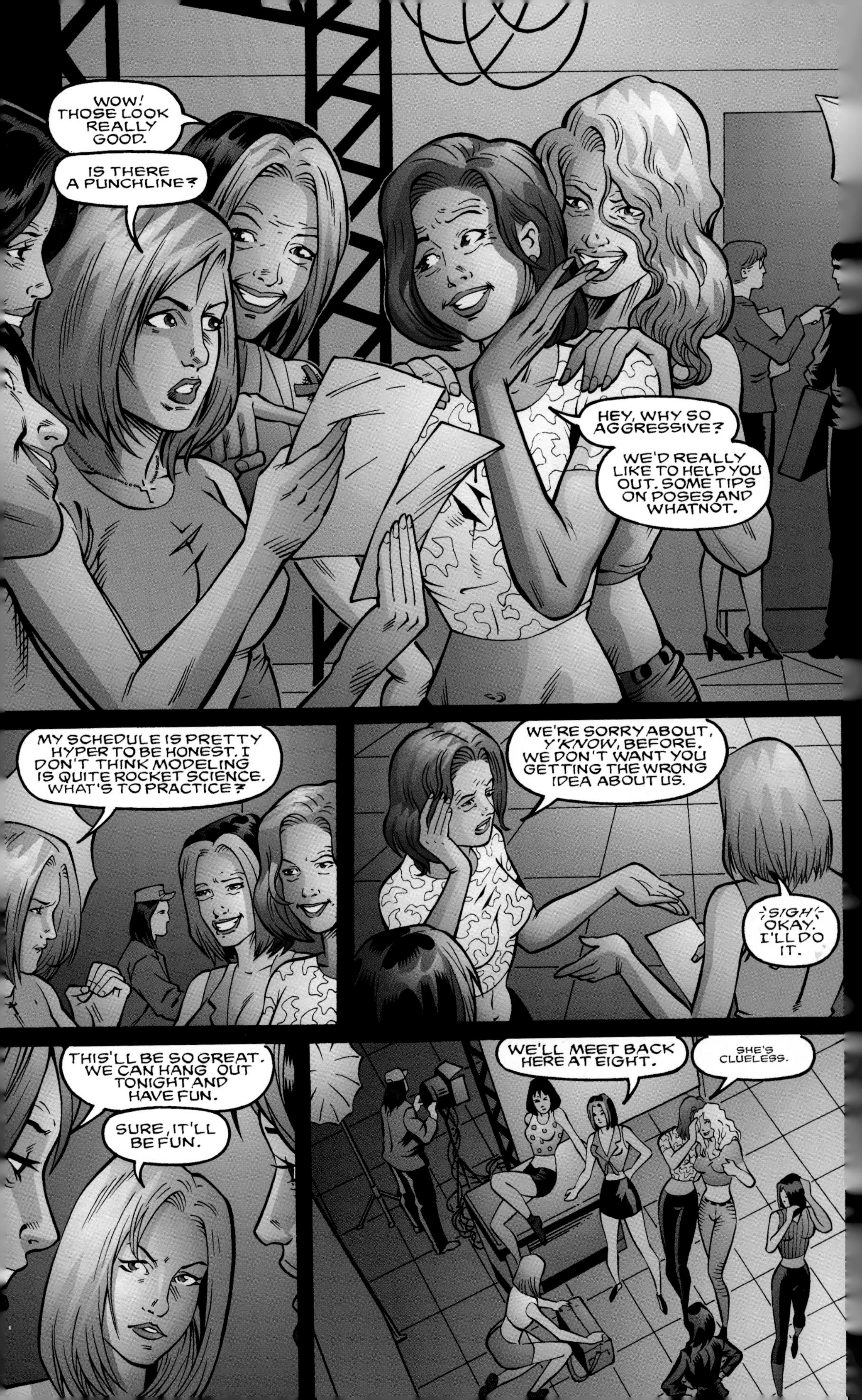
WOW! THOSE LOOK REALLY GOOD.
IS THERE A PUNCHLINE?
HEY, WHY SO AGGRESSIVE?
WE'D REALLY LIKE TO HELP YOU OUT. SOME TIPS ON POSES AND WHATNOT.
MY SCHEDULE IS PRETTY HYPER TO BE HONEST. I DON'T THINK MODELING IS QUITE ROCKET SCIENCE. WHAT'S TO PRACTICE?
WE'RE SORRY ABOUT, Y'KNOW, BEFORE. WE DON'T WANT YOU GETTING THE WRONG IDEA ABOUT US.
SIGH OKAY. I'LL DO IT.
THIS'LL BE SO GREAT. WE CAN HANG OUT TONIGHT AND HAVE FUN.
SURE, IT'LL BE FUN.
WE'LL MEET BACK HERE AT EIGHT.
SHE'S CLUELESS.

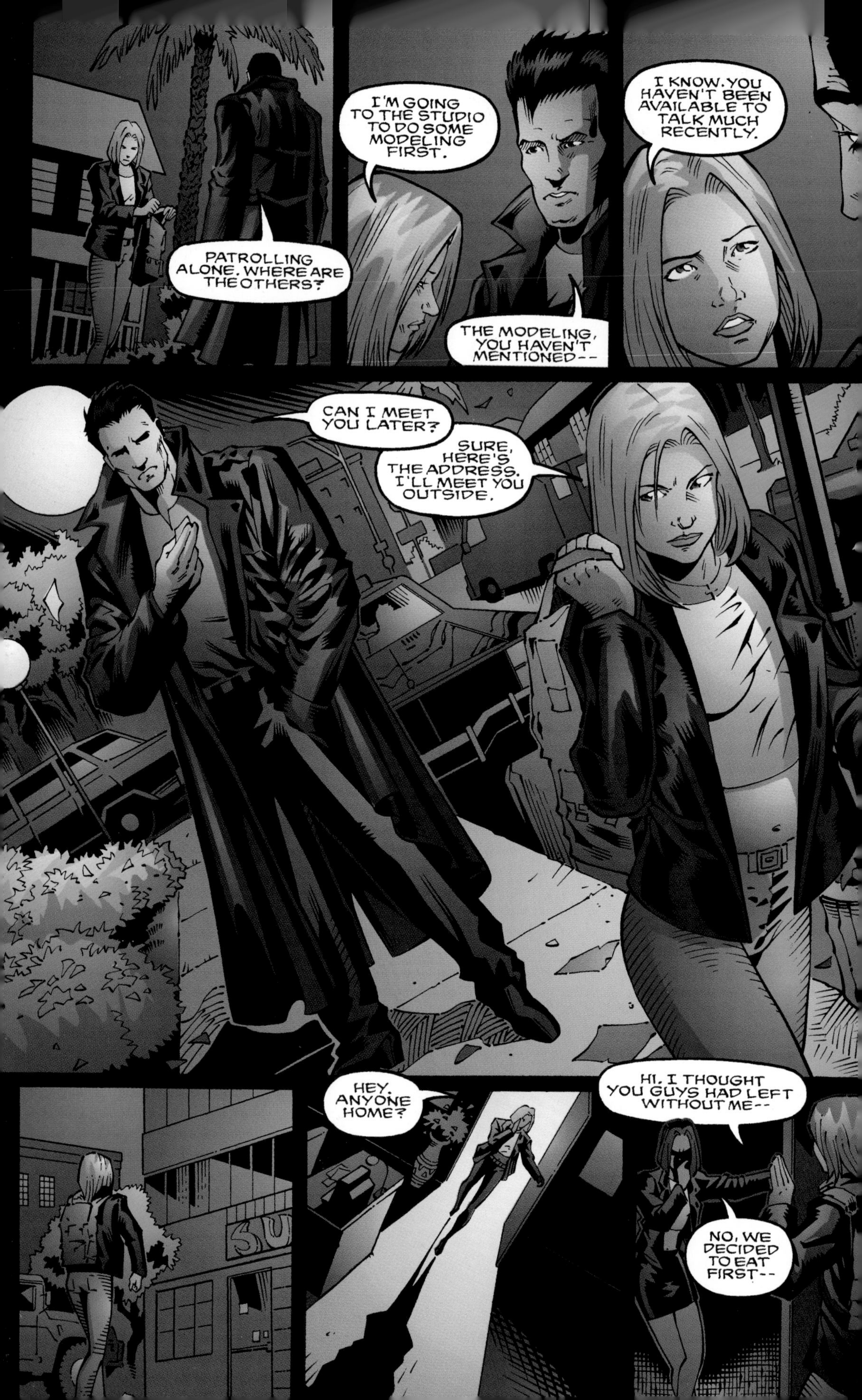
PATROLLING ALONE. WHERE ARE THE OTHERS?
I'M GOING TO THE STUDIO TO DO SOME MODELING FIRST.
THE MODELING, YOU HAVEN'T MENTIONED--
I KNOW. YOU HAVEN'T BEEN AVAILABLE TO TALK MUCH RECENTLY.
CAN I MEET YOU LATER?
SURE, HERE'S THE ADDRESS. I'LL MEET YOU OUTSIDE.
HEY. ANYONE HOME?
HI. I THOUGHT YOU GUYS HAD LEFT WITHOUT ME--
NO, WE DECIDED TO EAT FIRST--

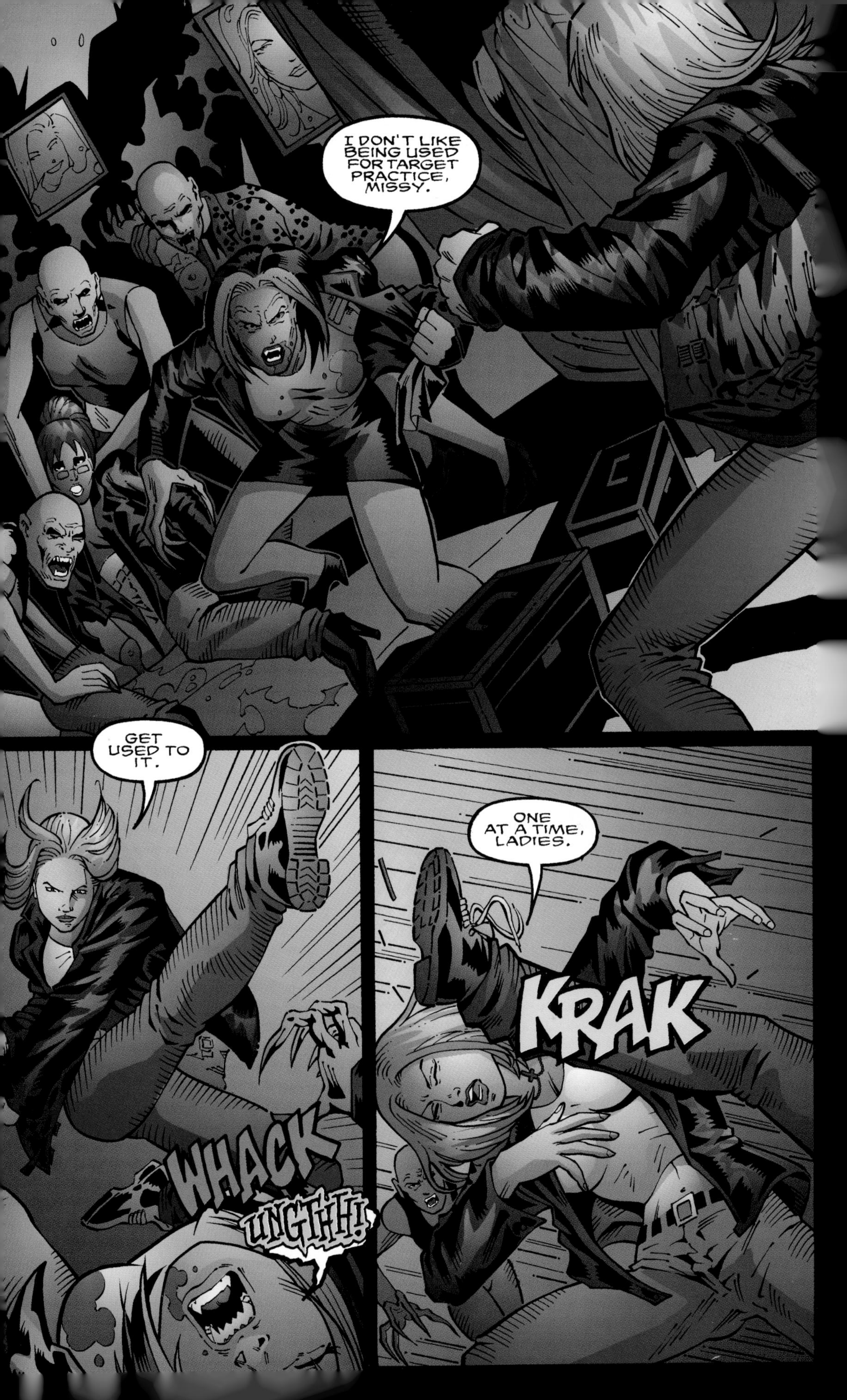
I DON'T LIKE BEING USED FOR TARGET PRACTICE, MISSY.
GET USED TO IT.
WHACK
UNGTHH!
ONE AT A TIME, LADIES.
KRAK

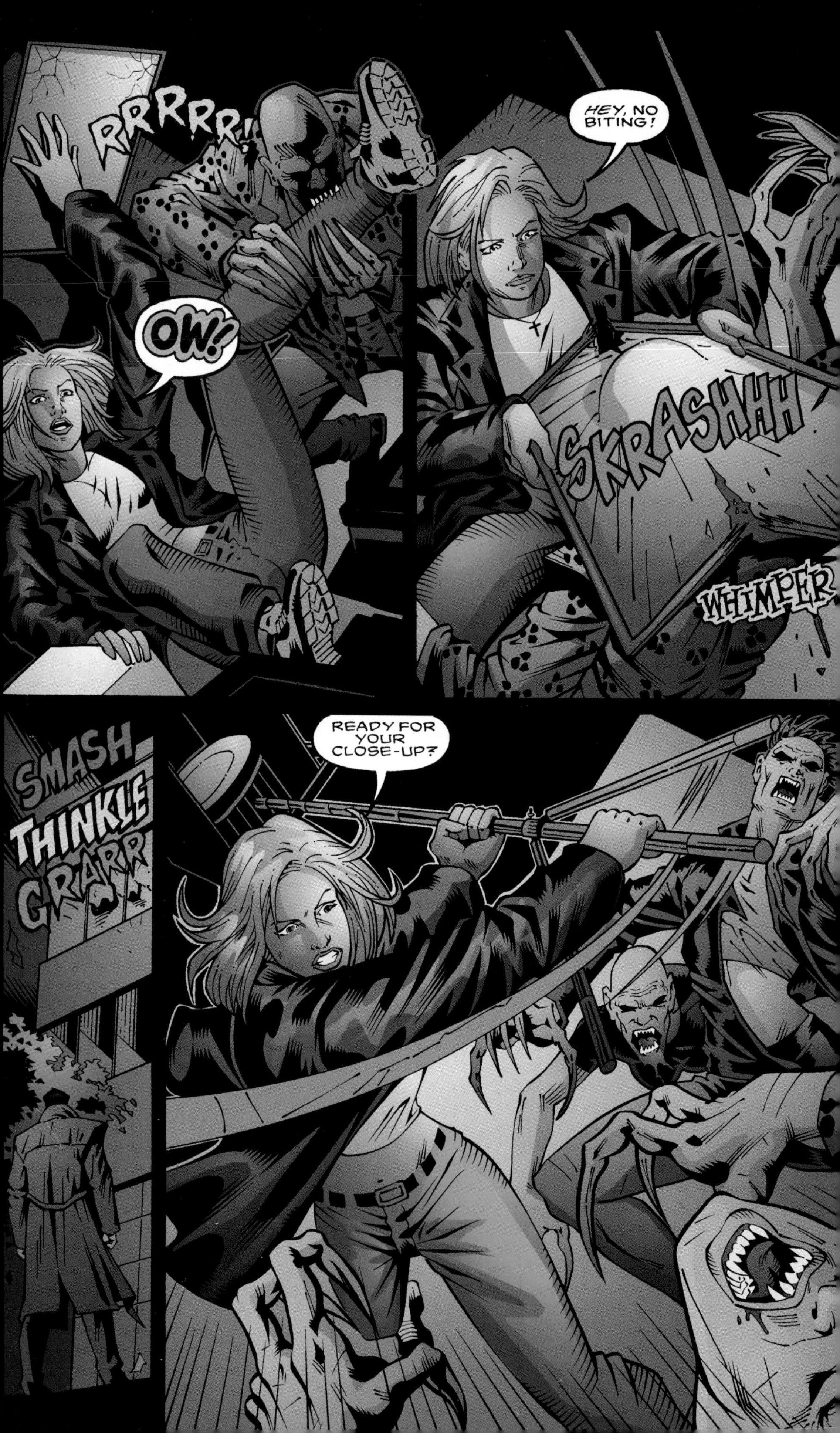
RRRRRR!
OW!!
HEY, NO BITING!
SKRASHHH
WHIMPER
SMASH
THINKLE
GRARR
READY FOR YOUR CLOSE-UP?

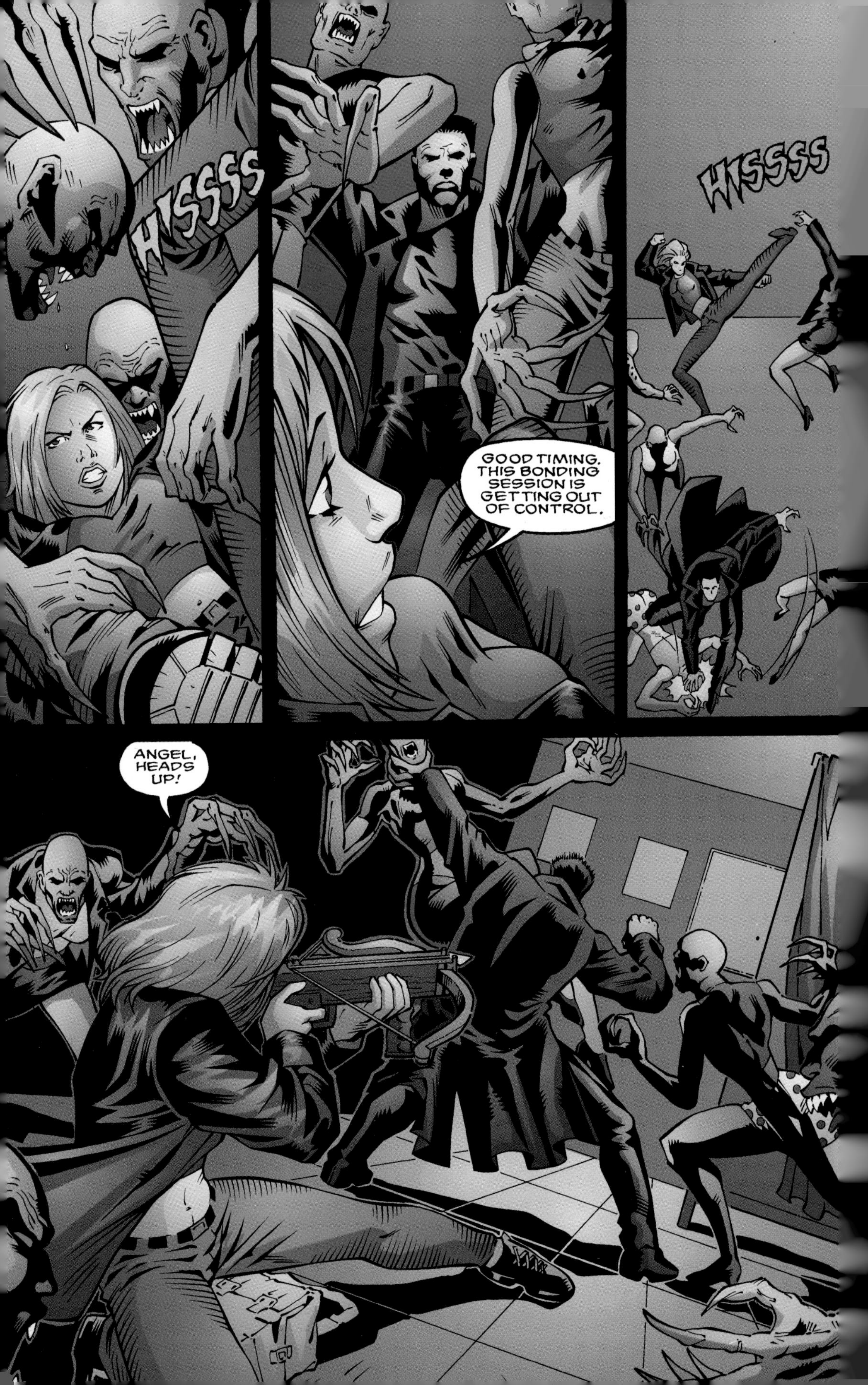
HISSSS
GOOD TIMING. THIS BONDING SESSION IS GETTING OUT OF CONTROL.
HISSSS
ANGEL, HEADS UP!

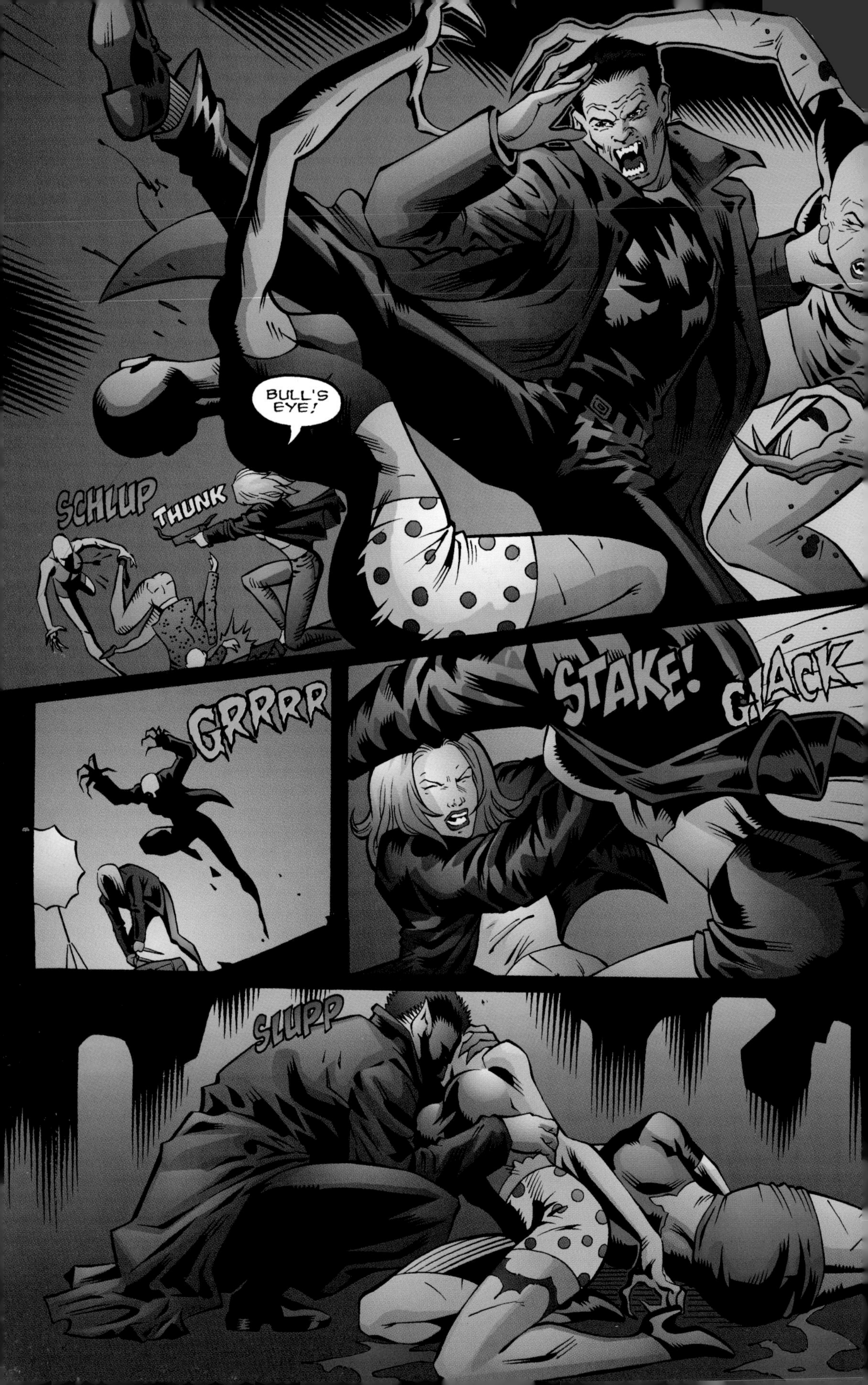
BULL'S EYE!
SCHLUP
THUNK
GRRRR
STAKE!
GLACK
SLUPP

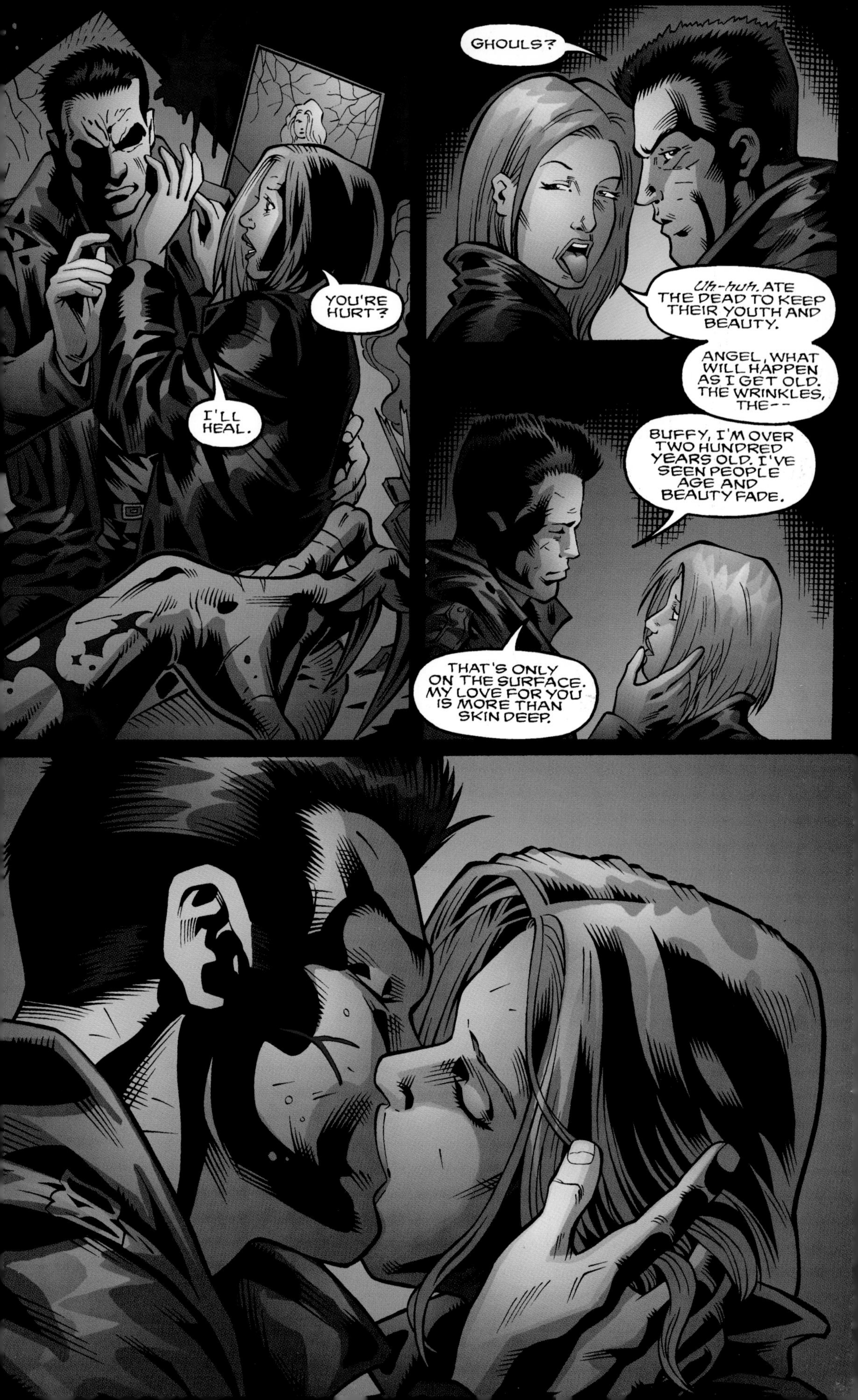
YOU'RE HURT?
I'LL HEAL.
GHOULS?
Uh-huh. ATE THE DEAD TO KEEP THEIR YOUTH AND BEAUTY.
ANGEL, WHAT WILL HAPPEN AS I GET OLD. THE WRINKLES, THE--
BUFFY, I'M OVER TWO HUNDRED YEARS OLD. I'VE SEEN PEOPLE AGE AND BEAUTY FADE.
THAT'S ONLY ON THE SURFACE. MY LOVE FOR YOU IS MORE THAN SKIN DEEP.

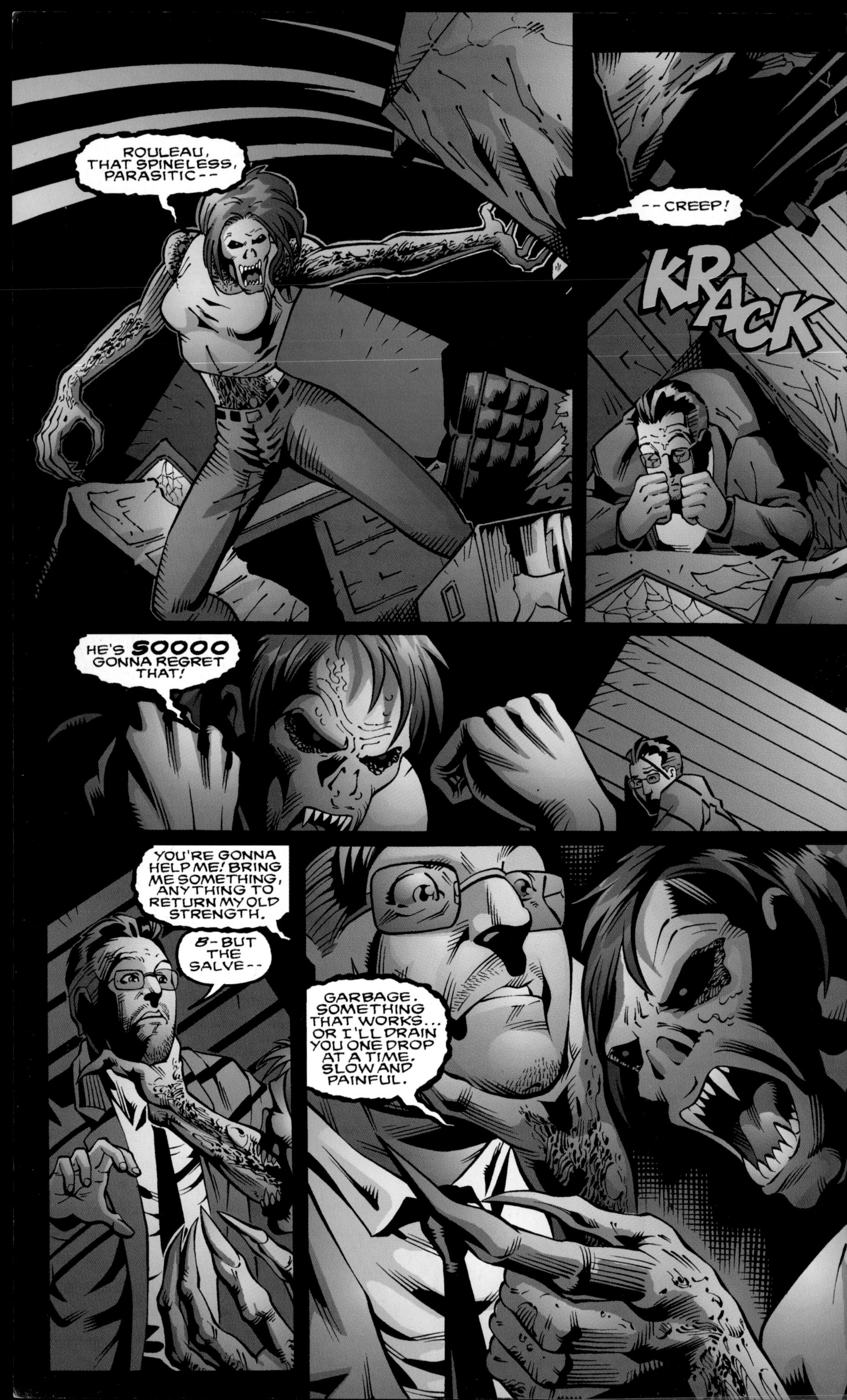
ROULEAU, THAT SPINELESS, PARASITIC--
--CREEP!
KRACK
HE'S SOOOO GONNA REGRET THAT!
YOU'RE GONNA HELP ME! BRING ME SOMETHING, ANYTHING TO RETURN MY OLD STRENGTH.
B-BUT THE SALVE--
GARBAGE. SOMETHING THAT WORKS... OR I'LL DRAIN YOU ONE DROP AT A TIME. SLOW AND PAINFUL.

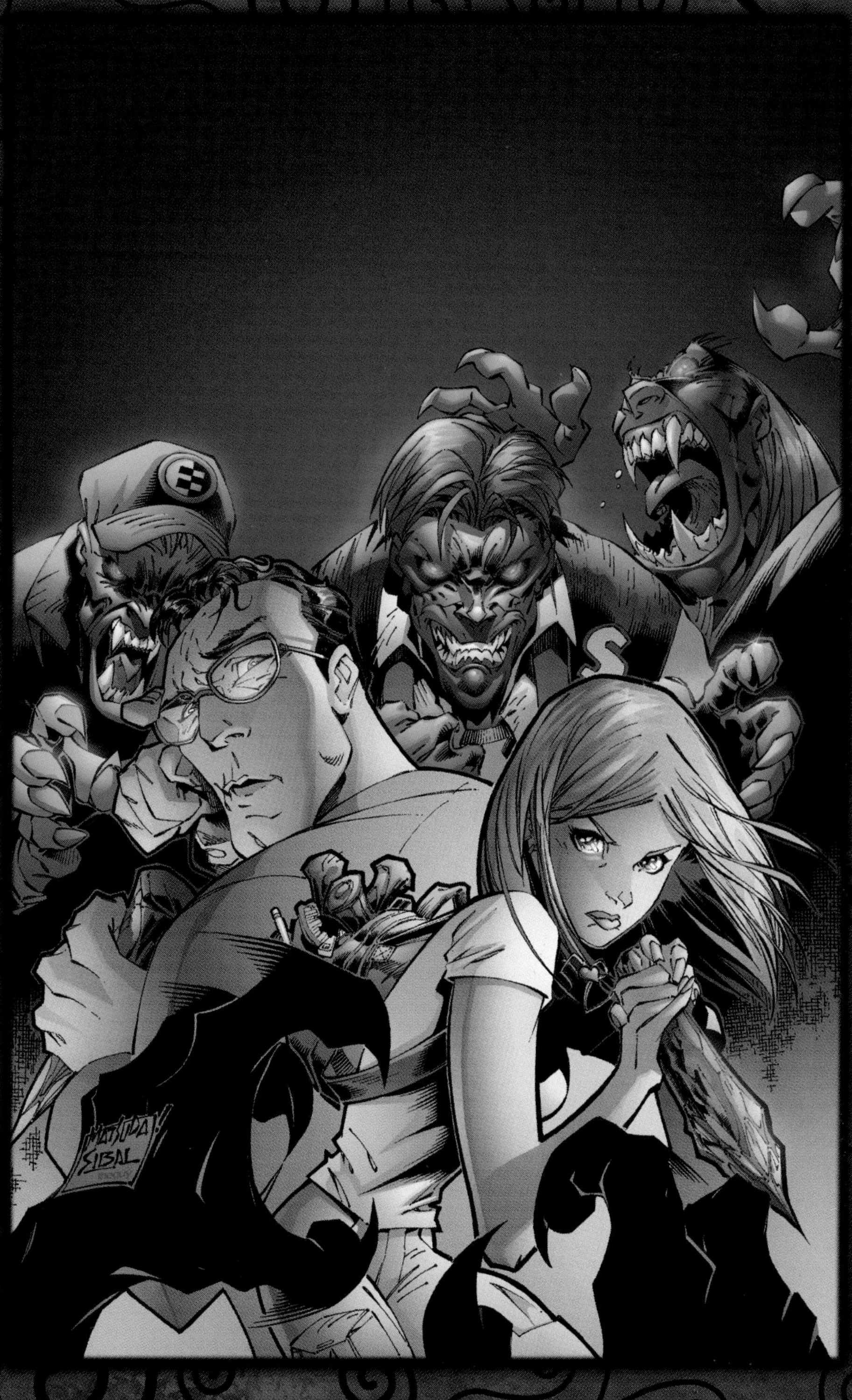
MATSUDA
SIBAL

Art by JEFF MATSUDA *and* JON SIBAL
Colors by GUY MAJOR

A BOY
NAMED SUE

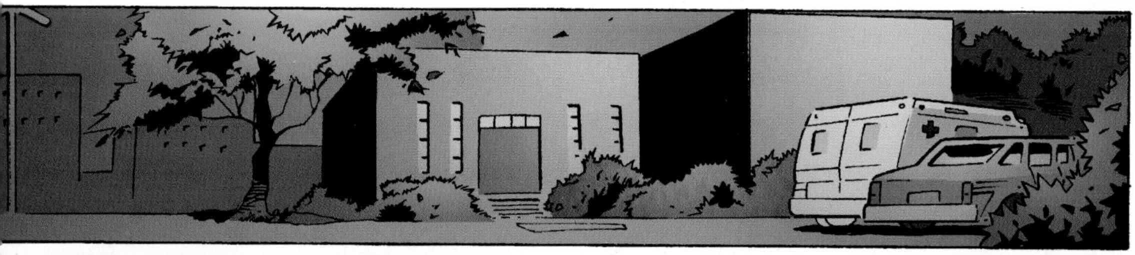

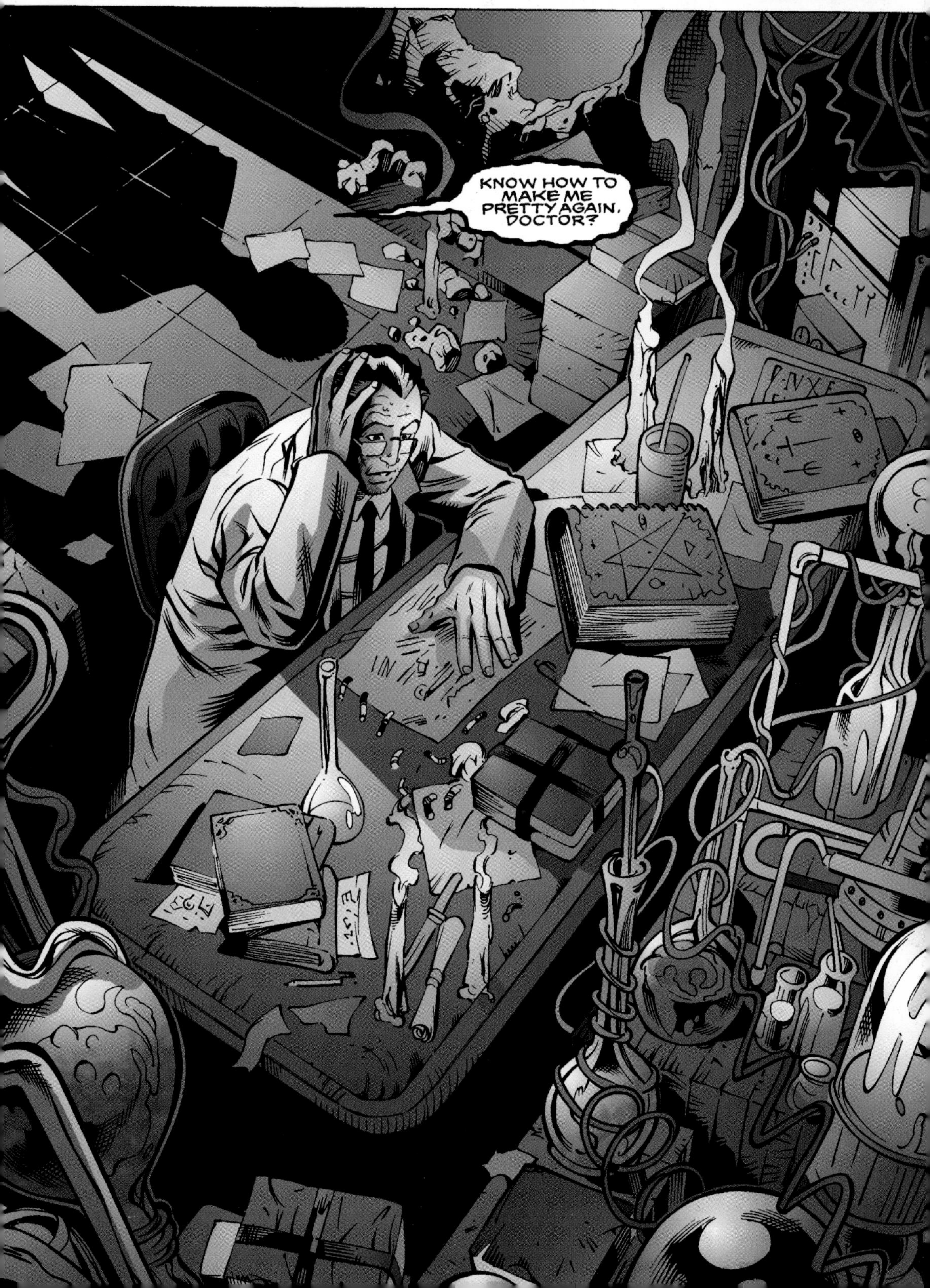
KNOW HOW TO MAKE ME PRETTY AGAIN, DOCTOR?

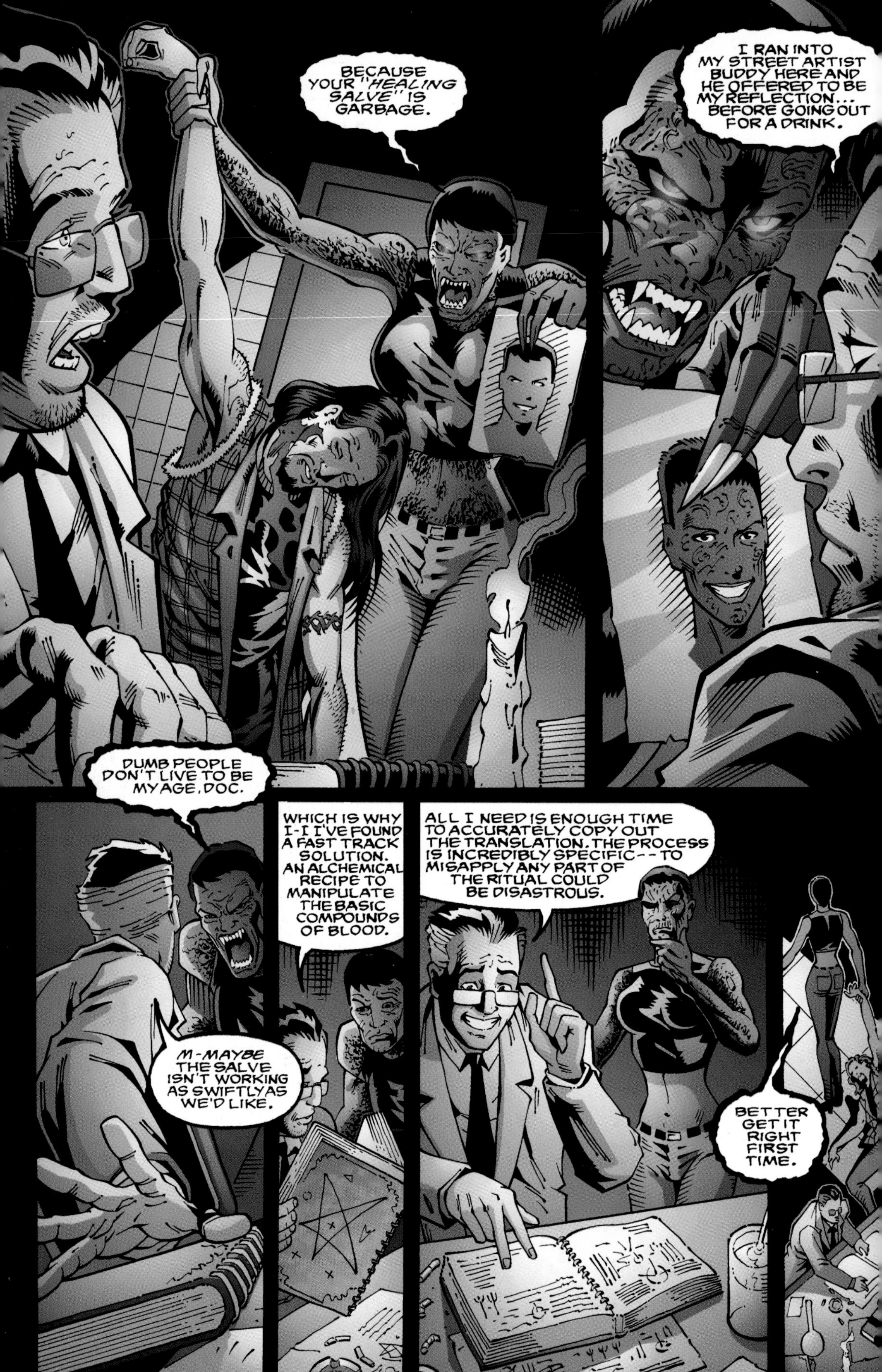
BECAUSE YOUR "HEALING SALVE" IS GARBAGE.
I RAN INTO MY STREET ARTIST BUDDY HERE AND HE OFFERED TO BE MY REFLECTION... BEFORE GOING OUT FOR A DRINK.
DUMB PEOPLE DON'T LIVE TO BE MY AGE, DOC.
M-MAYBE THE SALVE ISN'T WORKING AS SWIFTLY AS WE'D LIKE.
WHICH IS WHY I-I I'VE FOUND A FAST TRACK SOLUTION. AN ALCHEMICAL RECIPE TO MANIPULATE THE BASIC COMPOUNDS OF BLOOD.
ALL I NEED IS ENOUGH TIME TO ACCURATELY COPY OUT THE TRANSLATION. THE PROCESS IS INCREDIBLY SPECIFIC--TO MISAPPLY ANY PART OF THE RITUAL COULD BE DISASTROUS.
BETTER GET IT RIGHT FIRST TIME.

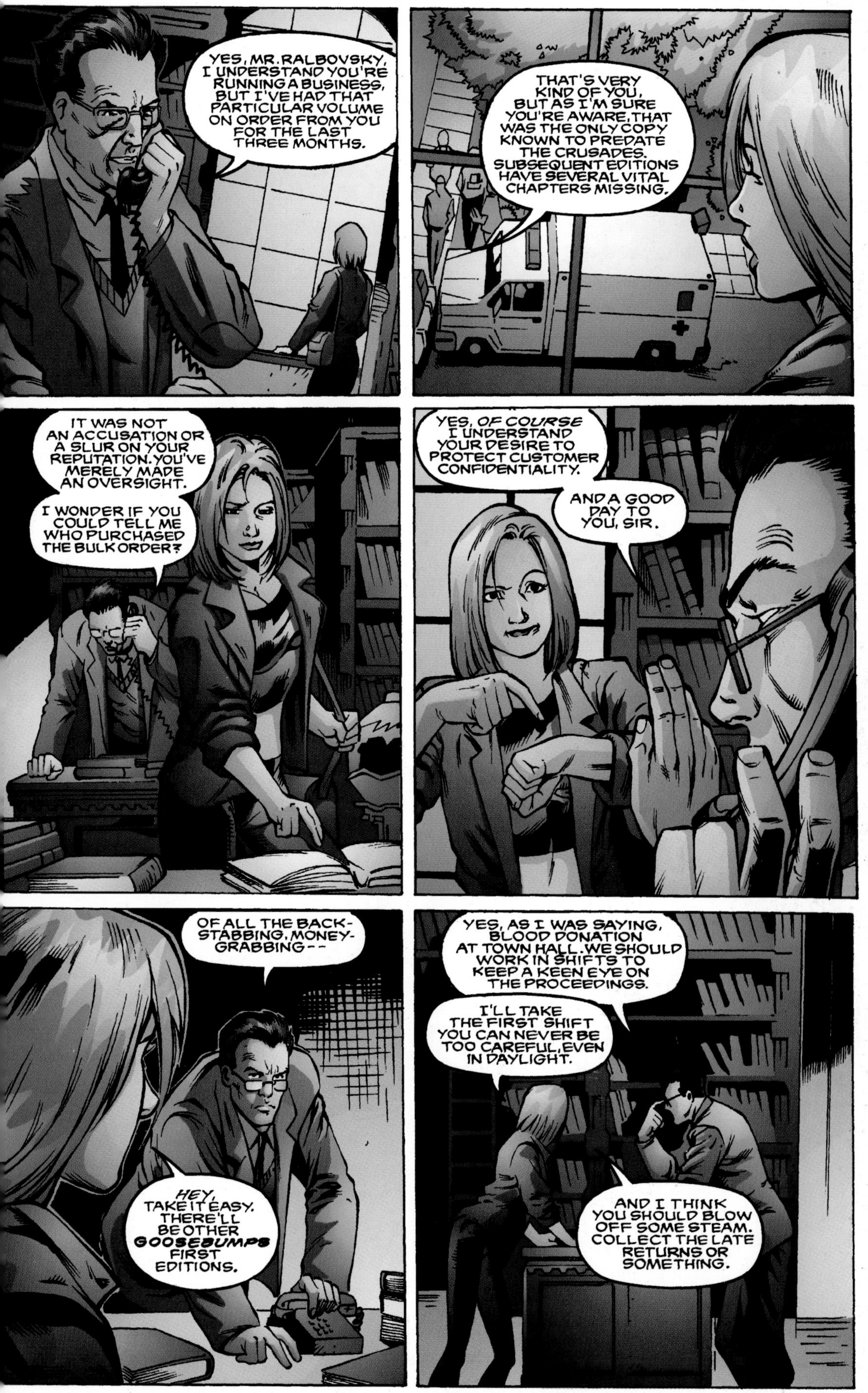
YES, MR. RALBOVSKY, I UNDERSTAND YOU'RE RUNNING A BUSINESS, BUT I'VE HAD THAT PARTICULAR VOLUME ON ORDER FROM YOU FOR THE LAST THREE MONTHS.
THAT'S VERY KIND OF YOU, BUT AS I'M SURE YOU'RE AWARE, THAT WAS THE ONLY COPY KNOWN TO PREDATE THE CRUSADES. SUBSEQUENT EDITIONS HAVE SEVERAL VITAL CHAPTERS MISSING.
IT WAS NOT AN ACCUSATION OR A SLUR ON YOUR REPUTATION. YOU'VE MERELY MADE AN OVERSIGHT.
I WONDER IF YOU COULD TELL ME WHO PURCHASED THE BULK ORDER?
YES, OF COURSE I UNDERSTAND YOUR DESIRE TO PROTECT CUSTOMER CONFIDENTIALITY.
AND A GOOD DAY TO YOU, SIR.
OF ALL THE BACK-STABBING, MONEY-GRABBING--
HEY, TAKE IT EASY. THERE'LL BE OTHER GOOSEBUMPS FIRST EDITIONS.
YES, AS I WAS SAYING, BLOOD DONATION AT TOWN HALL. WE SHOULD WORK IN SHIFTS TO KEEP A KEEN EYE ON THE PROCEEDINGS.
I'LL TAKE THE FIRST SHIFT YOU CAN NEVER BE TOO CAREFUL, EVEN IN DAYLIGHT.
AND I THINK YOU SHOULD BLOW OFF SOME STEAM. COLLECT THE LATE RETURNS OR SOMETHING.

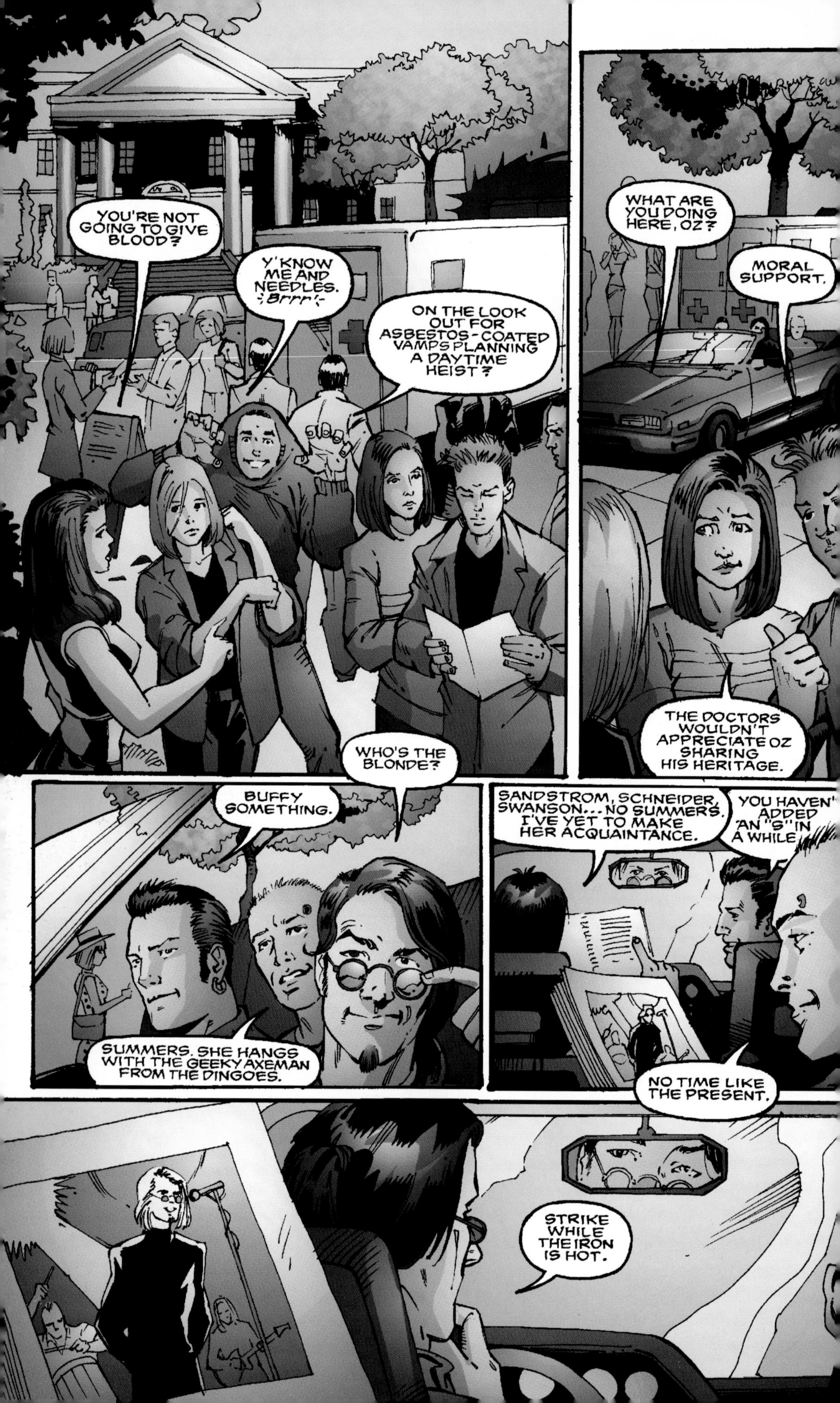
YOU'RE NOT GOING TO GIVE BLOOD?
Y'KNOW ME AND NEEDLES. Brrr!
ON THE LOOK OUT FOR ASBESTOS-COATED VAMPS PLANNING A DAYTIME HEIST?
WHAT ARE YOU DOING HERE, OZ?
MORAL SUPPORT.
THE DOCTORS WOULDN'T APPRECIATE OZ SHARING HIS HERITAGE.
WHO'S THE BLONDE?
BUFFY SOMETHING.
SUMMERS. SHE HANGS WITH THE GEEKY AXEMAN FROM THE DINGOES.
SANDSTROM, SCHNEIDER, SWANSON... NO SUMMERS. I'VE YET TO MAKE HER ACQUAINTANCE.
YOU HAVEN' ADDED AN "S" IN A WHILE
NO TIME LIKE THE PRESENT.
STRIKE WHILE THE IRON IS HOT.

WE'RE CALLED DOUBLE-CROSS AND WE'RE HEADLINING THE BRONZE TONIGHT. CATCH US NOW, BEFORE WE'RE ALL OVER MTV.

BUFFY SUMMERS, RIGHT? I DON'T THINK WE'VE EVER MET.

LET ME GUESS, THE LEAD SINGER OF DOUBLE-CROSS?

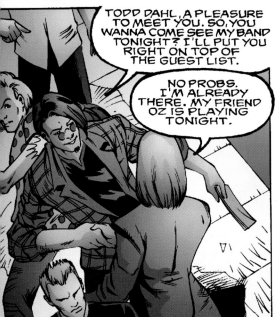

TODD DAHL, A PLEASURE TO MEET YOU. SO, YOU WANNA COME SEE MY BAND TONIGHT? I'LL PUT YOU RIGHT ON TOP OF THE GUEST LIST.

NO PROBS. I'M ALREADY THERE. MY FRIEND OZ IS PLAYING TONIGHT.

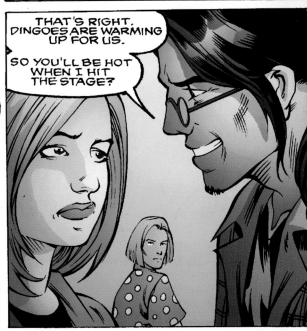

THAT'S RIGHT. DINGOES ARE WARMING UP FOR US.

SO YOU'LL BE HOT WHEN I HIT THE STAGE?

IF THE A/C'S WRECKED.

DAHL, TODD?

THAT'S MY CALL. SEE YOU TONIGHT.

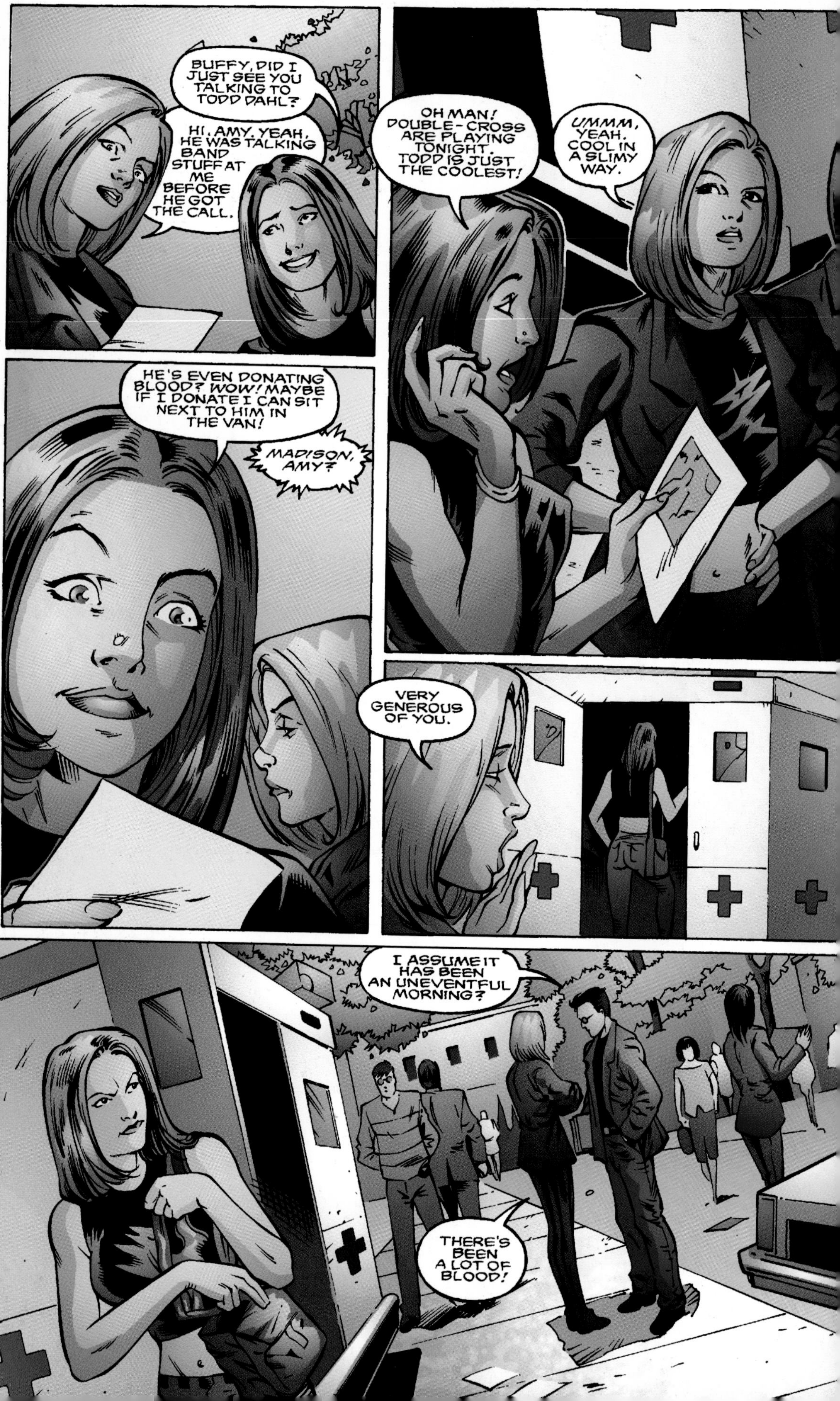

BUFFY, DID I JUST SEE YOU TALKING TO TODD DAHL?
HI, AMY. YEAH, HE WAS TALKING BAND STUFF AT ME BEFORE HE GOT THE CALL.
OH MAN! DOUBLE-CROSS ARE PLAYING TONIGHT. TODD IS JUST THE COOLEST!
UMMM, YEAH. COOL IN A SLIMY WAY.
HE'S EVEN DONATING BLOOD? WOW! MAYBE IF I DONATE I CAN SIT NEXT TO HIM IN THE VAN!
MADISON, AMY?
VERY GENEROUS OF YOU.
I ASSUME IT HAS BEEN AN UNEVENTFUL MORNING?
THERE'S BEEN A LOT OF BLOOD!

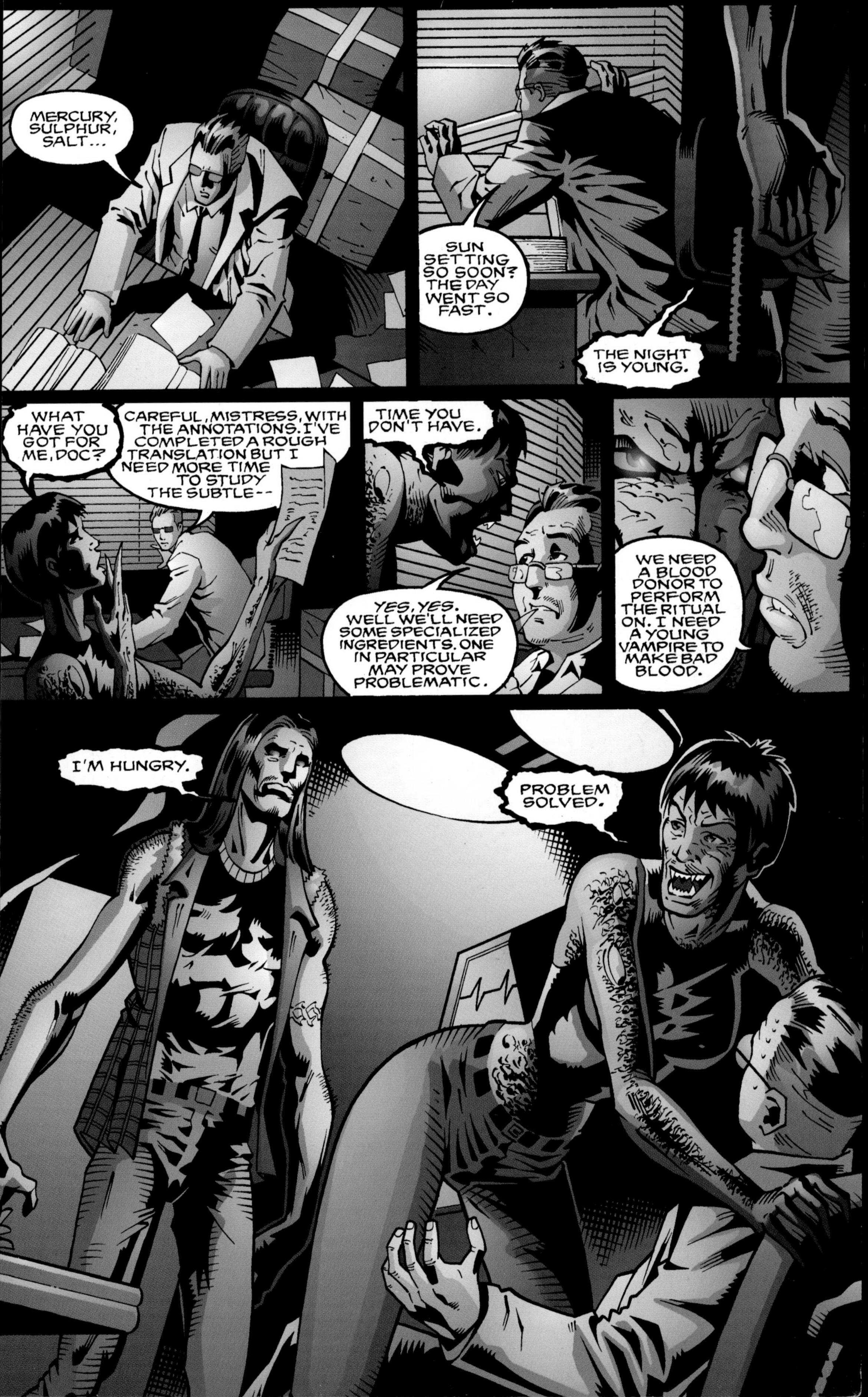
MERCURY, SULPHUR, SALT...
SUN SETTING SO SOON? THE DAY WENT SO FAST.
THE NIGHT IS YOUNG.
WHAT HAVE YOU GOT FOR ME, DOC?
CAREFUL, MISTRESS, WITH THE ANNOTATIONS. I'VE COMPLETED A ROUGH TRANSLATION BUT I NEED MORE TIME TO STUDY THE SUBTLE--
TIME YOU DON'T HAVE.
YES, YES. WELL WE'LL NEED SOME SPECIALIZED INGREDIENTS. ONE IN PARTICULAR MAY PROVE PROBLEMATIC.
WE NEED A BLOOD DONOR TO PERFORM THE RITUAL ON. I NEED A YOUNG VAMPIRE TO MAKE BAD BLOOD.
I'M HUNGRY.
PROBLEM SOLVED.

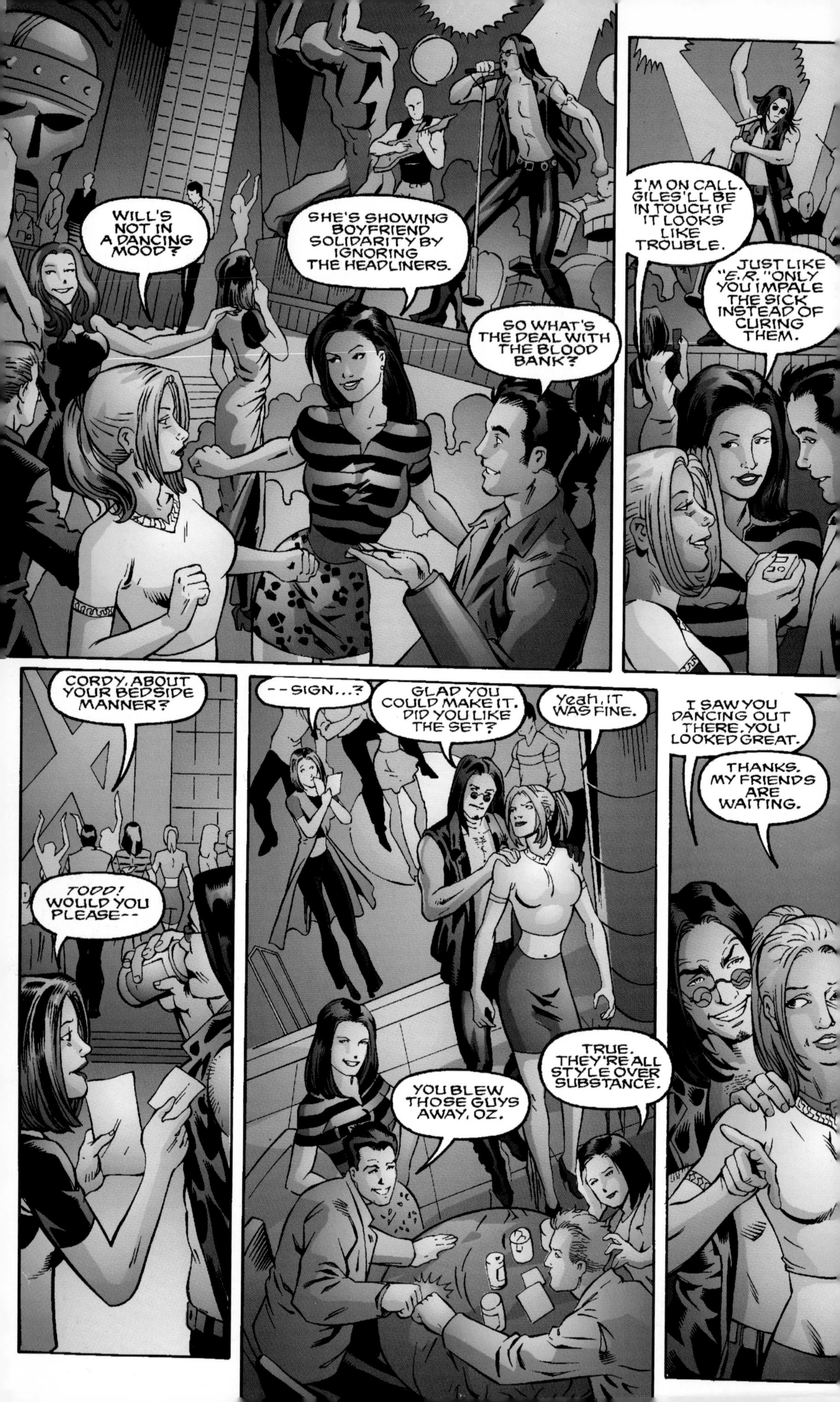
WILL'S NOT IN A DANCING MOOD?
SHE'S SHOWING BOYFRIEND SOLIDARITY BY IGNORING THE HEADLINERS.
SO WHAT'S THE DEAL WITH THE BLOOD BANK?
I'M ON CALL. GILES'LL BE IN TOUCH IF IT LOOKS LIKE TROUBLE.
JUST LIKE "E.R." ONLY YOU IMPALE THE SICK INSTEAD OF CURING THEM.
CORDY, ABOUT YOUR BEDSIDE MANNER?
TODD! WOULD YOU PLEASE--
--SIGN...?
GLAD YOU COULD MAKE IT. DID YOU LIKE THE SET?
Yeah, IT WAS FINE.
YOU BLEW THOSE GUYS AWAY, OZ.
TRUE. THEY'RE ALL STYLE OVER SUBSTANCE.
I SAW YOU DANCING OUT THERE. YOU LOOKED GREAT.
THANKS. MY FRIENDS ARE WAITING.

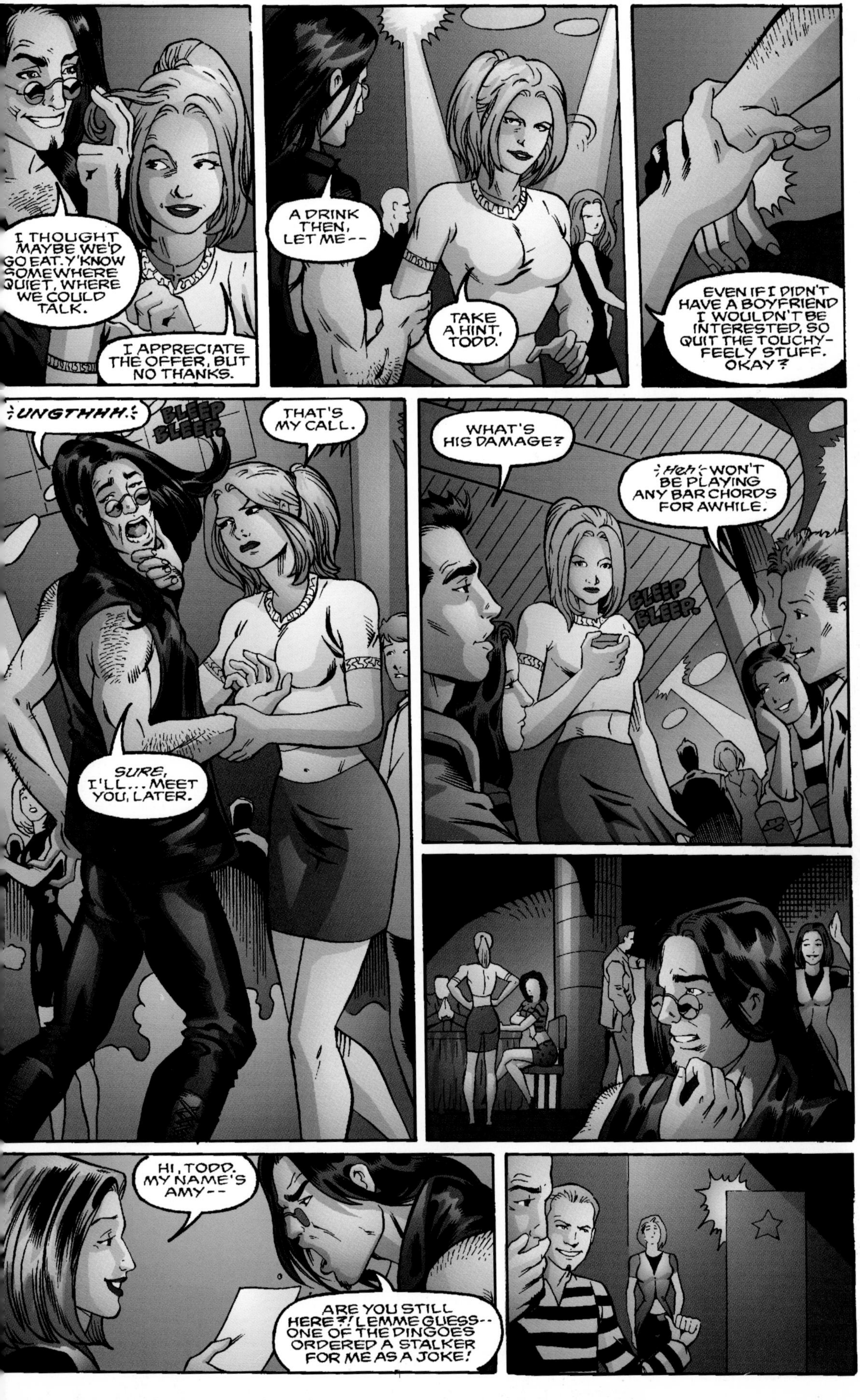

I THOUGHT MAYBE WE'D GO EAT. Y'KNOW SOMEWHERE QUIET, WHERE WE COULD TALK.
I APPRECIATE THE OFFER, BUT NO THANKS.
A DRINK THEN, LET ME--
TAKE A HINT, TODD.
EVEN IF I DIDN'T HAVE A BOYFRIEND I WOULDN'T BE INTERESTED, SO QUIT THE TOUCHY-FEELY STUFF. OKAY?
UNGTHHH.
BLEEP BLEEP.
THAT'S MY CALL.
SURE, I'LL... MEET YOU, LATER.
WHAT'S HIS DAMAGE?
Heh WON'T BE PLAYING ANY BAR CHORDS FOR AWHILE.
BLEEP BLEEP.
HI, TODD. MY NAME'S AMY--
ARE YOU STILL HERE?! LEMME GUESS-- ONE OF THE DINGOES ORDERED A STALKER FOR ME AS A JOKE!

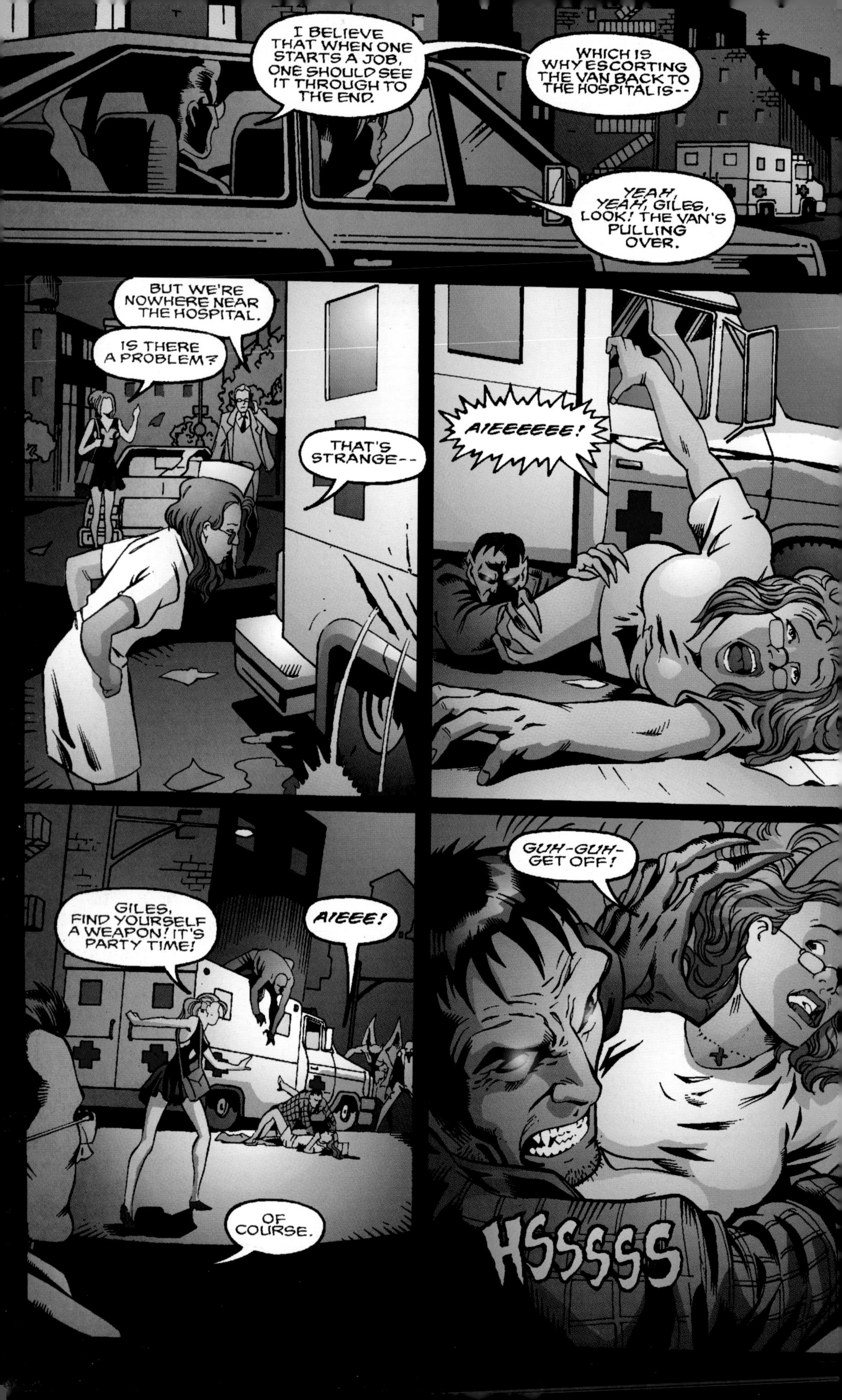
I BELIEVE THAT WHEN ONE STARTS A JOB, ONE SHOULD SEE IT THROUGH TO THE END.
WHICH IS WHY ESCORTING THE VAN BACK TO THE HOSPITAL IS--
YEAH, YEAH, GILES, LOOK! THE VAN'S PULLING OVER.
BUT WE'RE NOWHERE NEAR THE HOSPITAL.
IS THERE A PROBLEM?
THAT'S STRANGE--
AIEEEEEEE!
GILES, FIND YOURSELF A WEAPON! IT'S PARTY TIME!
AIEEE!
OF COURSE.
GUH-GUH-GET OFF!
HSSSSS

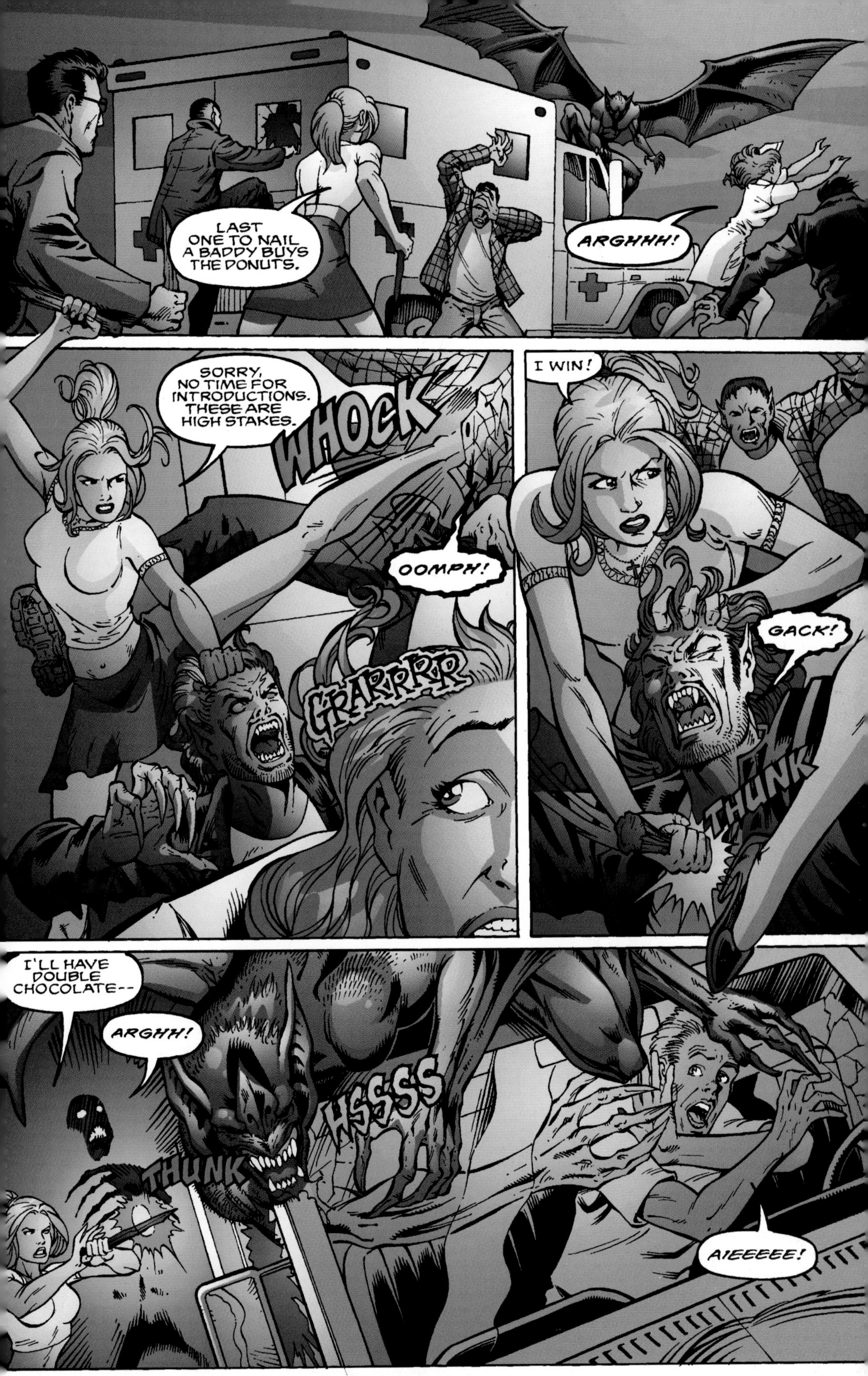
LAST ONE TO NAIL A BADDY BUYS THE DONUTS.
ARGHHH!
SORRY, NO TIME FOR INTRODUCTIONS. THESE ARE HIGH STAKES.
WHOCK
OOMPH!
GRARRRR
I WIN!
GACK!
THUNK
I'LL HAVE DOUBLE CHOCOLATE--
ARGHH!
HSSSS
THUNK
AIEEEEE!

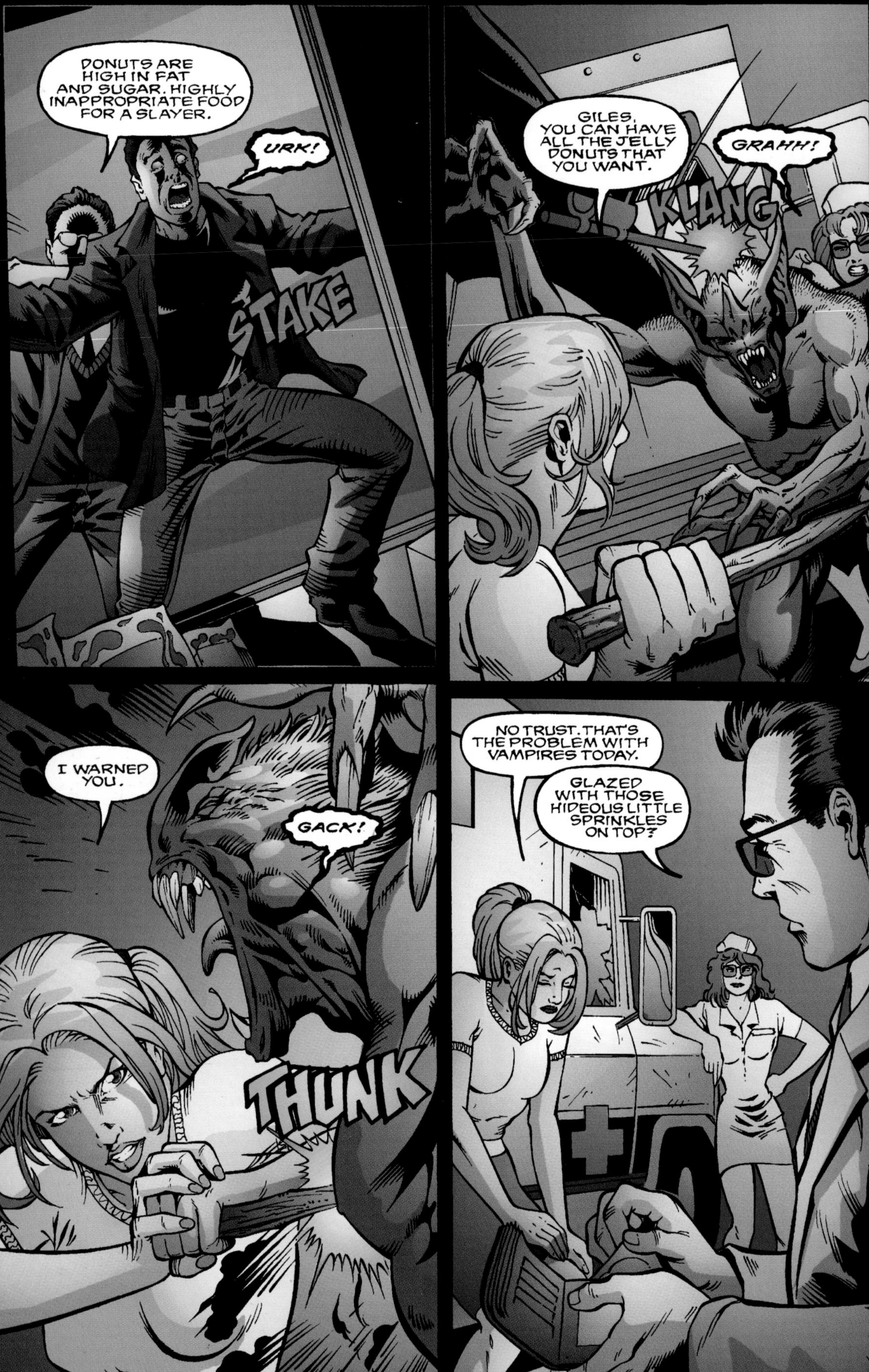
DONUTS ARE HIGH IN FAT AND SUGAR. HIGHLY INAPPROPRIATE FOOD FOR A SLAYER.
URK!
STAKE
GILES, YOU CAN HAVE ALL THE JELLY DONUTS THAT YOU WANT.
GRAHH!
KLANG
I WARNED YOU.
GACK!
THUNK
NO TRUST. THAT'S THE PROBLEM WITH VAMPIRES TODAY.
GLAZED WITH THOSE HIDEOUS LITTLE SPRINKLES ON TOP?

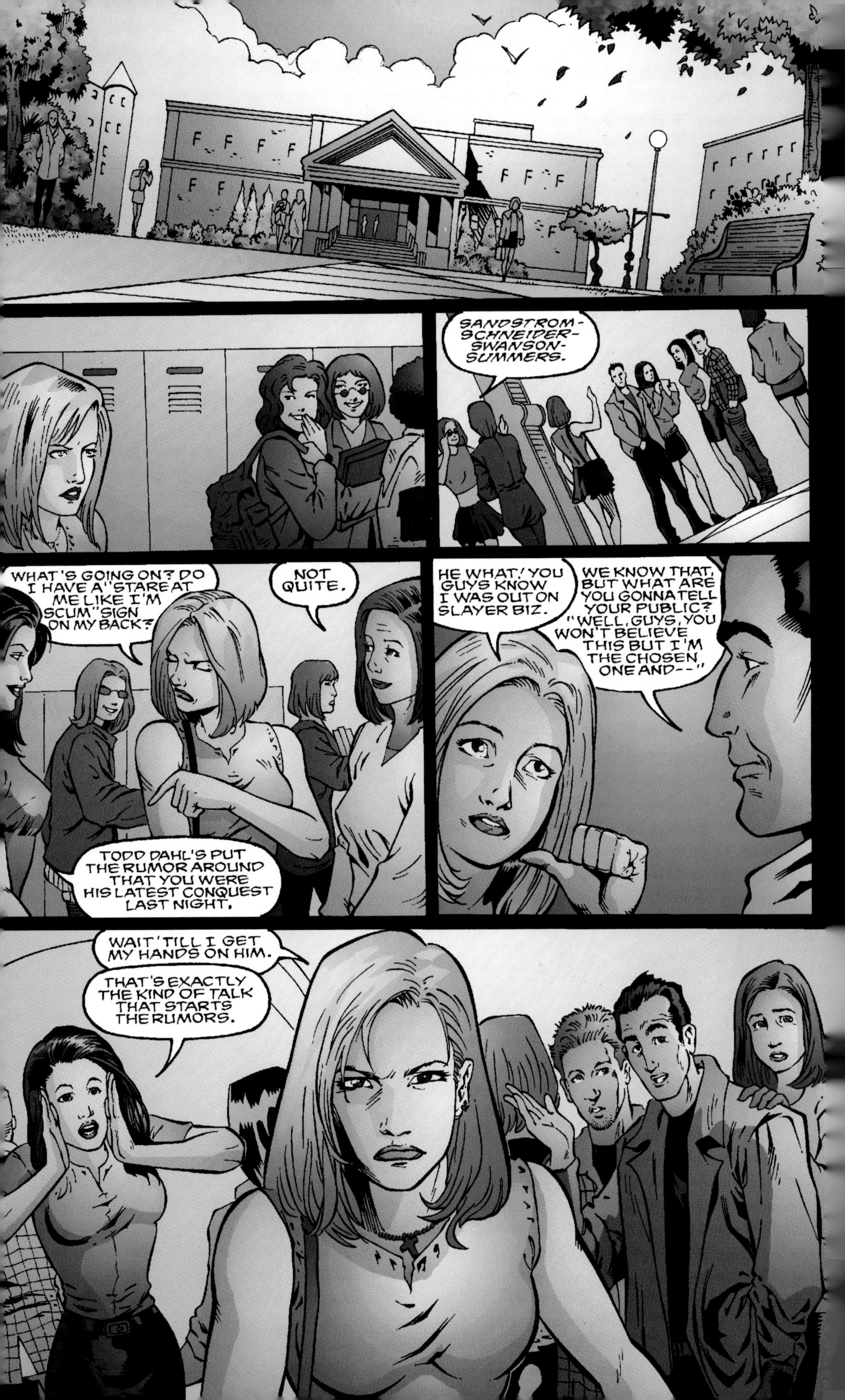
SANDSTROM-SCHNEIDER-SWANSON-SUMMERS.
WHAT'S GOING ON? DO I HAVE A "STARE AT ME LIKE I'M SCUM" SIGN ON MY BACK?
NOT QUITE.
TODD DAHL'S PUT THE RUMOR AROUND THAT YOU WERE HIS LATEST CONQUEST LAST NIGHT.
HE WHAT! YOU GUYS KNOW I WAS OUT ON SLAYER BIZ.
WE KNOW THAT, BUT WHAT ARE YOU GONNA TELL YOUR PUBLIC? "WELL, GUYS, YOU WON'T BELIEVE THIS BUT I'M THE CHOSEN ONE AND--"
WAIT 'TILL I GET MY HANDS ON HIM.
THAT'S EXACTLY THE KIND OF TALK THAT STARTS THE RUMORS.

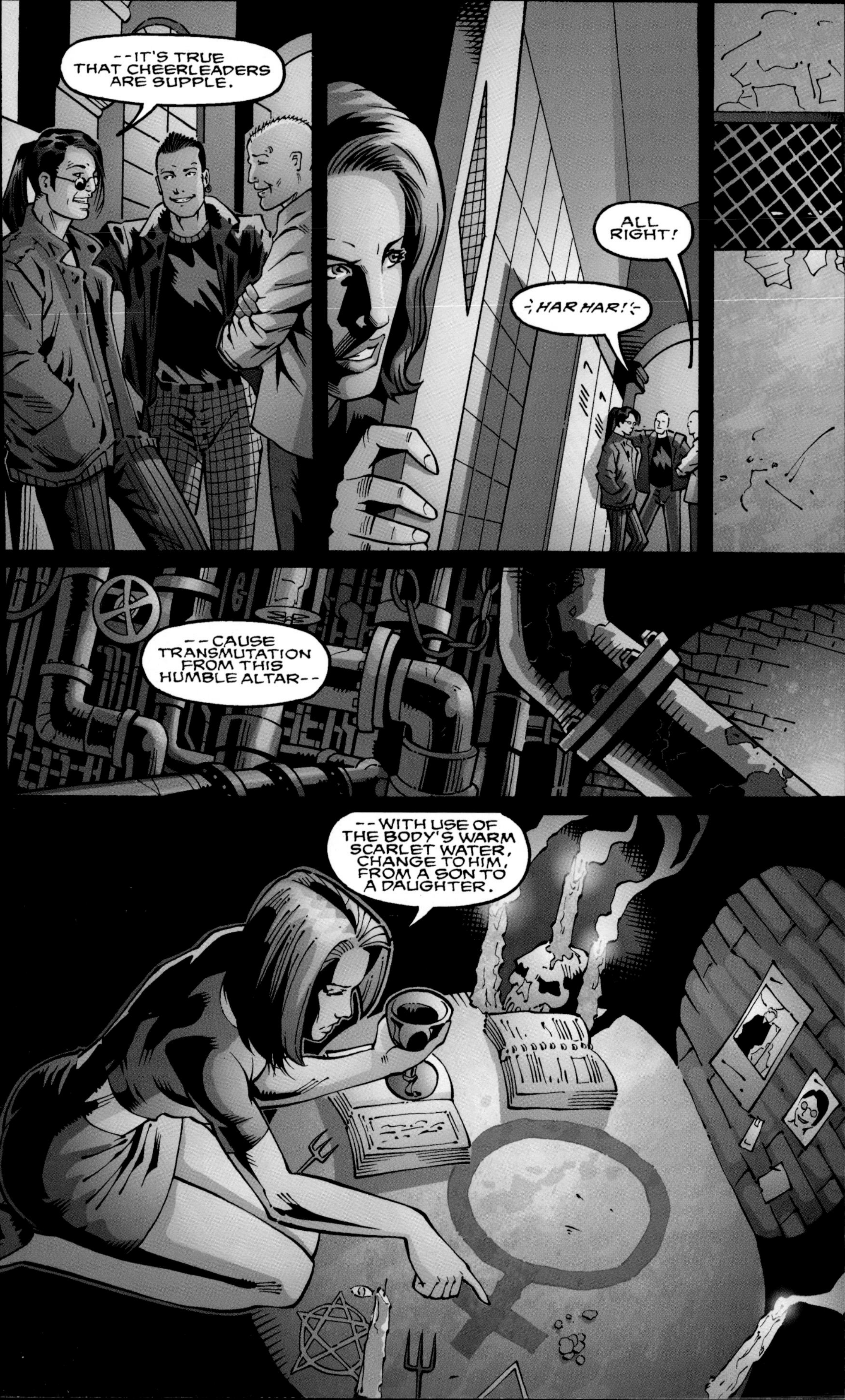
--IT'S TRUE THAT CHEERLEADERS ARE SUPPLE.
ALL RIGHT!
HAR HAR!
--CAUSE TRANSMUTATION FROM THIS HUMBLE ALTAR--
--WITH USE OF THE BODY'S WARM SCARLET WATER, CHANGE TO HIM, FROM A SON TO A DAUGHTER.

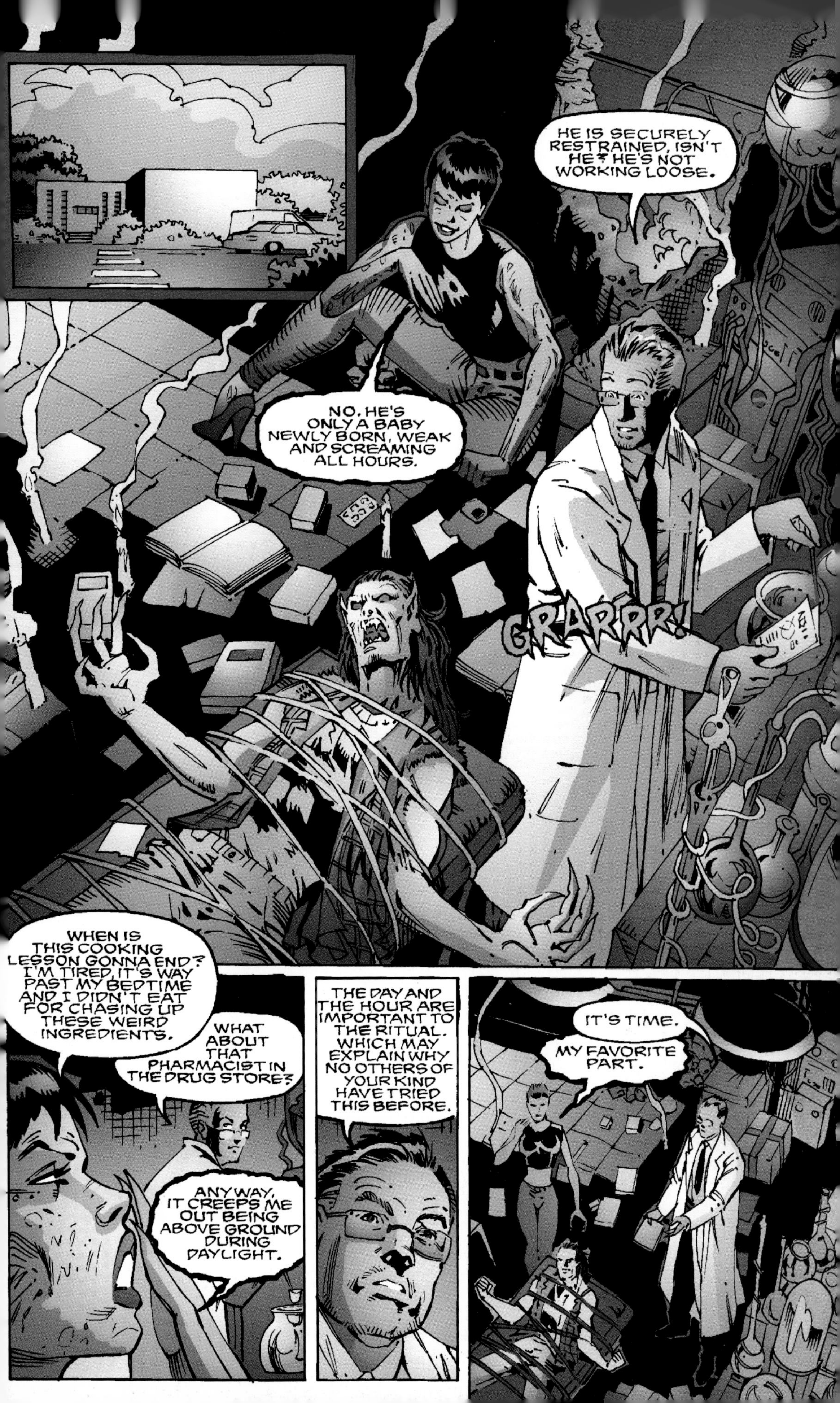

HE IS SECURELY RESTRAINED, ISN'T HE? HE'S NOT WORKING LOOSE.
NO. HE'S ONLY A BABY NEWLY BORN, WEAK AND SCREAMING ALL HOURS.
GRARRR!
WHEN IS THIS COOKING LESSON GONNA END? I'M TIRED, IT'S WAY PAST MY BEDTIME AND I DIDN'T EAT FOR CHASING UP THESE WEIRD INGREDIENTS.
WHAT ABOUT THAT PHARMACIST IN THE DRUG STORE?
ANYWAY, IT CREEPS ME OUT BEING ABOVE GROUND DURING DAYLIGHT.
THE DAY AND THE HOUR ARE IMPORTANT TO THE RITUAL. WHICH MAY EXPLAIN WHY NO OTHERS OF YOUR KIND HAVE TRIED THIS BEFORE.
IT'S TIME.
MY FAVORITE PART.

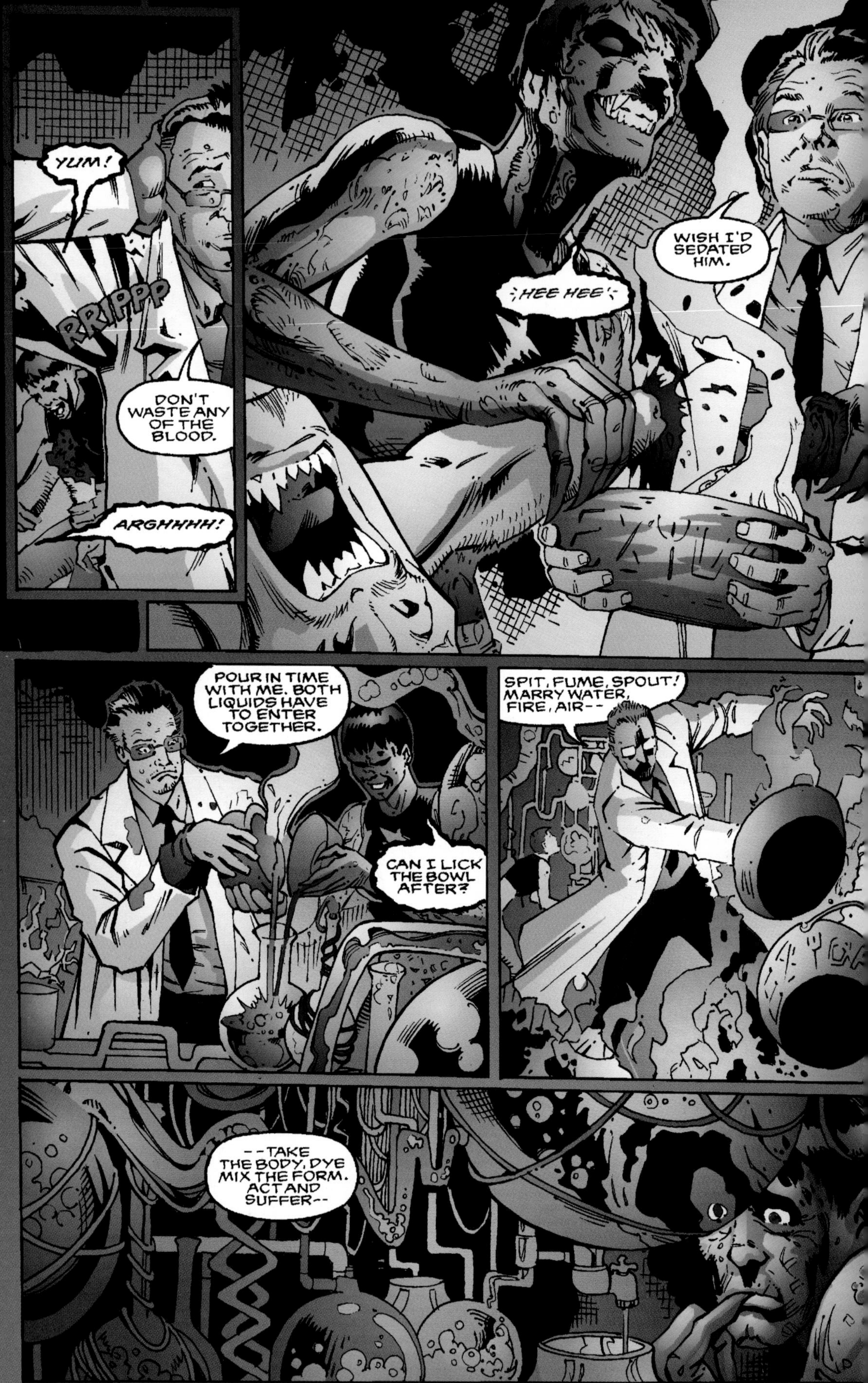
YUM!
RRIPPP
DON'T WASTE ANY OF THE BLOOD.
ARGHHHH!
HEE HEE
WISH I'D SEDATED HIM.
POUR IN TIME WITH ME. BOTH LIQUIDS HAVE TO ENTER TOGETHER.
CAN I LICK THE BOWL AFTER?
SPIT, FUME, SPOUT! MARRY WATER, FIRE, AIR--
--TAKE THE BODY, DYE MIX THE FORM. ACT AND SUFFER--

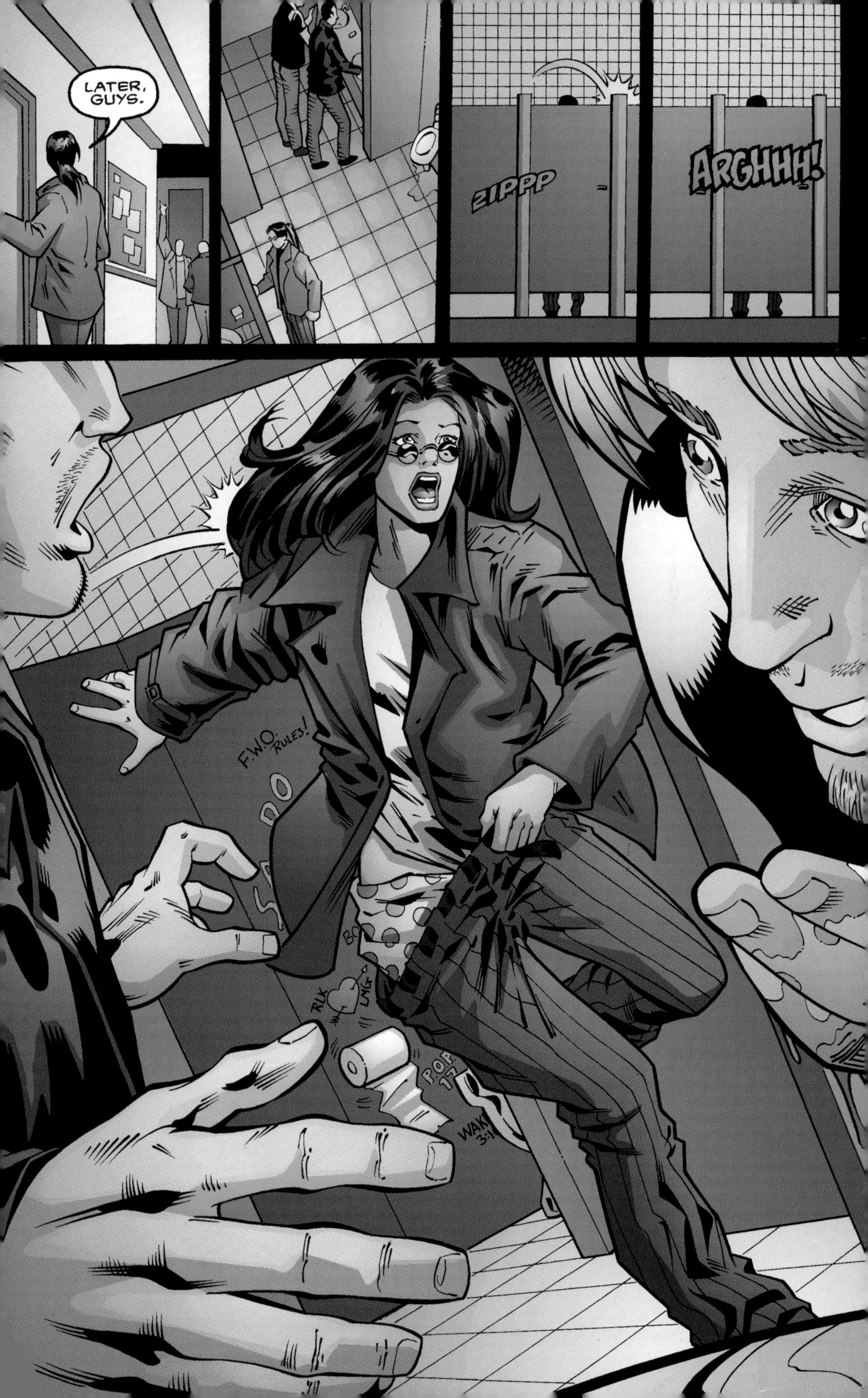
LATER, GUYS.
ZIPPP
ARGHHH!
F.W.O. RULES!

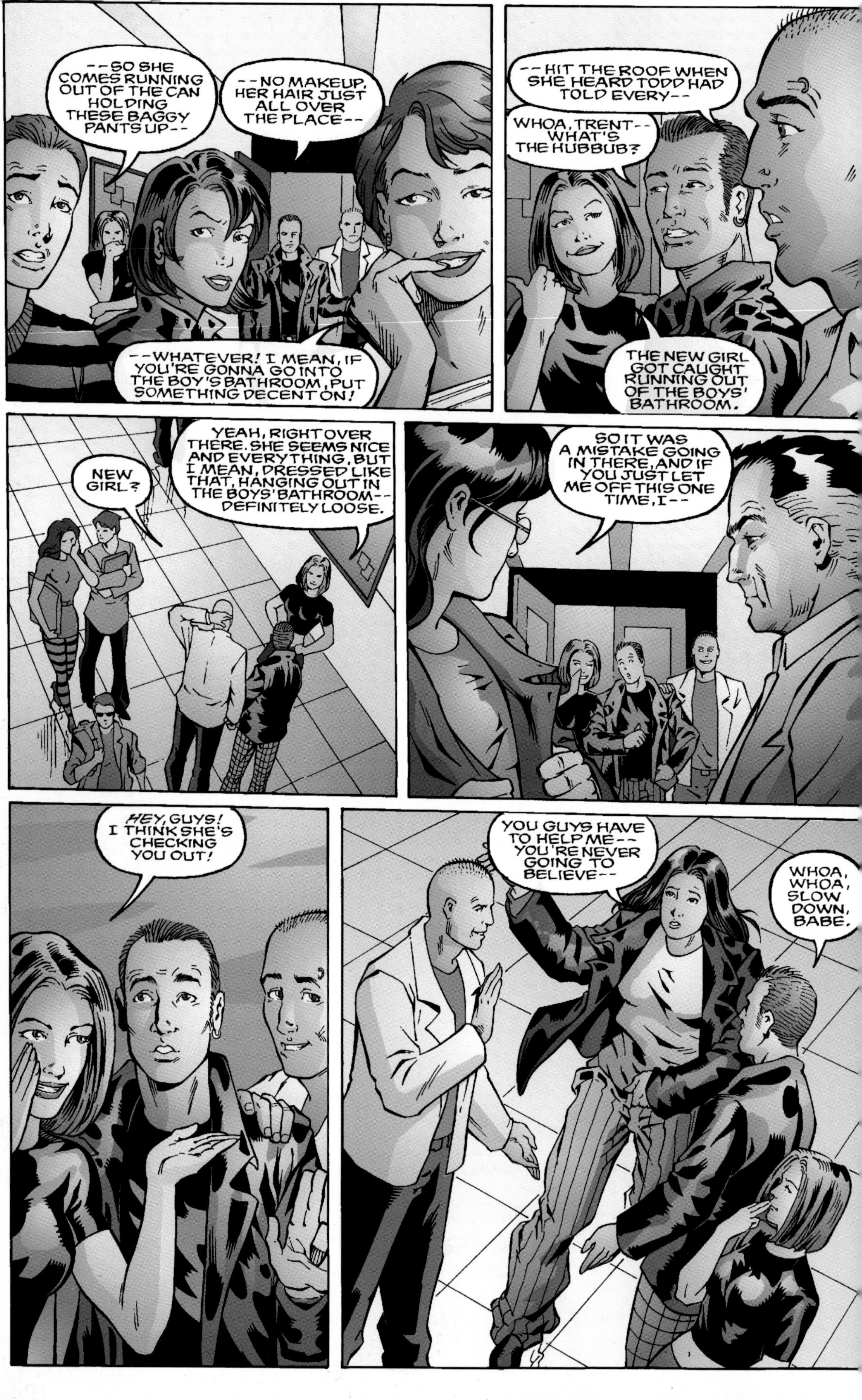
--SO SHE COMES RUNNING OUT OF THE CAN HOLDING THESE BAGGY PANTS UP--
--NO MAKEUP, HER HAIR JUST ALL OVER THE PLACE--
--WHATEVER! I MEAN, IF YOU'RE GONNA GO INTO THE BOY'S BATHROOM, PUT SOMETHING DECENT ON!
--HIT THE ROOF WHEN SHE HEARD TODD HAD TOLD EVERY--
WHOA, TRENT--WHAT'S THE HUBBUB?
THE NEW GIRL GOT CAUGHT RUNNING OUT OF THE BOYS' BATHROOM.
NEW GIRL?
YEAH, RIGHT OVER THERE. SHE SEEMS NICE AND EVERYTHING, BUT I MEAN, DRESSED LIKE THAT, HANGING OUT IN THE BOYS' BATHROOM--DEFINITELY LOOSE.
SO IT WAS A MISTAKE GOING IN THERE, AND IF YOU JUST LET ME OFF THIS ONE TIME, I--
HEY, GUYS! I THINK SHE'S CHECKING YOU OUT!
YOU GUYS HAVE TO HELP ME--YOU'RE NEVER GOING TO BELIEVE--
WHOA, WHOA, SLOW DOWN, BABE.

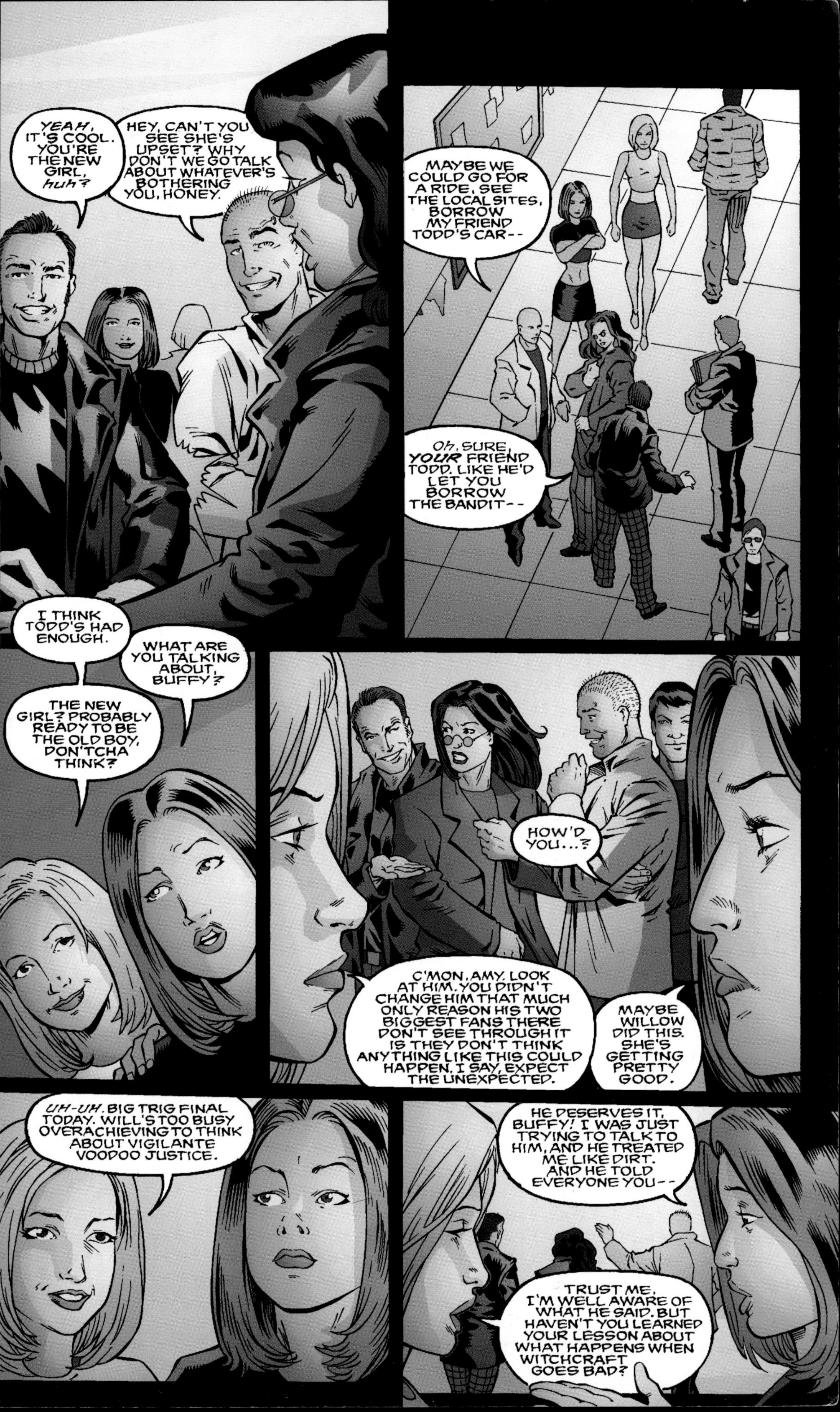

YEAH, IT'S COOL. YOU'RE THE NEW GIRL, huh?
HEY, CAN'T YOU SEE SHE'S UPSET? WHY DON'T WE GO TALK ABOUT WHATEVER'S BOTHERING YOU, HONEY.
MAYBE WE COULD GO FOR A RIDE, SEE THE LOCAL SITES, BORROW MY FRIEND TODD'S CAR--
Oh, SURE, YOUR FRIEND TODD. LIKE HE'D LET YOU BORROW THE BANDIT--
I THINK TODD'S HAD ENOUGH.
WHAT ARE YOU TALKING ABOUT, BUFFY?
THE NEW GIRL? PROBABLY READY TO BE THE OLD BOY, DON'TCHA THINK?
HOW'D YOU...?
C'MON, AMY. LOOK AT HIM. YOU DIDN'T CHANGE HIM THAT MUCH ONLY REASON HIS TWO BIGGEST FANS THERE DON'T SEE THROUGH IT IS THEY DON'T THINK ANYTHING LIKE THIS COULD HAPPEN. I SAY, EXPECT THE UNEXPECTED.
MAYBE WILLOW DID THIS. SHE'S GETTING PRETTY GOOD.
UH-UH. BIG TRIG FINAL TODAY. WILL'S TOO BUSY OVERACHIEVING TO THINK ABOUT VIGILANTE VOODOO JUSTICE.
HE DESERVES IT, BUFFY! I WAS JUST TRYING TO TALK TO HIM, AND HE TREATED ME LIKE DIRT. AND HE TOLD EVERYONE YOU--
TRUST ME. I'M WELL AWARE OF WHAT HE SAID. BUT HAVEN'T YOU LEARNED YOUR LESSON ABOUT WHAT HAPPENS WHEN WITCHCRAFT GOES BAD?

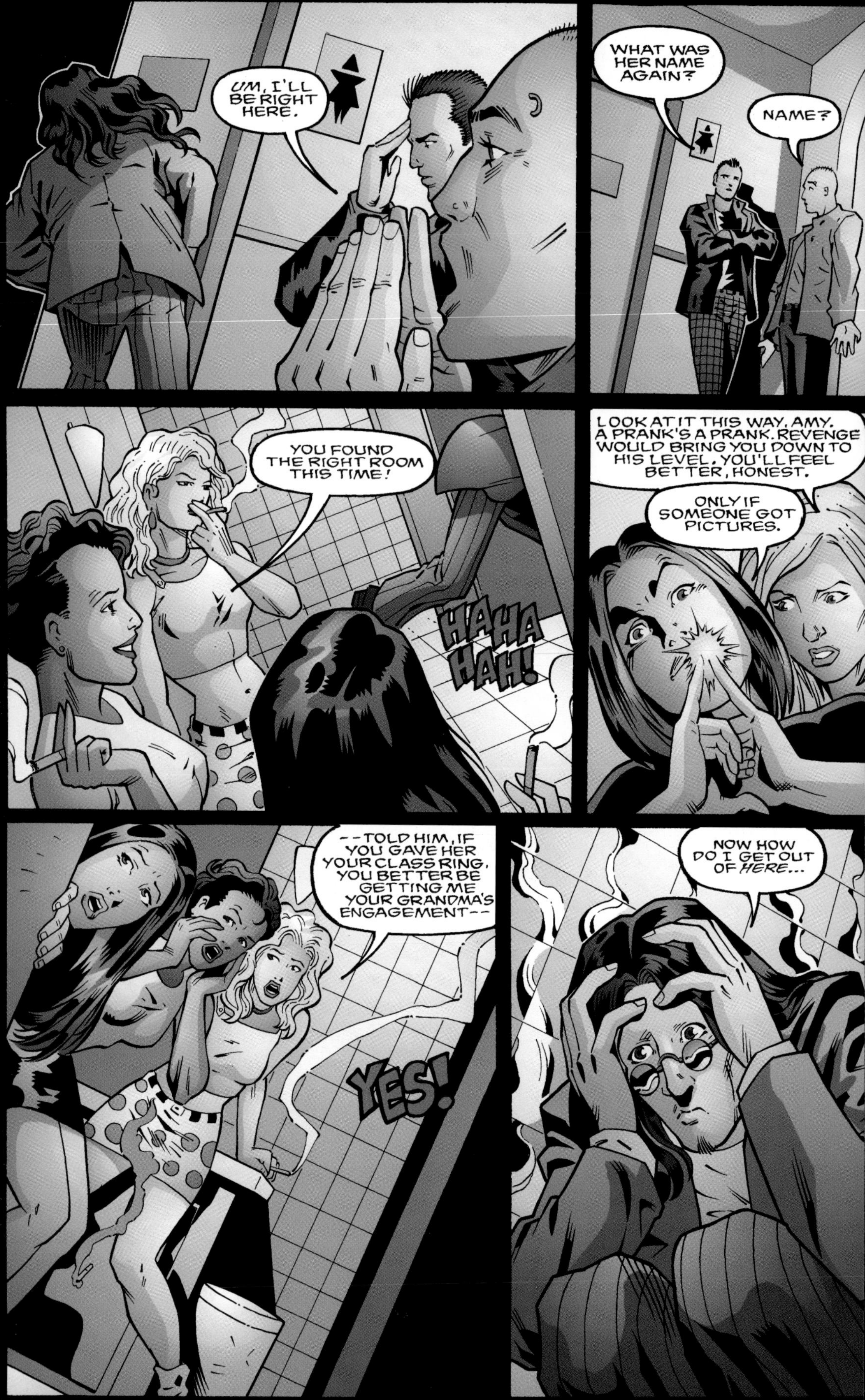
UM, I'LL BE RIGHT HERE.
WHAT WAS HER NAME AGAIN?
NAME?
YOU FOUND THE RIGHT ROOM THIS TIME!
HAHA HAH!
LOOK AT IT THIS WAY, AMY. A PRANK'S A PRANK. REVENGE WOULD BRING YOU DOWN TO HIS LEVEL. YOU'LL FEEL BETTER, HONEST.
ONLY IF SOMEONE GOT PICTURES.
--TOLD HIM, IF YOU GAVE HER YOUR CLASS RING, YOU BETTER BE GETTING ME YOUR GRANDMA'S ENGAGEMENT--
YES!
NOW HOW DO I GET OUT OF *HERE*...

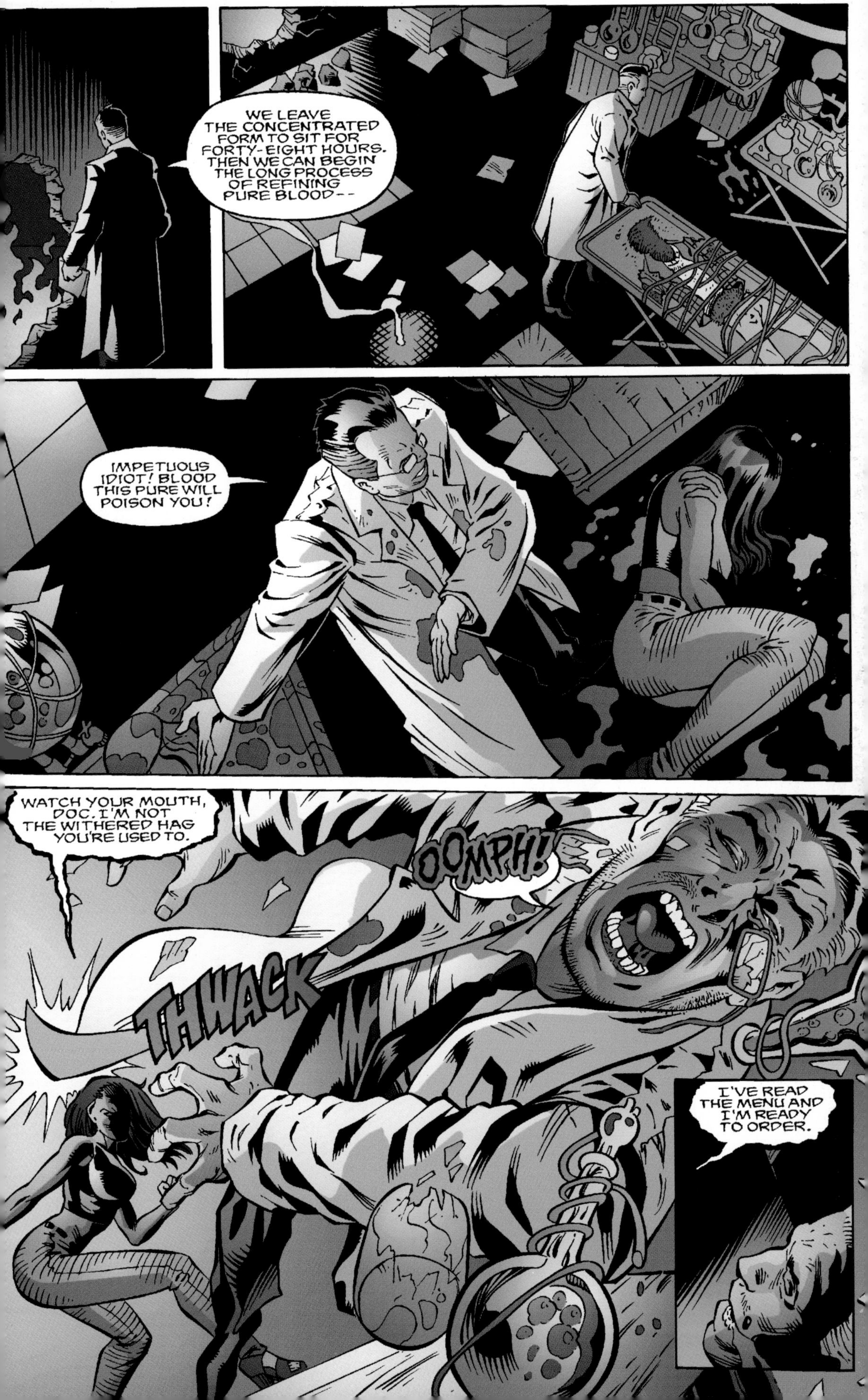
WE LEAVE THE CONCENTRATED FORM TO SIT FOR FORTY-EIGHT HOURS. THEN WE CAN BEGIN THE LONG PROCESS OF REFINING PURE BLOOD--
IMPETUOUS IDIOT! BLOOD THIS PURE WILL POISON YOU!
WATCH YOUR MOUTH, DOC. I'M NOT THE WITHERED HAG YOU'RE USED TO.
OOMPH!!
THWACK
I'VE READ THE MENU AND I'M READY TO ORDER.

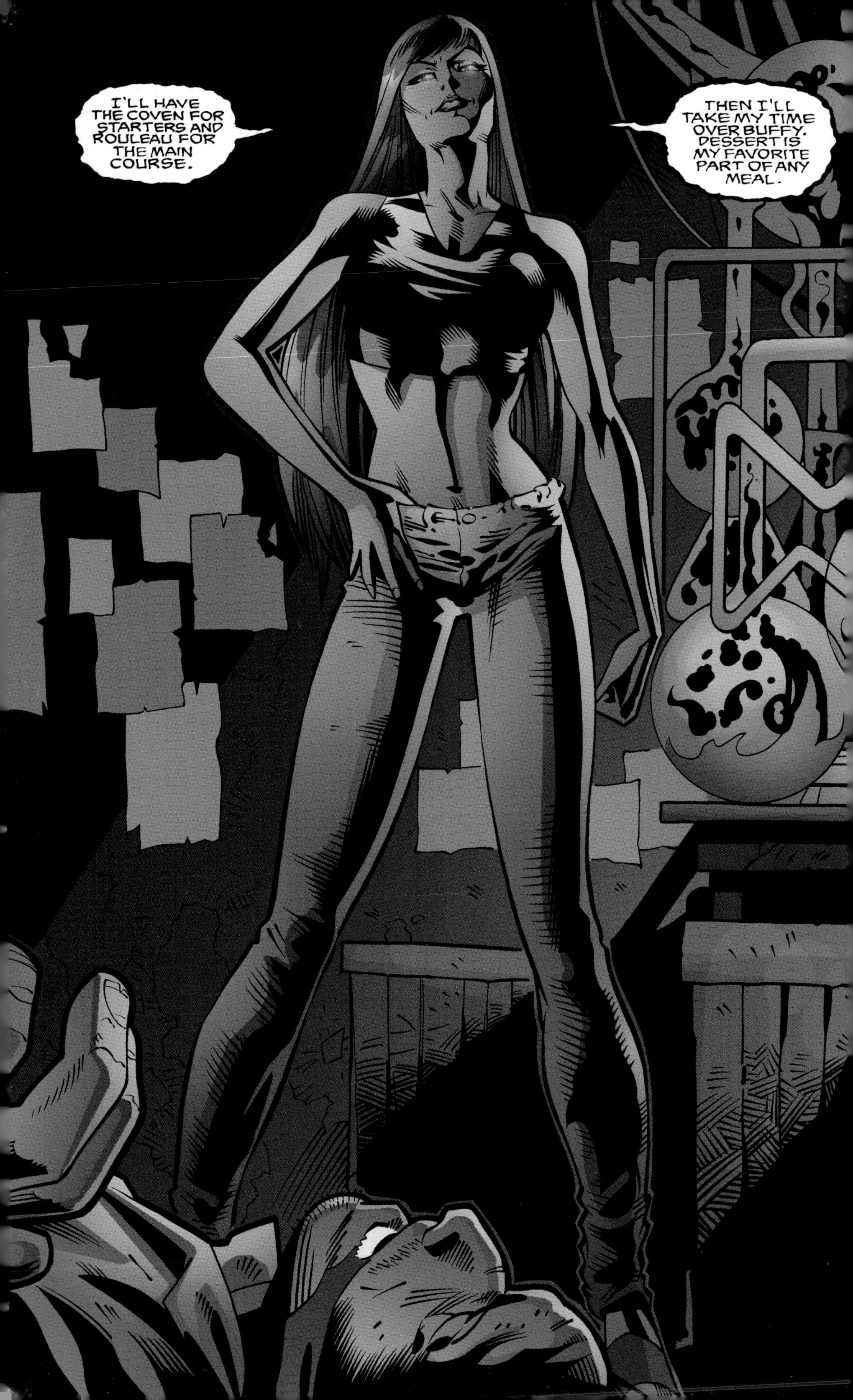
I'LL HAVE THE COVEN FOR STARTERS AND ROULEAU FOR THE MAIN COURSE.
THEN I'LL TAKE MY TIME OVER BUFFY. DESSERT IS MY FAVORITE PART OF ANY MEAL.

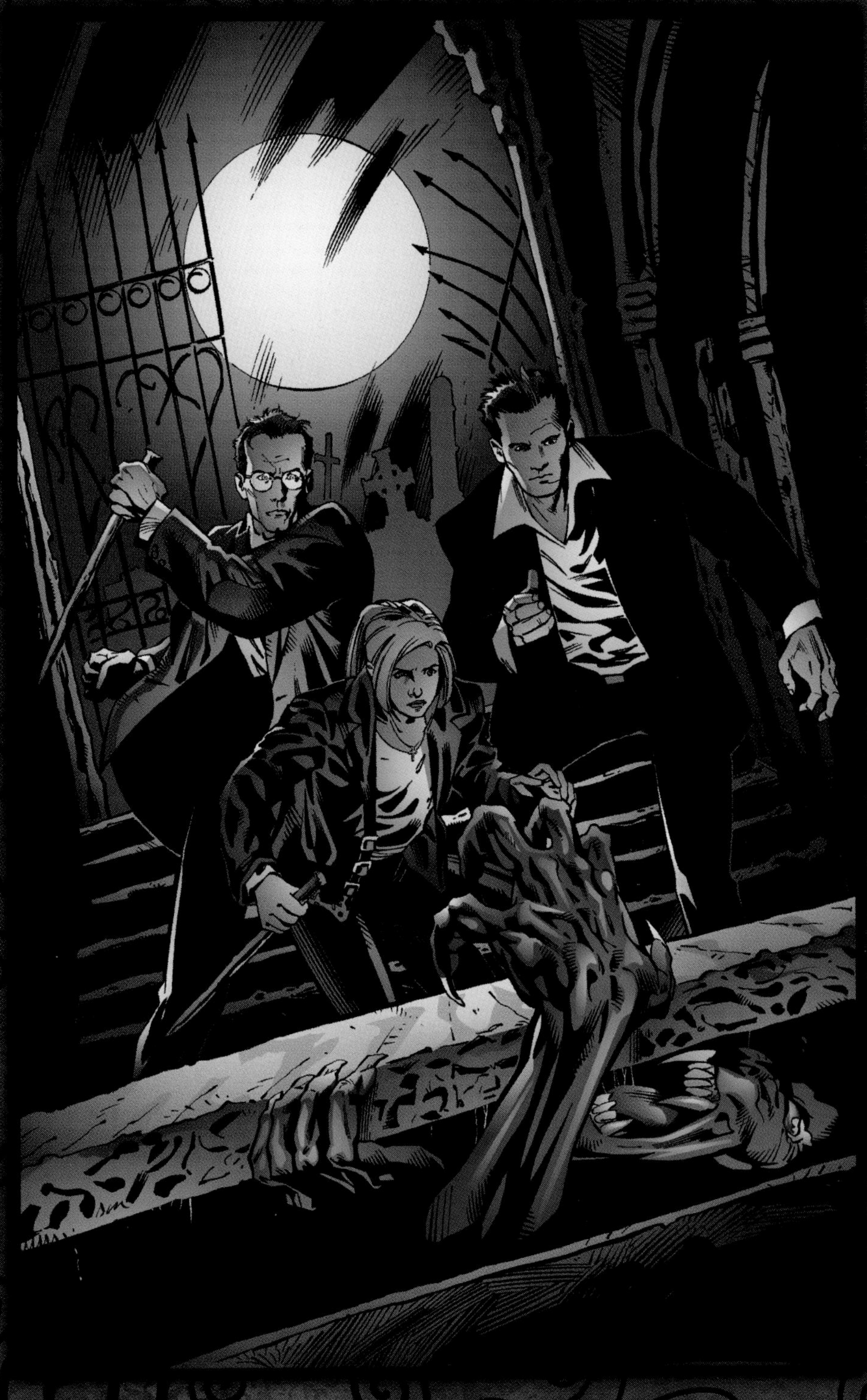

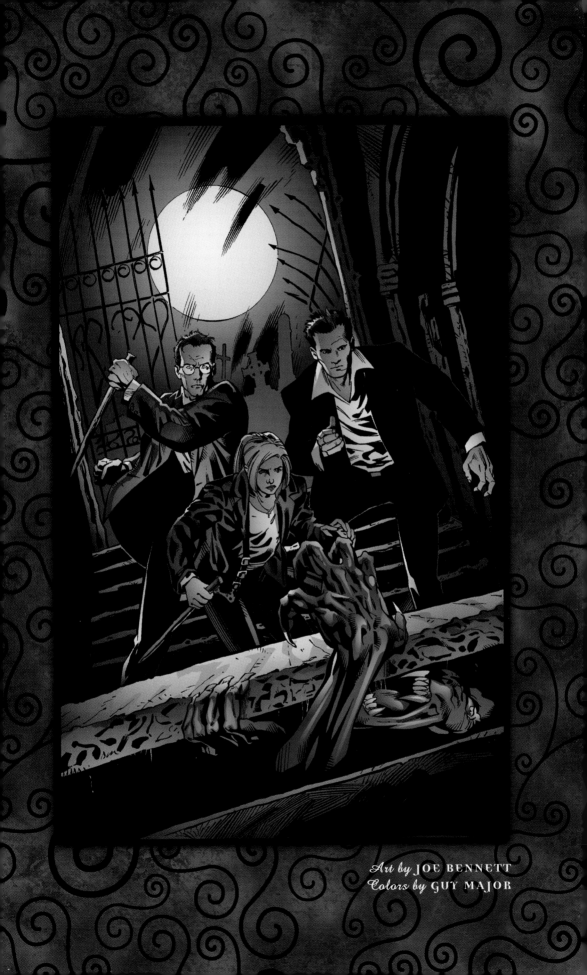

Art by JOE BENNETT
Colors by GUY MAJOR

HELLO,MOON

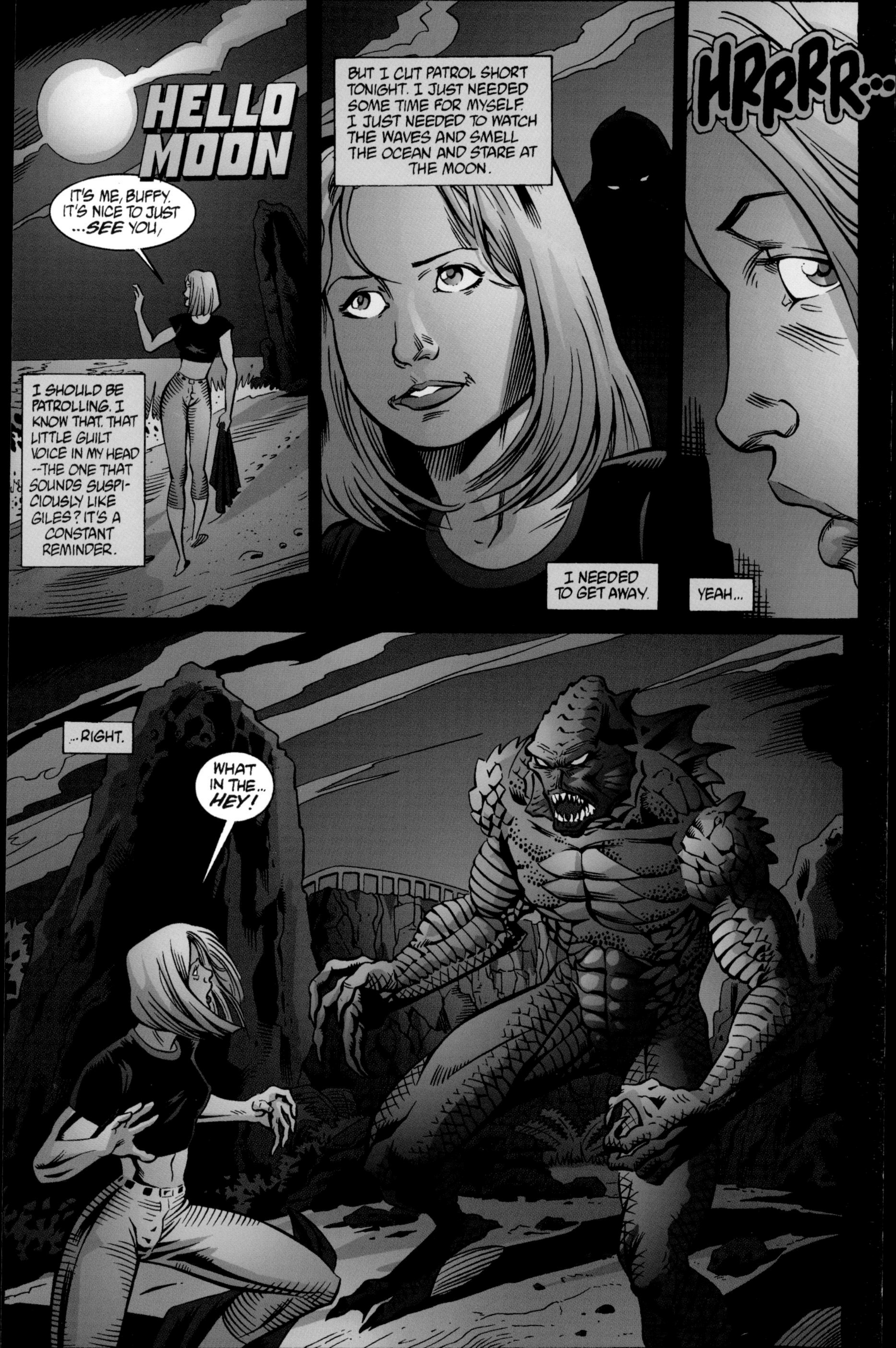
HELLO MOON
IT'S ME, BUFFY. IT'S NICE TO JUST ...SEE YOU,
I SHOULD BE PATROLLING. I KNOW THAT. THAT LITTLE GUILT VOICE IN MY HEAD --THE ONE THAT SOUNDS SUSPICIOUSLY LIKE GILES? IT'S A CONSTANT REMINDER.
BUT I CUT PATROL SHORT TONIGHT. I JUST NEEDED SOME TIME FOR MYSELF. I JUST NEEDED TO WATCH THE WAVES AND SMELL THE OCEAN AND STARE AT THE MOON.
I NEEDED TO GET AWAY.
HRRRR...
YEAH...
...RIGHT.
WHAT IN THE... HEY!

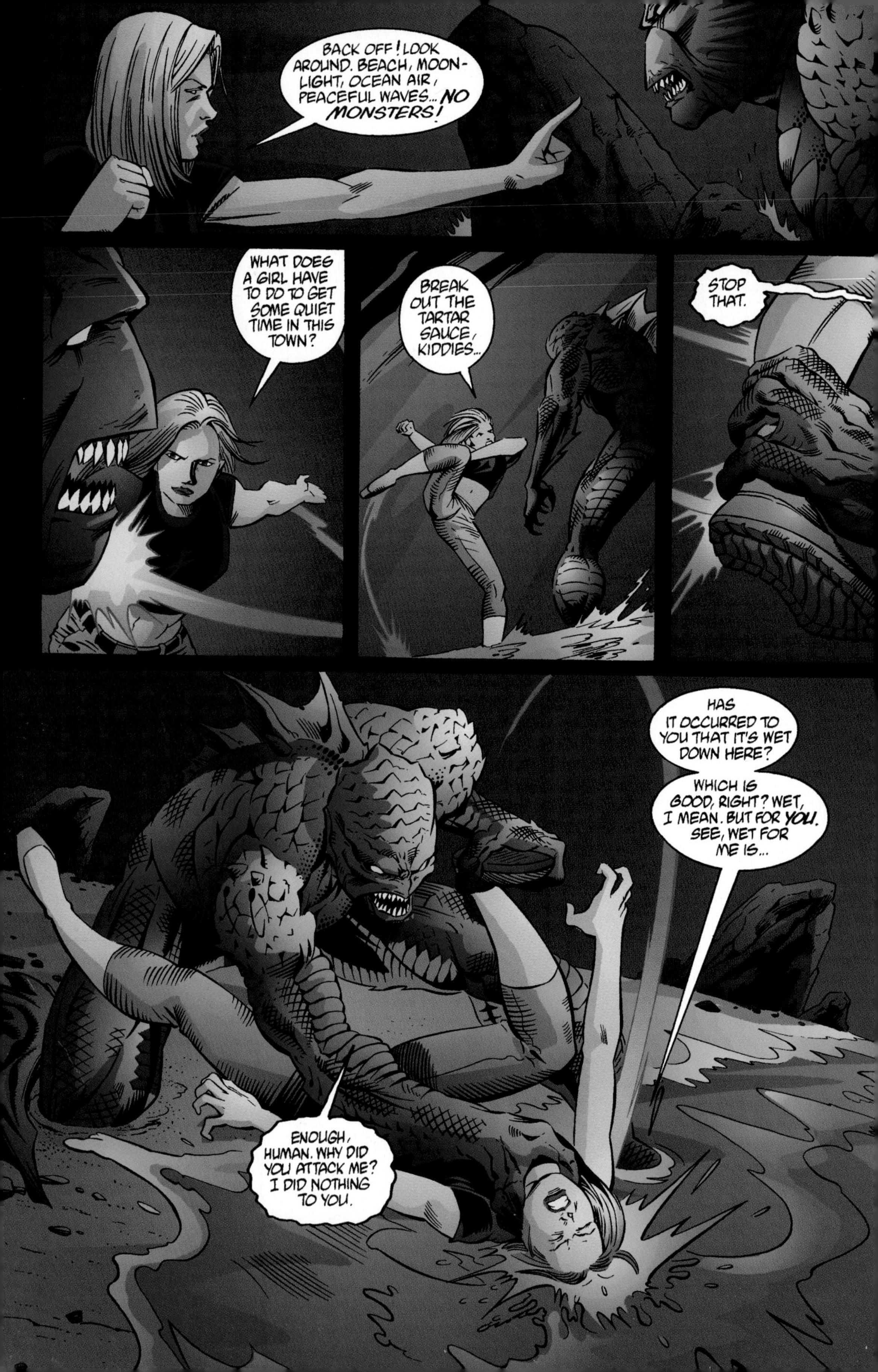
BACK OFF! LOOK AROUND. BEACH, MOON-LIGHT, OCEAN AIR, PEACEFUL WAVES... NO MONSTERS!
WHAT DOES A GIRL HAVE TO DO TO GET SOME QUIET TIME IN THIS TOWN?
BREAK OUT THE TARTAR SAUCE, KIDDIES...
STOP THAT.
HAS IT OCCURRED TO YOU THAT IT'S WET DOWN HERE?
WHICH IS GOOD, RIGHT? WET, I MEAN. BUT FOR YOU. SEE, WET FOR ME IS...
ENOUGH, HUMAN. WHY DID YOU ATTACK ME? I DID NOTHING TO YOU.

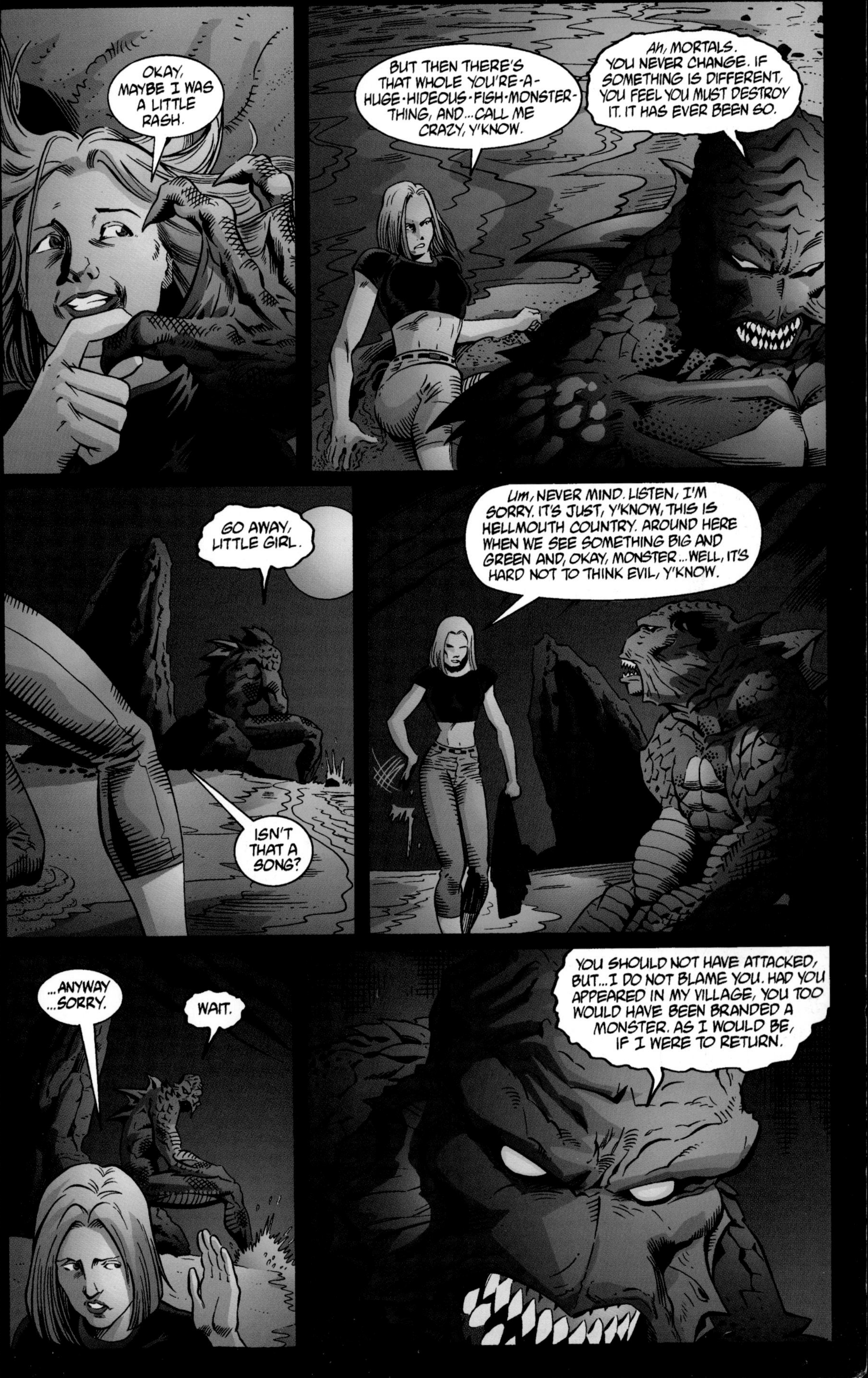
OKAY, MAYBE I WAS A LITTLE RASH.
BUT THEN THERE'S THAT WHOLE YOU'RE-A-HUGE-HIDEOUS-FISH-MONSTER-THING, AND...CALL ME CRAZY, Y'KNOW.
AH, MORTALS. YOU NEVER CHANGE. IF SOMETHING IS DIFFERENT, YOU FEEL YOU MUST DESTROY IT. IT HAS EVER BEEN SO.
GO AWAY, LITTLE GIRL.
ISN'T THAT A SONG?
UM, NEVER MIND. LISTEN, I'M SORRY. IT'S JUST, Y'KNOW, THIS IS HELLMOUTH COUNTRY. AROUND HERE WHEN WE SEE SOMETHING BIG AND GREEN AND, OKAY, MONSTER...WELL, IT'S HARD NOT TO THINK EVIL, Y'KNOW.
...ANYWAY ...SORRY.
WAIT.
YOU SHOULD NOT HAVE ATTACKED, BUT...I DO NOT BLAME YOU. HAD YOU APPEARED IN MY VILLAGE, YOU TOO WOULD HAVE BEEN BRANDED A MONSTER. AS I WOULD BE, IF I WERE TO RETURN.

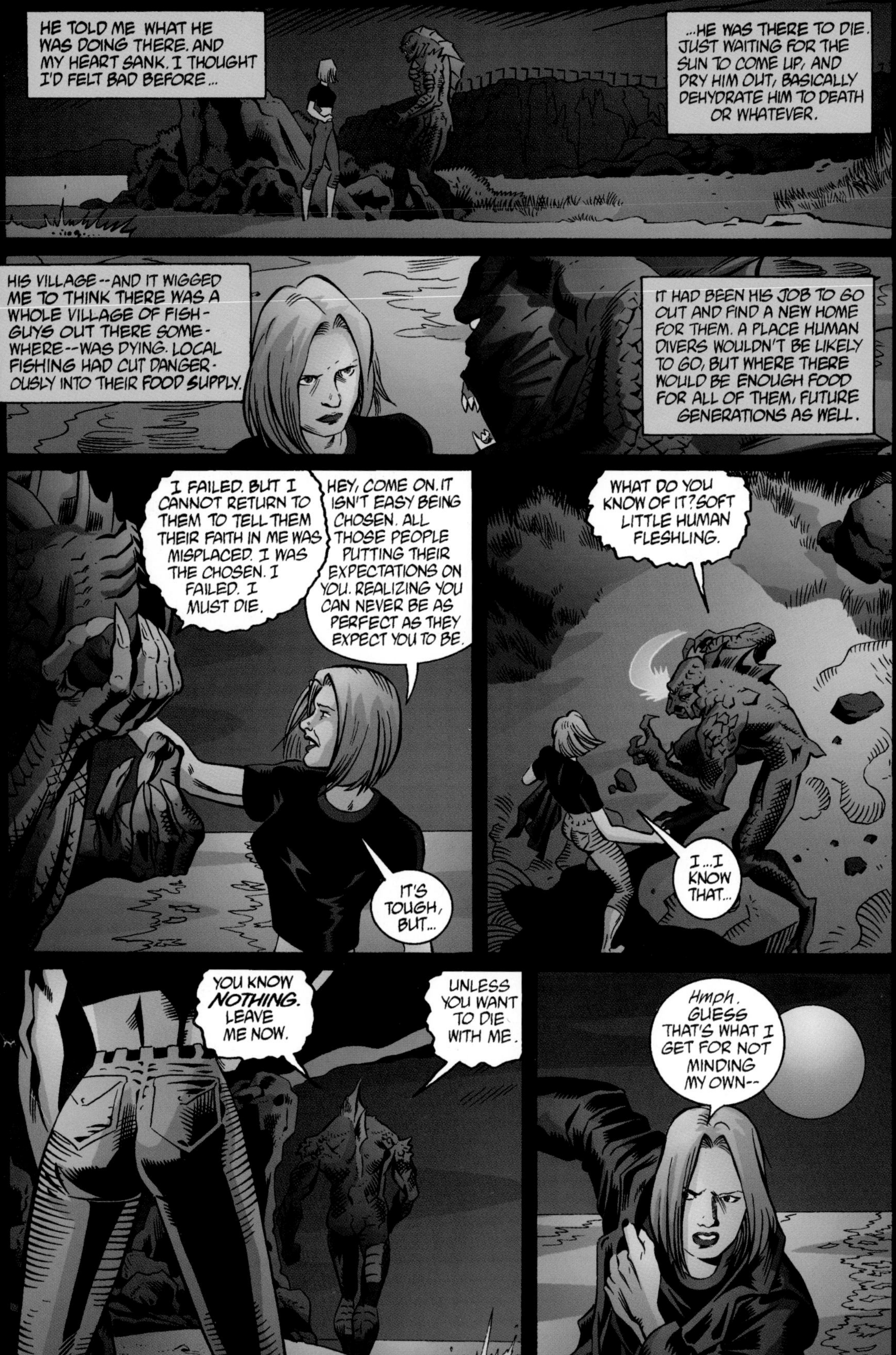
HE TOLD ME WHAT HE WAS DOING THERE. AND MY HEART SANK. I THOUGHT I'D FELT BAD BEFORE...
...HE WAS THERE TO DIE. JUST WAITING FOR THE SUN TO COME UP, AND DRY HIM OUT, BASICALLY DEHYDRATE HIM TO DEATH OR WHATEVER.
HIS VILLAGE--AND IT WIGGED ME TO THINK THERE WAS A WHOLE VILLAGE OF FISH-GUYS OUT THERE SOME-WHERE--WAS DYING. LOCAL FISHING HAD CUT DANGER-OUSLY INTO THEIR FOOD SUPPLY.
IT HAD BEEN HIS JOB TO GO OUT AND FIND A NEW HOME FOR THEM. A PLACE HUMAN DIVERS WOULDN'T BE LIKELY TO GO, BUT WHERE THERE WOULD BE ENOUGH FOOD FOR ALL OF THEM, FUTURE GENERATIONS AS WELL.
I FAILED. BUT I CANNOT RETURN TO THEM TO TELL THEM THEIR FAITH IN ME WAS MISPLACED. I WAS THE CHOSEN. I FAILED. I MUST DIE.
HEY, COME ON. IT ISN'T EASY BEING CHOSEN. ALL THOSE PEOPLE PUTTING THEIR EXPECTATIONS ON YOU. REALIZING YOU CAN NEVER BE AS PERFECT AS THEY EXPECT YOU TO BE.
IT'S TOUGH, BUT...
WHAT DO YOU KNOW OF IT? SOFT LITTLE HUMAN FLESHLING.
I...I KNOW THAT...
YOU KNOW NOTHING. LEAVE ME NOW.
UNLESS YOU WANT TO DIE WITH ME.
Hmph. GUESS THAT'S WHAT I GET FOR NOT MINDING MY OWN--

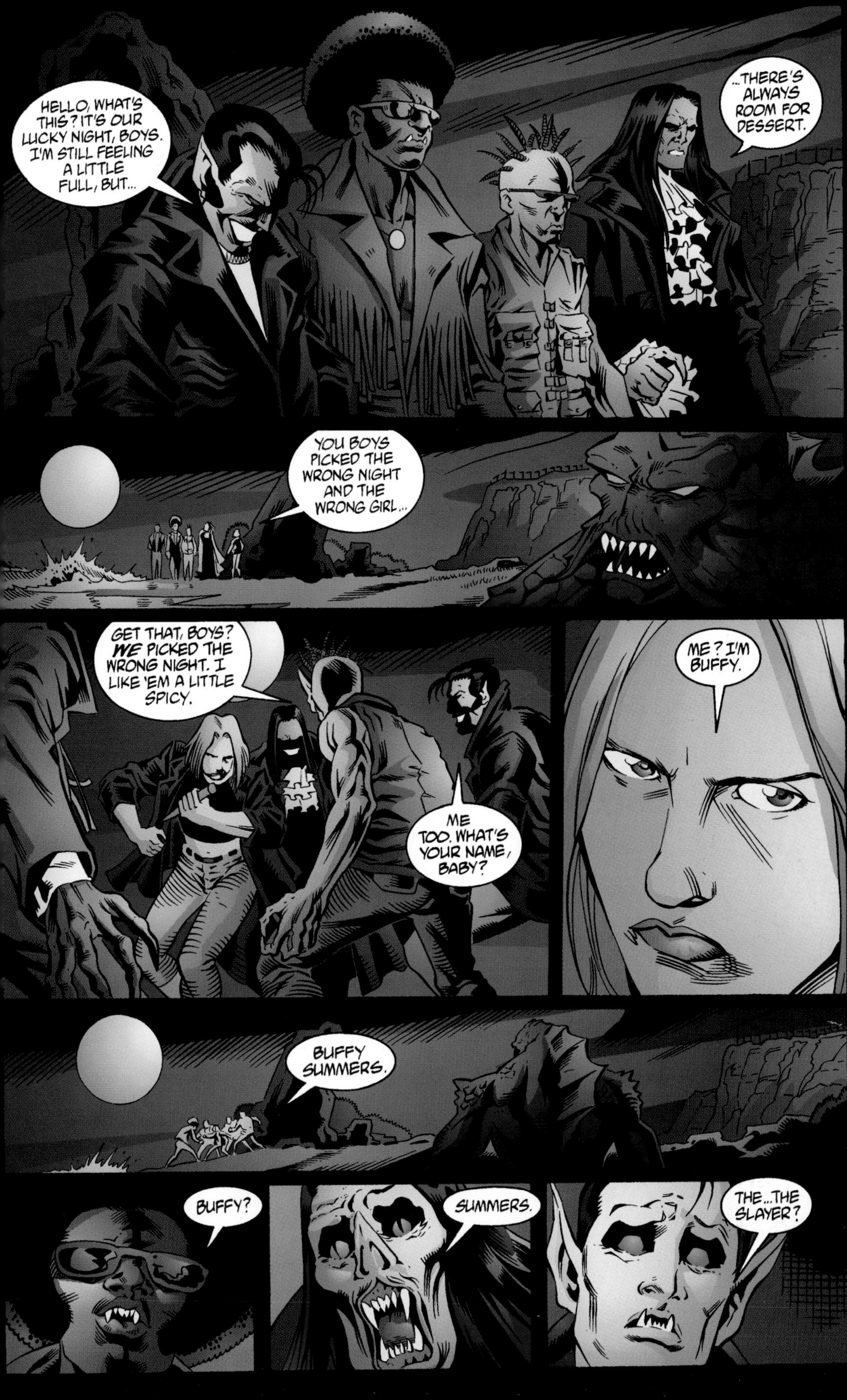
HELLO, WHAT'S THIS? IT'S OUR LUCKY NIGHT, BOYS. I'M STILL FEELING A LITTLE FULL, BUT...
...THERE'S ALWAYS ROOM FOR DESSERT.
YOU BOYS PICKED THE WRONG NIGHT AND THE WRONG GIRL...
GET THAT, BOYS? WE PICKED THE WRONG NIGHT. I LIKE 'EM A LITTLE SPICY.
ME TOO. WHAT'S YOUR NAME, BABY?
ME? I'M BUFFY.
BUFFY SUMMERS.
BUFFY?
SUMMERS.
THE...THE SLAYER?

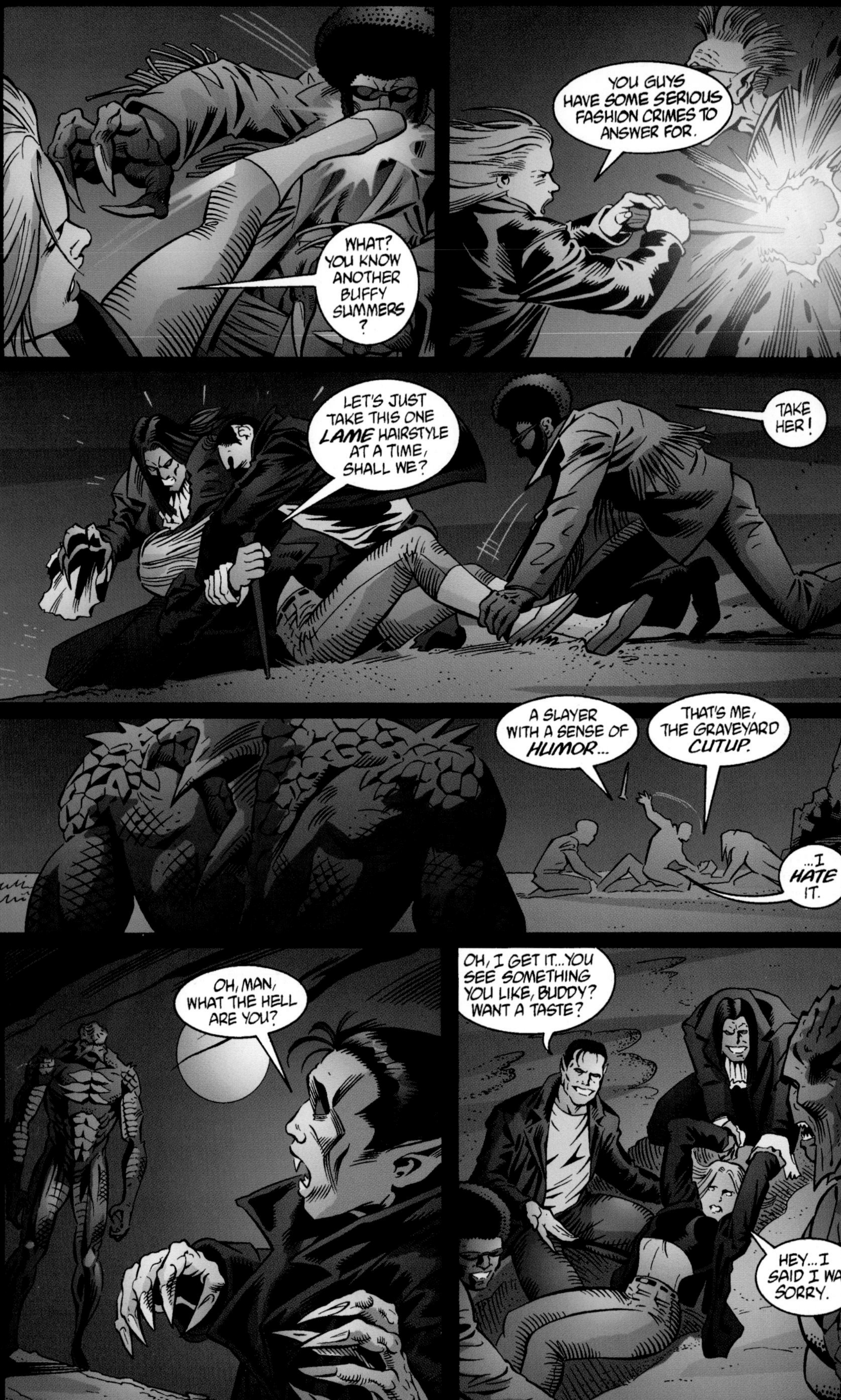
WHAT? YOU KNOW ANOTHER BUFFY SUMMERS?
YOU GUYS HAVE SOME SERIOUS FASHION CRIMES TO ANSWER FOR.
LET'S JUST TAKE THIS ONE LAME HAIRSTYLE AT A TIME, SHALL WE?
TAKE HER!
A SLAYER WITH A SENSE OF HUMOR...
THAT'S ME, THE GRAVEYARD CUTUP.
...I HATE IT.
OH, MAN, WHAT THE HELL ARE YOU?
OH, I GET IT... YOU SEE SOMETHING YOU LIKE, BUDDY? WANT A TASTE?
HEY... I SAID I WAS SORRY.

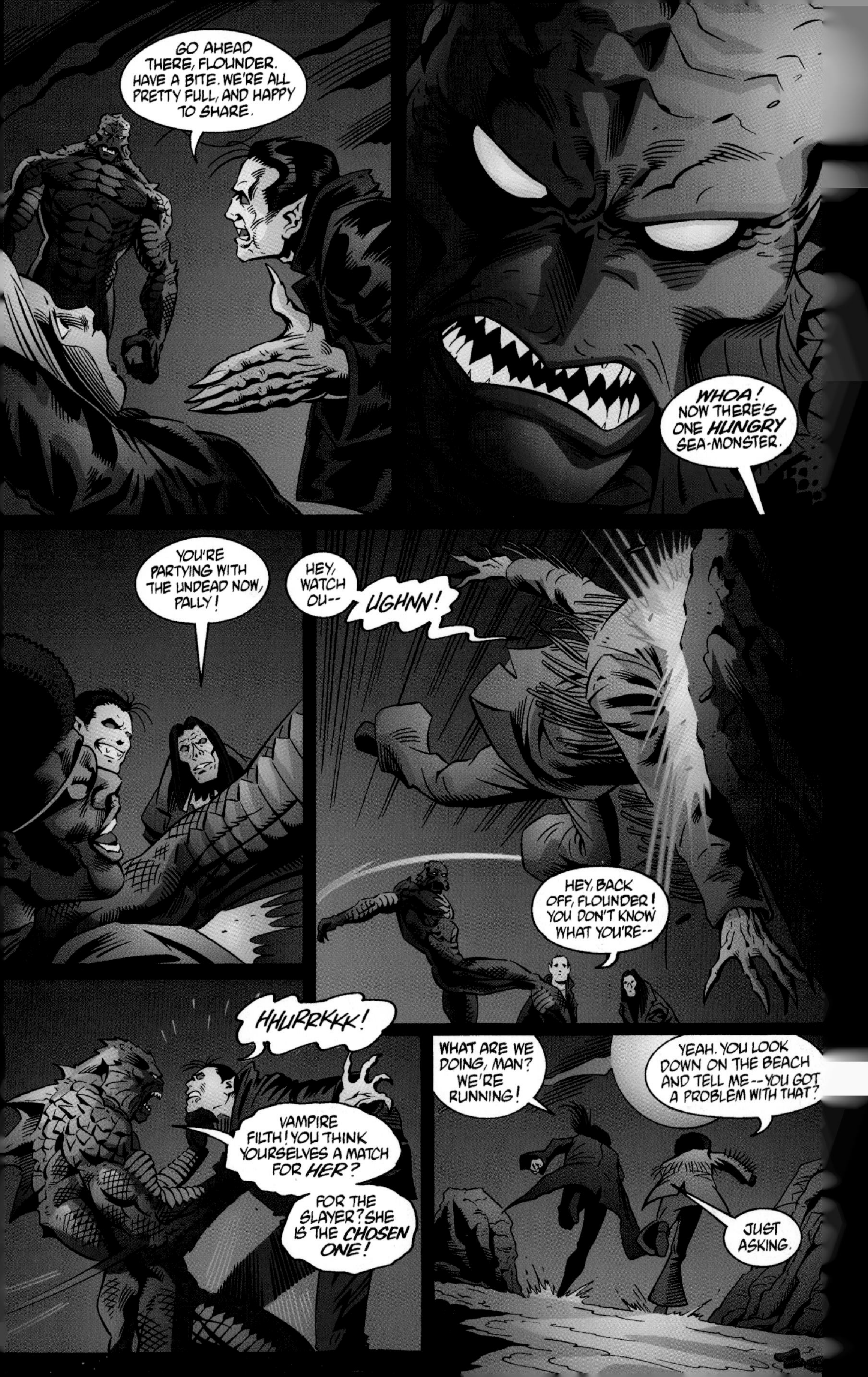
GO AHEAD THERE, FLOUNDER. HAVE A BITE. WE'RE ALL PRETTY FULL, AND HAPPY TO SHARE.
WHOA! NOW THERE'S ONE HUNGRY SEA-MONSTER.
YOU'RE PARTYING WITH THE UNDEAD NOW, PALLY!
HEY, WATCH OU--
UGHNN!
HEY, BACK OFF, FLOUNDER! YOU DON'T KNOW WHAT YOU'RE--
HHURRKKK!
VAMPIRE FILTH! YOU THINK YOURSELVES A MATCH FOR HER?
FOR THE SLAYER? SHE IS THE CHOSEN ONE!
WHAT ARE WE DOING, MAN? WE'RE RUNNING!
YEAH. YOU LOOK DOWN ON THE BEACH AND TELL ME--YOU GOT A PROBLEM WITH THAT?
JUST ASKING.

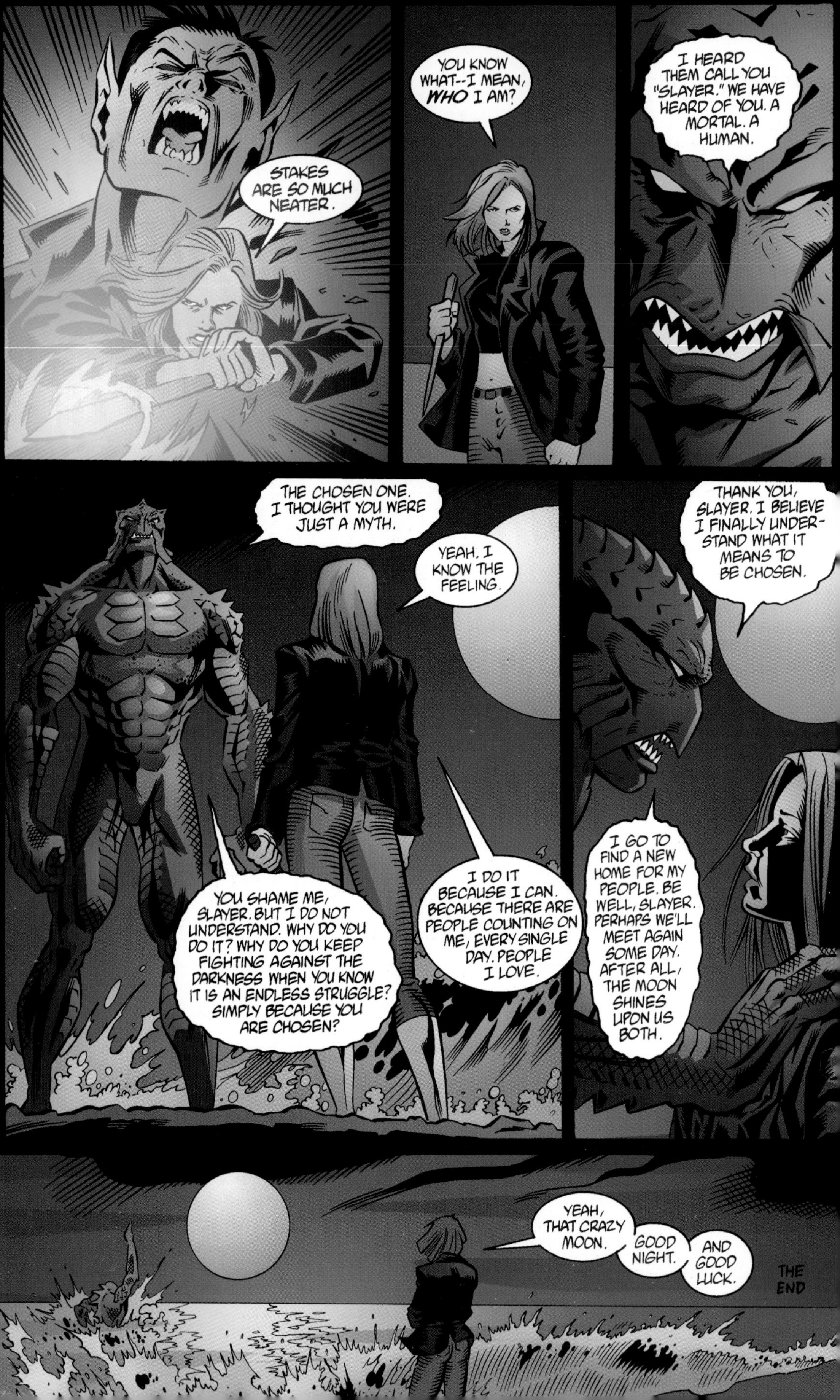
STAKES ARE SO MUCH NEATER.
YOU KNOW WHAT--I MEAN, WHO I AM?
I HEARD THEM CALL YOU "SLAYER." WE HAVE HEARD OF YOU. A MORTAL. A HUMAN.
THE CHOSEN ONE. I THOUGHT YOU WERE JUST A MYTH.
YEAH, I KNOW THE FEELING.
YOU SHAME ME, SLAYER. BUT I DO NOT UNDERSTAND. WHY DO YOU DO IT? WHY DO YOU KEEP FIGHTING AGAINST THE DARKNESS WHEN YOU KNOW IT IS AN ENDLESS STRUGGLE? SIMPLY BECAUSE YOU ARE CHOSEN?
I DO IT BECAUSE I CAN. BECAUSE THERE ARE PEOPLE COUNTING ON ME, EVERY SINGLE DAY. PEOPLE I LOVE.
THANK YOU, SLAYER. I BELIEVE I FINALLY UNDERSTAND WHAT IT MEANS TO BE CHOSEN.
I GO TO FIND A NEW HOME FOR MY PEOPLE. BE WELL, SLAYER. PERHAPS WE'LL MEET AGAIN SOME DAY. AFTER ALL, THE MOON SHINES UPON US BOTH.
YEAH, THAT CRAZY MOON.
GOOD NIGHT.
AND GOOD LUCK.
THE END